Casting Shade

A Welcome to Amoresville Book

Brandy Ayers

Contents

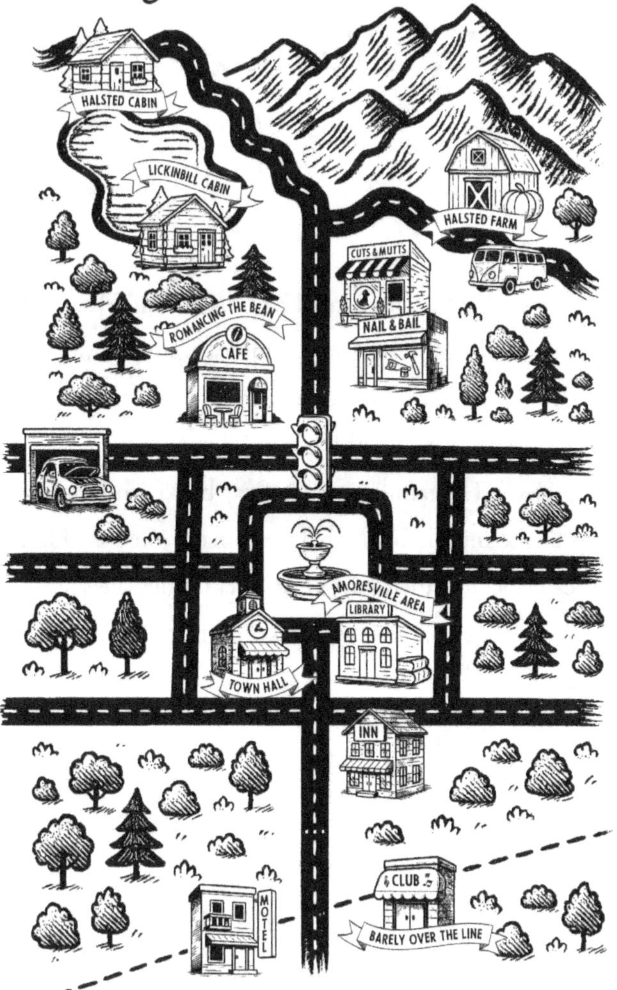

WELCOME TO
Amoresville
HALSTED CABIN
LICKINBILL CABIN
HALSTED FARM
ROMANCING THE BEAN
CAFE
CUTS & MUTTS
NAIL & BAIL
AMORESVILLE AREA
LIBRARY
TOWN HALL
INN
MOTEL
CLUB
BARELY OVER THE LINE

Chapter 1
Ten Years Ago

Delia

The halls of Amoresville Area High School are buzzing more than usual today. Not that that means a whole lot. Nothing new ever happens here. Someone probably got a new tractor and drove it to school or something dumb like that.

"DeeDee!" The familiar voice of my best friend pulls me to a stop in the middle of the hall. In a flash of color, Harley is practically tackling me to the floor. Thankfully, she's like a foot shorter than me so I manage to keep on my feet. "Have you heard?"

"Heard what?"

"There is a new kid!"

"Seriously? I haven't heard about a new family in town." Usually I'm the first to know anything in my group of friends. My mom owns the local coffee shop, Romancing the Bean. She has since I hit high school and she decided us kids could fend for ourselves enough for her to stop being a stay-at-home mom. That place quickly became the center of all town gossip. Since I work there after school most days, I get first dibs on all the juicy stuff.

"That's the thing, there is no new family. It's Mayor LickMy-Ball's nephew. He grew up in New York City, can you believe it?"

"Ugh, he must be awful if he's a freaking Lickinbill." The Lickinbill family has a long history of hating my mother's side of the family. Both our families have been in the town since it was founded. My ancestors were the first to settle here all the way back during the Revolutionary War. This is an annoying fact every single history teacher I've ever had loves to try to talk to me about. Mom has even come to my classes to give an oral history of my family. *So* embarrassing.

"I haven't seen him yet, but I hear he is hot."

I give Harley a disbelieving look. There is no way someone related to rat-faced Mayor Lickinbill is hot. "Why is he here? I thought his mom swore to never step foot in Amoresville ever again."

Mom loves to talk about how epic it was when Mayor Lickinbill's sister basically gave everyone in town the middle finger at her high school graduation then left town never looking back. But even managing to escape the physical town doesn't save you from the Amoresville rumor mill. The stories I've heard about Mary Lickinbill range from she's a druggie in New York City to she met a prince and now lives in a penthouse on Time Square. But I never heard a word about a kid.

Harley's face loses some of its enthusiasm. "His mom died. I heard Old Lady Winchester talking about it in the office when I got here." Harley is chronically late to the point the office ladies don't even ask her for a note anymore. "Apparently she was in a car crash a month ago. The guy had to stay at a foster home for a month while they tried to find his next of kin."

That might be the saddest thing I've ever heard. My family means everything to me. Sure, my brothers are a pain in my ass, but I can't imagine losing them in one day. Just the idea makes a pit open in my stomach.

The shrill ring of the first period bell rips through the air, pulling me from my thoughts. "Shit, if I'm late to Honors English again Mrs. Wheeler is going to make me write a thousand-word essay on the importance of punctuality. See you at lunch?"

Harley nods and starts sprinting in the opposite direction. Despite being one of the smartest people I know, Harley is in all remedial classes, mostly because she gives zero shits about school. Sometimes I think I'm the only reason she even comes to school. During our freshman year, they threatened to hold her back if she didn't get her grades up in the final quarter. She pulled all straight A's for the last three months of school. There was no way she would accept not being in the same grade as me.

I turn and run, too. Thankfully, years of chasing my brothers around the fields of our farm have made me crazy fast.

Just as I *Tokyo-drift* it around the last corner, I'm knocked off my feet in a flurry of papers and books.

"Ooph," a deep voice grunts in the general area of whatever it was that is blocking the hallway and causes me to eat dirt. "Oh shit, sorry. Are you okay?"

I adjust my glasses so I can see the hand held out to me from above. The hand is attached to a long arm which in turn is attached to some very broad shoulders. Above all of that is a boy I've never seen before. A cute boy. A really freaking cute boy with slightly too long dark brown hair that matches his equally dark eyes. He's wearing loose fitting khakis and a t-shirt covered in animated characters I've never heard of, and thick rimmed black glasses.

The second I take his hand, a sensation I've never felt before zaps through my body. I've had crushes on boys before, but they never felt like this. I've known every guy in this school since we were in kindergarten, and it's hard to get worked up over someone you saw eating paste when you were seven.

He pulls me to stand and I'm surprised to see he is significantly taller than me. Maybe even taller than my oldest brother who is away at college.

"Are you okay?" He tilts his head slightly, looking concerned.

I shake my head, clearing my mind, but he must take it the wrong way.

"Oh shit, what's wrong, did you hurt something?"

"No, I mean yes, I'm fine. Not hurt. Just surprised."

He nods and tries to smile a little, but it looks like it takes way too much effort.

"I'm Delia." I hold my hand out and he takes it, giving it a small shake.

"Wesley. You can call me Wes."

* * *

Wesley

The last few months have been a never-ending parade of the darkest shit you can imagine. But suddenly, just standing in the middle of the hall in my new school, a little ball of light has crashed through the muck.

I should let go of Delia's hand. We've finished our introductions, it's the normal thing to do. But for some reason, loitering in the hall holding this girl's hand feels like the only thing keeping me together.

Another warning bell's shrill tone pierces the air.

"Miss Halsted, you are late again. You know what that means." An older woman seems to appear in the doorway as if she had been waiting for the opportunity to pounce. She has silver-gray hair pulled into a tight bun that pulls at her scalp. She looks at Delia with unmitigated loathing. This must be Mrs. Wheeler. Uncle Burt let me know she is a friend of his and would make sure I got settled, as if that would comfort me. "And you must be Mr. Lickinbill."

Everything inside me recoils at that name being attached to me. "Goldman. Not Lickinbill."

"Well, either way, I do not tolerate tardiness. As Miss Halsted very well knows." She looks down her pug-like nose at Delia in obvious distaste.

Halsted, the name makes everything around me screech to a stop. It explains the teacher's obvious dislike for the pretty girl that ran into me. She's a member of the family my uncle seems to hate more than anything in the world. I believe his exact words were, "*a bunch of delinquent outsiders that think they run the town without doing any work.*"

"Oh, she's only late because the office asked her to show me to your class. It was all my fault." The words pop out of my mouth, everything inside me needing to prove I am not like my uncle.

This seems to confound Mrs. Wheeler. She looks between us, confused that there might be a connection between the nephew of the town mayor and the daughter of his sworn enemy. Plus, I still haven't let go of her hand. Honestly, it all seems a little petty. I barely even knew my next door neighbors in Brooklyn, let alone bothered to get to know them well enough to form a vendetta.

"Well, okay, both of you come in and take your seats."

I bend down, finally letting go of her hand, and pick up the books and papers that went flying after our collision, handing them back to Delia as she looks at me with a conflicted expression. "Halsted, huh? I heard your family is trouble."

She smirks. "I'm sure you did."

"Good thing I'm a big fan of trouble."

Never in my life have I said something so cool in the exact moment I needed a good line. It seems to land with my audience, because she smiles, a blush rushing up her cheeks as she ducks her head letting the strawberry blonde hair fall around her face.

Without responding, Delia rushes into class, taking a seat in the back corner, as far from Mrs. Wheeler's desk as she could possibly get.

I follow behind, like the girl holds an invisible leash that is dragging me in after her.

"Mr. Lick—I mean Goldman." The teacher places her hand on my shoulder, preventing me from following Delia further. "Word of advice: if you want to succeed at this school, you will stay away from that one and her friends."

I shrug and take the only open seat in the room, right in front of the teacher's desk. But every few minutes I can't help but look back at the corner, at the girl everyone insists I shouldn't talk to.

Chapter 2

Delia

How can a single, tri-folded piece of paper feel so heavy?

I read the letter again, in complete disbelief.

Beneath my feet the floor pulses, not because of the pounding of my heart, but because the club is in full swing on the other side of my office door. Not twenty feet away there are half-naked women twirling around poles while men throw money at them. I love each and every single one of those women as if they were my own family.

Which is why I refold the letter carefully, open the top drawer of my desk, and shove it all the way to the back before slamming the drawer closed again.

But I swear I can still feel it in there, with its life changing words. So I open the drawer again, grab the letter, and march over to the safe hidden behind one of the paintings on the wall from my short stint thinking I could be an artist. The beeps of the combination as I enter feel like salvation. I pop open the door and throw the paper into the safe, stacking the wads of cash that running a strip club requires on top. Then the contracts and important paperwork on top of that.

There. That should do it.

I close the door to the safe once again and swing the painting back into place. The swirls of color that at one point I truly thought meant I was destined to be a world-famous painter mix together as my eyes mist over. I won't cry. There is no need to cry. This changes nothing.

Because in Amoresville, nothing changes.

Case in point, my best friend since birth bursts through the door in a tsunami of color, glitter, and bare flesh. I jump a little at her dramatic entrance.

"Hey, Jumpy, what's your deal?" She drapes herself over the pleather couch against the opposite wall.

All she wears is a G-string, impossibly high platform stilettos, and a smile. But at this point I'm more used to seeing her naked than clothed, so it isn't a big deal. This is what happens when you go into business with your best friend to open a strip club. You get real used to seeing each other in various stages of undress. Although I haven't graced the stage in years. Not since the first years we were open.

"No deal. I just drank too much coffee today." Truth. That's what happens when your mom runs the local coffee shop and is trying out a new latte recipe.

"No such thing." Harley crosses her legs, twirling one of her pink extensions around a finger. Today her hair is down and curled into big looping waves around her shoulders. She changes hair like I change hobbies.

We both get bored very easily. But never of each other.

"Something is off about you, is it the election signs posted on every fucking sign in this goddamn town?"

Ugh. They don't help.

I cross the room and plop down on the couch next to my friend. Unlike her, I'm dressed in a crisp business suit, tailored to perfectly flatter my ample curves. Beneath the jacket, I wear nothing but a black lace bra, but with it buttoned up, nothing is exposed.

"I ripped down ten more on my way into the cafe today. We're going to need to have another bonfire soon."

Harley guffaws out her over-the-top laugh. "Dude, you have to stop bothering with stealing them. No matter how many you take down, Burt is going to just replace them. He's like the kraken of election managers. For every piece of propaganda you rip down he'll replace it with four."

"Fucking Burt."

Harley nods in agreement.

Suddenly the thoughts swirling in my head feel too heavy, so I drop it down onto her shoulder. "Walking around town and seeing Wesley's stupid face everywhere is torture."

"His stupid hot face," she mutters.

I respond with a hard pinch to her muscular thigh. "Ouch, bitch! Yes, he is an asshole, but you cannot deny that Wesley Goldman is hot as fuck."

"Says the girl that had a crush on Quasimodo from the Hunchback cartoon."

My head bounces as she shrugs. "Guilty as charged. You can't let him get to you. The closer we get to the election the more he's going to be out and about in town peddling for votes."

"He doesn't even have an opponent. Why can't he just stay in his little library and shut the fuck up? Let the natural course of things play out like it always does in this town."

Harley lays her head on top of mine. "Honey, I hate to say it, but it isn't going to get better once he's elected. As mayor he is going to be everywhere, just like his uncle and every Lickinbill before him."

Nausea twists in my stomach, because she's right. For as long as there has been an official town government in Amoresville, there have been Lickinbills leading. Why couldn't my ancestors have had more ambition? But nooooo, the Halsteds and Louises just wanted to farm and run their businesses in peace. Sometimes being a member of the oldest family in the area is downright annoying.

"Okay, changing the subject. There is a big spender out there tonight. You should probably come out and make an appearance." Harley picks her head up, giving my leg a firm pat while tilting her shoulder up so I have no choice but to find my own spine again.

"Ugh, yay, nothing like having to schmooze with a slimy rich asshole to distract me from another slimy not-so-rich asshole."

"It is what it is." Harley stands from the couch and reaches down to grip my hand, pulling me up to standing. "I'm the talent and the beauty, and you are the brains in this venture."

"Um, rude. I have talent and beauty, too."

Harley wobbles her hand up and down. "Meh."

"Get out there and make me some more money, you witch." I spin her around by her shoulders and slap her ass.

"Oh baby, are you finally turning bi with me? Don't worry, I'll walk you through eating pussy for the first time. It's much easier than sucking cock, trust me."

"If only it was that easy. There is nothing worse than only being attracted to men. It is seriously the worst."

My dating history is woefully sad. A few boys when I was younger, a security guard that worked here a few years ago, which was a huge mistake, and hookups here and there. But every single one has just driven home my belief that the only good men in the world are the ones I'm related to, which leaves me shit out of luck in the romance department.

"Truth. This is why I try to ignore that half of myself entirely." Harley loops her arm through mine. Even in her insane platform heels, she's still a couple inches shorter. "If only I could stop getting wet at the sight of Tom Hiddelston in his Loki costume, I could go full lesbian."

I lead the way out of the office and onto the main floor of Club Barely Over the Line with Harley strutting behind me. It's like as soon as we cross the threshold between my private office and the rest of the club a switch flips in us both. Harley turns back into the bubble headed bimbo that rakes in the biggest tips of any dancer in the whole place. I turn into the badass bitch that has turned this place from a shitty, worn-down warehouse to one of the most sought-after clubs in Pennsylvania.

Truthfully, looking around I can't help but feel pride right in lock step with the overwhelming sense of being trapped. When Harley and I took possession of the warehouse, it was nothing but a rusty, half-collapsing building that used to manufacture glass in the nineties. When we opened, we had a stage made from leftover pallets and the seating was nothing but folding tables and chairs. We served beer from kegs and hired guys from the local fire station to act as security for less than minimum wage. Honestly, it was probably half illegal.

But now that same building gleams with crystal chandeliers, a chrome bar kept impeccably clean by our mixologists, leather benches and chairs (easier for cleaning) and a huge stage in the middle.

Harley nods in the direction of the man occupying our VIP area. He sits in one of the club chairs and gives half-assed smiles to the men surrounding him, obviously trying to impress him with jokes that I don't need to hear to know are probably at the expense of the very women entertaining them.

Three of our newest hires are draped across the laps of some of his lackeys, not giving lap dances, but just acting as their companions for the evening. Yet the man himself doesn't have a woman near him. Odd.

One quick tug of my suit jacket and I strut over to the roped-off area. My head of security gives me a subtle nod and unclips the rope, allowing me to climb the two steps up to the platformed seating area. The VIP section has the best view of the main stage, but also its own pole in case they want a personal show. Unlike the seating in the rest of the club, the chairs up here could double as thrones. There is something about a leather club chair that makes a man feel more important. Like he's fucking Henry the Eighth with his court serving at his feet. It tends to loosen grips on wallets.

Without hesitation, I walk up to the man—his eyes track my every move. He's handsome in a Zaddy kind of way. Salt-and-pepper hair neatly trimmed, not a strand out of place. Clean shaved, manicured nails. He wears tailored suit pants and a crisp white shirt. The shiny loafers on his feet probably cost more than all my dancers will make in their shift tonight combined.

"Hello, I'm Delia Halsted, owner of the club." I hold my hand out for him to shake, but when he takes it he turns it so he can kiss the back. I'm sure he thinks it is a slick move, but more than anything it sends the sensation of worms crawling over my skin up my arms.

"Bill Olsen. Patron of the arts. Dance is a special interest of mine." His eyes slip past my face as he takes in the main stage behind me. From the song currently playing, I know it'll be

Harley on the spotlight pole. I know every song she dances to by heart, can practically see the moves she will be performing at that very moment in my head. "This may be my new favorite venue to support."

Ugh, this guy is the fucking worst. "Well, we appreciate your business. Is there a dancer that has caught your eye in particular that I can introduce?"

"Mmmm, you have many talented artists."

Don't roll your eyes. Don't roll your eyes. Don't roll your eyes.

"I would enjoy a conversation with the young lady currently on the stage." Well, at least he has good taste. But also, young lady? Harley and I are both pushing twenty-seven.

"A man with good taste, I will have Harley head over as soon as she finishes her act." Judging by the chorus of "Cherry Bomb" by the Runaways currently booming through the club, she should be hanging upside down from the pole right now. The boob job she got just a few years ago defies gravity. I have no doubt she will lighten this man's wallet significantly by the time he leaves for the night. No one is better than Harley at prying money out of an asshole's grip.

"I wouldn't mind if you wanted to have a conversation with me in the meantime." He uncrosses his legs, manspreading like a fucking expert, making his meaning more than clear.

"Unfortunately, I don't converse in that manner. But I will make sure to send over a bottle of Macallan for you to enjoy while you wait." Fucking rich douchbags love to think they know whiskey. They choke down that nasty shit like it will make their dicks bigger.

He gives me a condescending smile and nod, hooking his ankle back over his knee now that he knows I won't be mounting his lap.

I turn, making sure to put a little less shake in my strut as I head over to the bar. I catch Harley's eye as she dismounts the pole with a seductive roll over her body. One flick of my eyes in the big spender's direction and she rolls her eyes, knowing she will need to pretend to find the guy interesting for the rest of the night.

Just another night pretending like men aren't the absolute fucking worst.

Chapter 3

Wesley

I swore I wouldn't do this again. It's been years since I gave into the temptation. But here I am, once again, sitting in my car on the small hill just on the edge of the Amoresville town line.

Across the street, the lights of Club Barely Over the Line shine like a lighthouse guiding men home. More like to their demise. Or at least their bank accounts. I have never once stepped inside the doors. And never plan to. Not because I think it is immoral or dirty. I've actually heard it is a pretty classy place. My elderly neighbor, Mrs. Winchester, is a frequent patron of the dance classes they offer to the community during the day, and she speaks very highly of the place. True, I have had to turn down her offers of a demonstration of her latest moves far too many times, but at least she is staying active at her age.

The reason I will never enter the front door of the only strip club in a two-hour radius is because the owner's family is my family's sworn enemy.

Also, I am in love with her.

Yeah, it's complicated.

When she first opened the club, I used to sit on this very spot and make sure she got home safe every single night. Or more often than not, every morning. I didn't trust the guys she got to act as security, especially since I often saw them in the parking lot with dancers, getting way more than a lap dance.

But I couldn't keep it up forever. Sitting in my car every night until three a.m. then needing to open the library by eight a.m. each morning just wasn't sustainable. Plus, she would have quite literally had my balls if she knew I was looking out for her.

Some days I wished I would get caught so I could just see her up close.

It's been five years since I stopped pulling the Batman act, but like any other addict, all I needed was one slip to be right back in the thick of my obsession. For me, that one push was seeing the pure anger on her face the day Uncle Burt, mayor of the town and enemy of all Halsteds, announced I would be running to serve as the next mayor of Amoresville.

The fire in her eyes. The way she stared right at me for the first time in years, even if it was with undiluted vitriol. It was like a hit of the strongest drug and I couldn't say no. All I want is for her to look at me again. To cause a reaction that isn't her looking right past me as if I don't exist.

The pull to sit up on this hill came roaring back. Not to protect, she's got that covered with the expensive security team she hired a few years back. No, I simply want a glimpse of her. I don't deserve a single thing from her after what I did when we were dumbass teenagers. After what my family has tried to do to hers over the years. But I can't help but wish anyway.

The back door to the club opens and the air in my lungs solidifies like cement. There she is. *Fuck.* How can one woman be so fucking gorgeous. She's tall, only a couple inches shorter than my six feet two inches. She's curvy, the transition from chest to waist to hips generous enough to give me whiplash. She's wearing a suit tonight, black but crisp and tailored to show off those curves while keeping it classy.

She unbuttons the jacket and my breath comes rushing back out so fast my vision goes blurry for a second. There is no shirt under the jacket. Just a bra that I'm not close enough to see the detail on. She props her hands on her hips, pushing the jacket back so the bare skin of her soft stomach is exposed to the night air. She tilts her head back, long strawberry blonde pulled up into a high ponytail swinging down between her shoulder blades.

I shouldn't be here. Shouldn't be watching her take a moment to herself. A moment she believes to be totally private. Yet I also can't tear myself away. I'll take any little snippet of Delia that I can; including creeping on her from across the street and accidentally seeing her rip down the ridiculous election signs Burt insists on hanging on every flat surface in town.

The parking lot out front is packed, so full in fact some cars are parked in the grass, too. But the back parking lot is totally fenced off with a gate that only opens if you have a key card.

Club Barely Over the Line is the only gentleman's club within two hours of Amoresville. The next closest club is over the border in Canada. As a result, people come from all over northern Pennsylvania for a little adult entertainment. Honestly, it was a little shocking to see how quickly the place blew up in popularity. So much so that there were definitely some problems at first. Guys that thought they were owed more than a dance. Dancers that didn't follow the rules. Even rumors of drugs at one point.

But Delia shut all that shit down, fast. Within a year of opening they had garnered a reputation for catering to high-end clients. They also paid their dancers incredibly well, used local businesses for as much as they could, and even donated regularly to charities in town, always under the club name. I'm fairly certain they do it just to piss off my uncle.

After a few minutes, the back door opens once again and for a split second I see Delia slump back against the cinderblock wall, looking more defeated than I have ever seen her. But then she snaps her spine straight, rebuttons her blazer, and turns to a guy I don't recognize but is obviously one of the security guys.

He's huge, I think his muscles have muscles. They have a short exchange and a wild part of me wants to know what they are talking about. Is there a fire she needs to put out? Are they friendly? More than friendly?

The thought pisses me off more than it should.

Disgusted with myself, I look away, an old familiar sharp pain searing through my chest. A little too aggressively, I shove my key into the ignition and start up my jeep, ready to stop torturing myself now that I've seen her.

One deep breath and I lift my eyes, ready to leave this behind. I tell myself *this* is the last time, but I am nothing if not self-aware and know that is a complete lie. But my eyes lock on her face. Her face pointed in my direction, her hand shielding her eyes from my headlights, which I forgot were on high beams when I got here and turned off my car. I can't see the expression on her face. Can't tell if she recognizes my car or realizes who it is parked in the middle of the empty field that overlooks her back parking lot.

Inside my chest my heart slams against my ribs, in fear or excitement I'm not sure. There is a sad part of me that wants her to know I'm here. For her. That even after nearly ten years I still think of her daily. Would it piss her off? Yeah, without a doubt. But I'll take her anger over cold dismissal any day.

But the moment slips away all too soon and she turns to follow her employee back into the club.

"You are pathetic, man." My hands shake as the adrenaline seeps out of my body. "As pathetic as you were in high school."

Chapter 4
Ten Years Ago

Delia

It's been two days since the cute, slightly nerdy, sad boy showed up in school and every girl in the sophomore class collectively swooned. Including me.

Living in a tiny mountain town where everyone knows each other means there isn't much in the way of variety for love interests. Every boy in my class is either distantly related or I've known them since we were in diapers.

It also helps that Wes is tall, has incredible hair, and has this untouchable big city mystique about him. Everywhere I go kids are whispering about him, whether about the revelation that his mom—the one that ran away from home at eighteen and never looked back—was in fact gay and married to a woman; the general tragedy of his story; or about how cute he is. This town loves nothing more than a good story, and this one doesn't even need to be exaggerated in any way.

Despite being the most popular topic of conversation in the area, I almost never see Wesley talking to anyone.

This morning I was late to school thanks to the shitty old truck Orion drives breaking down once again. As a result, I had to sprint to class and managed to slip into Honors English just in time. It was seriously like something out of those old *Indiana Jones* movies my dad loves to make us watch when it's his night to pick.

I only had enough time to glance at Wes as I shuffled to the back of the room and slumped down into my chair, Mrs. Wheeler glaring at me the entire way.

Then after class she asked me to stay back and assigned me another essay about punctuality even though I was technically on time. So, I missed him during the period change too.

"Bitch, what are you looking at?" Harley steps up next to me, her lunch tray filled with two slices of pizza, two sodas, and a single apple that I am sure the lunch lady forced onto her and will inevitably end up in the trash can.

My eyes sweep around the cafeteria. Wes has to have this lunch period. Almost all the sophomores do, so I don't know why I couldn't find him yesterday. After a minute, I realize nearly all the heads in the place are swiveling to look at the table in the back corner, the one farthest away from any windows with a wobbly leg that no one ever sits at. Except today there is a boy slouched down, a hoodie pulled over his head and a book open in front of him.

"We're changing tables." Without waiting for her to respond, I march over to where Wes is sitting.

"Holy shit, oh my god, are we seriously going to go sit with Mayor LickMyBalls' nephew? Your mom is going to be *pissed* if she finds out," Harley whispers in my ear, trying to keep up with my much longer stride.

She's not wrong. Mom has always hated the Lickinbill family, but that hatred went nuclear after Burt got elected mayor. More like appointed since no one ran against him. His first order of business was to try and block Mom from opening her cafe. It had been in the works for months, almost ready to open, then he started saying she needed a special business license, sent health inspectors out, the whole deal. But Mom is nothing if not stubborn. She passed every test he threw at her, then ignored the insane business license he tried to say she needed. Turns out there isn't much he can do about it. So technically, my mom is running a speak-easy style cafe.

"Shut up, Harley. Mom would want me to be friendly to a new kid who has had a shit time." Also true. I just don't know which side of Mom would win out: the side that hates Burt with the fire of a thousand suns or the maternal woman who would want me to be kind to someone that so obviously needs it.

"Okay, your funeral, girl."

* * *

Wesley

Being the new kid is something I've never experienced before. It's something I would have been happy with never experiencing, but here I am.

Back in New York, I had gone to the same school with the same kids since kindergarten. Sure, just my grade had more kids than this entire school, but I at least I knew where I fit in there. If I were still in the before times, I'd be heading to lunch with my friends. We'd gather around a table in the cafeteria, talking about the latest video game releases or our favorite episodes of a manga that's been running for more than thirty years.

But at Amoresville High School, there doesn't seem to be a cliché for nerds who game and are obsessed with all things manga and anime. Or at least not that I've found yet in my second day of school. Instead, I sit alone at a table in the corner, head buried in a volume of *One Piece*, trying to pretend like I'm not constantly teetering on the edge of crying into the shitty pizza this cafeteria serves.

"Oh my God, could they have drawn that chick's tits any bigger?"

The table shakes as an unfamiliar, high-pitched voice interrupts my reading. Two trays are unceremoniously dropped onto the table, both also holding slices of pizza along with sodas and the fruit the lunch lady apparently makes everyone take.

"Holy crap, Harley, you cannot talk like that at school." *That* voice I recognize. Delia Halsted. She's in my first period Honors English class. She was late again this morning. I thought about waiting for her outside the door, but thought that might seem creepy. "Hey, Wes."

Finally I look up from my book, peeking out from the edge of my hoodie. "Hey, Crash."

Delia sits directly across from me, her red hair piled on top of her head in a messy twist. Next to her is a girl I haven't seen in my two days at this school. She has blonde hair cut in a severe bob, the ends dyed a bright pink, which combined with the alarmingly neon green dress she's wearing means it would be impossible for her to blend in anywhere.

"Who the hell is Crash?" Harley looks back and forth between her friend and me.

Delia looks like she is trying to hold back a smile. "I'm guessing I am, because I literally crashed into him in the halls before English yesterday."

I nod a little, smiling back at the girl I haven't been able to stop thinking about since she collided with me.

Apparently bored with our little interaction, Harley leans across the table, ogling my book. "Man, I might need to start reading manga, because I would absolutely bang those chicks." She practically shouts the words and several people nearby look over their shoulders to sneer at her.

Delia shakes her head and laughs. "Ignore her, Harley hasn't even kissed a girl yet let alone anything more than that."

Harley slumps down onto the table, her cheek resting against her arm that now lays flat across the table. "I know, there are like no bi-curious girls in this town, it is so fucking sad."

As fast as she deflated, Harley pops back up to lean across the table looking at me with a weird amazement. "You're from New York City, I bet there were tons of bisexuals and lesbians at your last school. Oh wait, wasn't your mom gay? That is so fucking cool."

"Harley! Are you incapable of keeping a thought inside of your head?" Delia smacks her friend's shoulder lightly.

"Oh right, sorry. You probably don't want to talk about your dead lesbian moms, sorry."

Everyone in my life has avoided talking about my parents since they died six months ago. Harley just talking about them in this totally inappropriate way is somehow a relief. So much so that I can't help but huff out a laugh.

"It's okay. Yes, my moms were gay. I hate to break it to you, but their sexual orientation did not make them any cooler than other parents."

Harley seems supremely disappointed by this nugget of information. "Well damn. Thanks for crushing my dreams."

"Any time."

"Seriously, ignore her. If she wasn't my best friend I would." Delia shoots her friend a mock angry expression, who in turn sticks her tongue out. "So, Wes, how is your second day going? Didn't see you at lunch yesterday."

Before I can answer, Harley once again pipes up far louder than I would like. "Did they make you go see the school shrink? We have the same counselor for the whole district, and most days I'm pretty sure she just plays Sudoku on her phone all day. She must be thrilled to have a student with actual trauma."

"Harley!" Delia must say her friend's name in that tone a lot. The two of them are kind of entertaining to watch.

"What? They made me go see Mrs. Scott when my dad got arrested for the second time. Of course they are going to make him go see her." She leans over the table and stage whispers, "If you shed a tear or two she will let you lay down in the nurse's office for like two periods to gather yourself."

Without even taking a breath she returns to her usual too loud register and continues her stream of consciousness conversation that I barely need to contribute to. "I heard your uncle told you to stay away from Delia and her brother. Did he say anything about me?"

I shake my head.

"Damn, I was hoping being the low-class kid of a deadbeat dad convict and single mom would get me some sort of warning from Mayor Burp. I'll have to work on increasing my bad girl rep."

Delia seems to take her own advice and ignore Harley, returning her focus to me. "Seriously, how has it been so far?"

I just shrug, because honestly everything has sucked since the day I came home from school to find two cops waiting outside my house to tell me my moms were hit by a drunk driver on the New Jersey turnpike on their way to spend a weekend away for their anniversary.

"What are you reading?" Delia seems to know I don't particularly want to talk about how I'm doing, so I appreciate the change in subject.

"*One Piece*, it's a manga with about a million chapters in the series. I'm trying to read them all before I turn seventeen this summer."

Harley has gotten distracted by something on her phone and is completely ignoring us now that we aren't paying attention to her.

"Oh wow, what's it about?" Delia leans over the table to glance at the book laying open in front of me. A few strands of hair fall down into her face, and for the second time in two days I notice the freckles that are scattered over her face; not just her nose and cheeks, but her forehead, chin, neck, everywhere.

I start to wonder where else she has freckles, but stop the thought in its tracks. I can't think about the only person who has talked to me at this school naked. Which is going to be hard because she is so pretty it makes my stomach hurt a little. I've had crushes before, I'm a sixteen-year-old boy after all, but nothing like this.

"Um, it's about a band of pirates exploring the ocean and looking for a treasure that will make them the king of pirates."

Delia's eyes light up. "I'm reading something about pirates, too." She reaches down into her bag and pulls out a well-worn book. She holds it up to show me the cover; it features a man in a half-ripped open white shirt, muscles rippling as he clasps a woman against his chest.

Harley starts laughing and grabs the book to look at. "Look at you two with your matching books. Only Wes is reading about pirates looking for treasure, and DeeDee is reading about this guy plundering a young mistress's hidden treasure."

Delia grabs the book back. "Shut up, it's not even that raunchy." But the way her cheeks glow bright red makes me think maybe it is.

"You like romances?"

She shrugs, but lifts her chin in defiance. "Romance gets a bad rap because 99 percent of the time it is written for women by women, but it takes skill to make a reader feel something deeply from just ink on paper."

"No shade from me. I'll read just about anything you put in front of me." I push my glasses back up my nose since they've drifted down a little too far. "By the way, is there a library in this town? Burt won't let me buy the next volume in the series, so I need to see if I can borrow it."

Harley scoffs a little, "Fucking Burp. What an asshole."

She's not wrong. Burt has to approve every withdrawal I take from the account that was set up with the life insurance money and the proceeds from the sale of the brownstone my moms owned in Brooklyn. I've only been living with him for a week and I can tell already he is going to be a hardass about what I can and can't buy. Apparently manga is indecent and he doesn't want me wasting my money on it.

Delia elbows her friend in the side. "Yeah, if you don't have anywhere to be after school, we can show you where it is."

I nod, looking down at my tray. Delia Halsted and I are going to the library together, something that should not excite me as much as it is.

Chapter 5

Delia

Pulling into the driveway I spent my youth playing in with my brothers is different now that we are all getting older. Knox has a wife, which is weird as hell to say even though their first anniversary is right around the corner.

Orion has a live-in girlfriend and treats her son like he is his own blood.

Here I am still single, still running the strip club I opened out of spite for our mayor. As much as I love my family, sometimes coming to these dinners feels like regressing to the same kid I was in high school. The black sheep social outcast of the family.

It doesn't matter that I own a business, have dozens of employees, and make amazing money; my brothers treat me like the same annoying little girl with chubby cheeks and stains on her knees that I was back then. It's both a comfort and annoying as hell.

Unlike our family dinners from three years ago, before June and Brigid showed up on the scene, when I push open the front door chaos greets me.

Orion is on the ground with his dog Spruce and what for all intents and purposes is his son, Mica. The kid is cute as hell, he even makes me think maybe someday I might want one just like him.

"DeeDee!" Mica spots me and comes running. He's almost two now and runs everywhere. I'm not sure he even knows how to walk.

For instance, right at this very minute he is running straight for me, arms stretched out for a hug that when it makes contact nearly knocks me over. I stumble back a couple inches as his arms wrap around my knees, effectively tying them together.

"Roar!" He points back to his dad and my brother, who is knee-crawling toward us with his elbows tucked into his sides and his hands held in front of him T-Rex style.

"Oh no! Is the dinosaur coming to get us?"

He looks up at me with wide happy eyes, a fake ass frown comically pulling down his face.

"Don't worry, kid, Auntie Dee's got this." I scoop him up in my arms and we go sprinting past Orion who reaches his arms out a few inches to try and get his son. "You can't have him, T-Rex, he's mine." I tuck Mica's little body against my chest and we both go charging into Orion's much bigger body, knocking him over.

Orion rolls onto his back and waves his tiny little T-Rex arms around like he can't get up, all the while Mica screeches with laughter.

"Okay, kids, dinner is ready. You too Mica." Even though I can't see Mom from where we are on the floor, I can hear the happiness in her voice. I know she still misses our dad, probably always will, but with each new addition to our family I have slowly watched her come more and more into herself.

I place Mica gingerly onto the floor and climb to my feet.

"Oh no, Delia, I'm so sorry." Brigid comes through the front door along with June. "Looks like Mica got something on your shirt."

I crane my neck around to try and see the back of my shoulder. Why did I think it was a good idea to wear a pristine white t-shirt? The beautiful fabric is now smeared in what looks like grape jelly.

"Sorry, sis. I let him have PB&J crackers to tide him over until dinner." Orion looks sheepishly at me. PB&J crackers were a staple in our house as kids. Literally just saltines with peanut butter and grape jelly smooshed between. It is a fucking messy snack, but so delicious.

"No big deal. It's just a shirt."

June skirts around me carrying a basket filled with fresh eggs in the crook of her elbow. "Do you want to borrow something?"

"Nah, I'm good, thanks though."

With that put to rest, we all go about shuffling around the huge dining room table that takes up half the first floor of Knox's old farmhouse. The place looks so different from when we were kids. June and Knox spent last winter painting nearly every room in the house. Now the place felt like walking into the middle of their love for each other. A soft robin's egg blue graces each wall with a mural of wispy daisies painted along the back wall. Pops of yellows and reds in the accessories make the place pop. I love it. But it also makes me sad that the home I knew really is gone now. True, I haven't lived here since Dad passed away and it became too painful to be here without him, but having the place looking the same felt like a touchstone I could return to time and again when I needed to feel anchored.

"Delia," June places a hand on my shoulder, the clean one, "you sure you don't want me to grab a shirt?" Her eyes are soft and her voice low.

"I'm sure, thanks."

As I sit at the table it occurs to me that we might actually run out of seats at the table someday soon. Mom sits at the head of the table, with Mica sitting in a highchair between her and Brigid. Then comes Orion, one arm suspiciously hidden beneath the table, most likely placed on his girlfriend's leg, which is both sweet and gross. I sit next to Orion, across from me is Meredith, June's mother and my business manager for the last year. She moved to town at the same time as her daughter, though their relationship is super complicated. June is next with a space open beside her for Knox, who is still carrying food to the table.

There is room for maybe three of four more people at the end of the table. I have no doubt eventually both my brothers will add more kids to the mix and those spaces will quickly be filled.

Will there even be room for my own additions someday? Do I want that? I honestly don't know.

The aroma of garlic and cheese wafts through the air, breaking me out of my increasingly depressing thoughts.

Knox hands a bowl of pasta to Mom and another to June. The next few minutes are spent dishing up the food, which looks freaking amazing. All three of the Halsted kids have our mother to thank for our cooking abilities. Roxanne Halsted made sure both her sons would be able to cook for themselves, she wouldn't stand for any patriarchal gender roles in her house. And since I wanted to do everything my brothers did, I got in on the fun too. Don't worry, Mom made sure to balance it out with lots of sports practices and time in the fields for me.

Days spent in the kitchen with Mom making pasta from scratch, canning tomato sauce, baking muffins, they are some of the best memories I have. I think it is why I still cook nearly all of my meals from scratch to this day. When I'm not at the club, researching some new hobby or business opportunity, or hanging out with Harley, you'll find me in the kitchen cooking up something new I found online.

By the time the food makes its way around to me, there are several conversations in full swing around the table. Mom and

June chat about the new chicken breeds they plan to get next spring. Knox sits between them shaking his head trying to look grumpy, but has the slightest hint of a smile curling up the sides of his mouth.

Brigid is trying to coax Mica into eating some of the pasta while Spruce sits at his feet hoping for some castoffs.

Orion and Meredith are deep in a conversation about business plans.

"I should be able to get the showroom up and running by early spring if everything goes according to plan," Orion twirls some pasta onto his fork and shovels it into his mouth.

"We might want to talk about increasing the prices of some of your pieces to account for the additional overhead." Meredith is a retired bank CFO, but she couldn't just sit around knitting in her retirement, so once she moved to town a couple years ago she took on a bunch of clients for tax season, then that turned into a full financial and business planning firm.

"Wait, you're opening a shop? Since when is Burt letting a Halsted get a business license in town?" The only reason Mom was able to open the cafe was because Burt hadn't yet been elected mayor when her plans started. His predecessor, another Lickinbill, wasn't quite as much of an asshole. Burt tried to block the café from opening, but didn't succeed.

Orion and Meredith exchange a look, and at the end of the table everyone falls silent.

"Well, Burt is only going to be mayor for a few months, honey, so things will be changing," Mom says cautiously.

"You guys are fooling yourselves if you think anything is going to be different when Wesley is mayor." I stab my fork into a piece of lettuce. "Same bullshit in a different package."

"Actually, Wesley has been talking a lot about how we can make the downtown more attractive to visitors, and part of that is more businesses," June chimes in. She took on a consulting role with Burt on increasing tourism in town when she moved here. She has actually done a lot to attract people from the bigger towns around the state. The fall festival is an especially big draw, the club even saw a bump in revenue that weekend. "I think he might actually be good for the town."

I look around the table and see Brigid is nodding her head, but Knox and Orion both stare at the table and Mom is a little too interested in how much Mica is or isn't eating.

"Wait, are you saying you guys actually *want* another fucking Lickinbill to be mayor of Amoresville? How many times have we sat at this very table—" I knock my knuckles against the wood "—and complained about *that* family killing the spirit of the town *our* family founded?"

"He's not a Lickinbill. Not really," Brigid adds, her voice brittle. For some reason she and Wesley formed a bit of a friendship when she moved to town. She and Mica are frequent attendees at Story Hour at the library where Wesley serves as town librarian. "He's a Goldman, and a good person. I think he'll make a good Mayor."

Beside me Orion shifts uncomfortably. He has just as much of a reason to hate Wesley as I do. Everything that went down back in high school changed the course of my brother's life as much as it did mine.

"Orion, you're okay with this?"

He sighs and slumps back in his chair. "It's not like it makes a difference. No one else is running. He's going to be mayor. It's been ten years, it might be time to just—" he shrugs and looks down at the edge of the table, picking at an imperfection in the wood grain "—let it go or something. Everything turned out fine in the end."

His gaze slides over to Brigid, the love of his life. Yeah, everything turned out fine for him. But I still can't trust a man with anything, let alone my heart after what Wesley pulled when we were sophomores. Not to mention the two years after when I had to see him every day in the halls at school.

"This is bullshit. We should have more than one option for mayor. Literally anyone could run against him and they would win."

Knox huffs and shakes his head. "Come on, Dee. You know that's not true. Not every Lickinbill has run unopposed and they still won."

"But how long has it been since anyone actually put up a good fight in one of these elections? Not since I've been voting age? About since you turned eighteen, Mom?"

Her soft green eyes look down at me with sadness. "You know the answer to that."

"Exactly. Spruce could run against Wesley in the election and would win."

"Hey, keep my dog out of this."

"Seriously, if the town could have learned to spell CuGo's name he would have won during the last election," I insist.

CuGo is the vicious Canada Goose who has lived on Knox's farm ever since some dumbass kids injured him by throwing rocks at a flock of geese as they flew overhead. The giant bird came down in one of the fields and Knox couldn't just let him starve to death, so he took him in and the rest is history. During the last election someone started a write-in campaign to get the goose elected mayor instead of Burt. But no one could agree on how to say or spell his name and half the votes were thrown out.

"Well, CuGo isn't running this year and the election is only a month away, so I think it's time you accepted Wesley is going to be mayor." Orion shrugs and they all turn back to their various conversations.

My mind, however, is still totally occupied with the injustice of yet another in a long line of Lickinbills getting to be mayor without even trying. Why should it be so fucking easy for them to just run this town like their own little puppet shows?

The posters plastered all over town with Wesley's stupid, and yes stupid hot because of course Harley is not wrong about that, face. He should have to fight to be mayor, not just walk into the position like he's being coronated instead of elected.

Maybe I can do something about it. Kick up a little dust. Dole out a little payback. Get justice for the town and me.

Chapter 6

Wesley

Despite living in Amoresville for over a decade, there is only one place I feel truly at home: the library. It is as true now as it was at sixteen when I lost my parents and landed on Burt's front porch.

Something about the quiet, being surrounded by stories—both true and fictional—makes each breath come easier and the roaring of thoughts in my head quiet to a dull murmur. Only one other thing has made me feel at ease since my life got turned upside down. But I ruined that.

"Mr. Goldman, what the—" the kid looks around the library, even going up onto his tiptoes to look over the other side of the desk. Joe leans forward, voice low "—hell." He slams the stack of books I recommended last week on the desk, the first five books in the *Animorphs* series. "Are you trying to traumatize me?"

I chuckle a little. "Sorry, kid, this is a canon event we all must go through. If it's too much, you can stop there." I take the stack of books I've been holding to the side all week and plop them right next to the first five. "Or, you can forge ahead and seal your fate."

His eyes slide over to the next five books. Joe is tall for his age, nine going on forty. Hair cut in a choppy bowl cut that I am fairly certain was self-performed, and I can't quite tell if the baggy clothes are a choice or a product of his circumstances. Joe's dad left a few years ago with stories of getting a job on an oil rig and he would send money home. The money never showed up and neither did his dad. His mom does the best she can from what I see, but she can't afford babysitters and still needs to work. So most afternoons Joe comes straight to the library from school. He reads like words are oxygen. I understand him probably more than he realizes.

"Ugh." He pulls the books closer and swings his ratty backpack around from his shoulder. "You know I can't stop now. But I'm sending you my therapy bills when I'm old like you."

I fight to hold my smile back. Who knew twenty-eight now qualified for geriatric status?

"Deal. Good news, there are like forty more where that came from. I'll see if I can track down the whole series, they aren't always easy to find."

"Thanks, man. Is the computer lab open?"

I nod and after he finishes stashing the books into his bag, he heads back to the room where we hold our weekly Minecraft night.

A ghost of a smile stays glued to my face as I absentmindedly scan in Joe's returns along with the stacks of books I pulled from the return bin outside. I organize the books on carts, ready for my part-timers to re-shelve them in the morning. Thankfully, I have a community member that comes in and volunteers their time for the Minecraft and Lego clubs, two things I never got into and would be completely useless at leading kids in activities. If there is one thing I've learned about kids since I originally got hired at the Amoresville Area Library, it is that they will call you on your bullshit so fast it will make you feel like you just got off the *Gravitron*.

Just as I get to work planning out the winter-themed events for December, the front doors swing open and the absolute last person I want to see comes walking in carrying an armful of yard signs with my face on them.

"Afternoon, Uncle Burt." I give him a tight smile, rounding the desk to take the signs from him. "I told you no more signs, this is completely unnecessary."

He gives me the same cartoonish frown I became all too familiar with as a teen. It's the *if only I had been in your life from the start you would have turned out so much better* expression. "Wesley, you need to take this seriously. Especially since you won't use the Lickinbill name on any of the signs. We need to build name recognition."

"I'm pretty sure the voters of our town will recognize my name since it will be the only one listed under *Mayor* on the ballot."

Burt started talking about me running for mayor over a year ago. In Amoresville, mayors can serve for three four-year terms. My uncle, the last in a long line of Lickinbills, is coming up to the last few months of his last term and seems to be getting more and more manic each day.

I don't consider myself an easily riled person, but the day he suggested I drop my mothers' last name in favor of the Lickinbill name, I nearly lost it on him. Goldman might not be the most common name in the town, but it was the name both my mothers carried. Burt hates it when I remind him of anything having to do with his sister Mary Goldman, formerly Lickinbill. It wasn't even a question when she met and married the love of her life that she would take the new last name. She was all too ready to ditch the name of the family that had shunned her as a teen when she came out as a lesbian.

If I had any other choice as a teenager, I would have gone literally anywhere else. But Burt was the last living family member I had left, and I wasn't allowed to try for emancipation at fifteen. Other reasons have kept me here into adulthood.

"Wesley, I need you to take this seriously. You are carrying on an important legacy."

So he keeps telling me. But I can't help the twist in my stomach that accuses me of betraying my mother by going along with my uncle's plan.

As I have learned over the years, it is usually easier to just go along with Burt's strict rules. I've learned how to gently steer him toward the slightly less insane side of the road over time. But outright fighting him on anything will just make his heels dig in even deeper.

"Sorry, Burt. I'll try to do better."

He gives me a swift nod. "Good, now go grab the rest from my car. There are more of these out in the trunk and a box with more flyers in the back seat. Someone keeps ripping them down or drawing inappropriate figures on them."

Honestly, I found the one of me with a very phallic-looking hot dog in my hand pretty inspired. There is no doubt in my mind who the vandal is; it can only be one of two people. Delia or Harley. Two names I never dare to bring up around Burt, so I just ignore the last comment and make my way out to get the rest of the election signs that I despise.

Burt has parked his shiny Lincoln at the curb, parked illegally with the flashers on. Not that it will matter; we have no police in town and next to no car traffic in the square. His trunk is already open, the sheer volume of signs lying there honestly taking me back a step.

There are dozens of yard signs with my stupid face on each and every one. Burt practically had to drag me to the photographer to get the headshots done. Quite the feat for a man five inches shorter and with about a hundred pounds less muscle.

"What are we looking at?" Brigid, the owner of the meta-physical crystal and herb shop down the street, and cause of many rants from my uncle, wheels her stroller up next to me. When she moved to town last year, Brigid and I became something between acquaintances and friends. I think if it weren't for the fact that her live-in boyfriend is a Halsted, we could be friends. "Oh my. Are there even that many houses in town?"

"Probably not." All the same, I pick up as many as I can muster and tuck them under one arm. "Can you pick up the rest and put them under my other arm?"

"Sure." Brigid locks the wheels on the stroller in place.

Mica points to the library and says clear as day, "Book."

"That's right, baby, we're going to pick out a couple new books to read since you were so good today."

"What do you think, Mica, still on your bear kick?" The last time they were in, Mica picked out three different versions of *Brown Bear Brown Bear*, even though his mom insisted they already had it at home. "I got some new options for you."

This is apparently his plan, because he starts clapping his hands and saying bear over and over.

Brigid shoves the rest of the signs under my arm and we make our way across the sidewalk. "Let me get the door for you."

It takes some work, but we manage to get me, all the signs, and the stroller through the door without any injuries or property damage.

"Hello, Burt." Despite the hell my uncle put her through when she was trying to open her business, Brigid is always nothing but nice to him. I think she pities him more than anything.

Burt nods at her but doesn't say a word.

"Well, I hear there are new books on bears upstairs for us to check out. Have a good day." She wheels around the desk back toward the elevator behind the non-fiction section that goes up to the second floor where we have the children's section.

"Why can't that woman never wear something with color. It's all black all the time. Not very ladylike." Burt scrunches his brow up as he watches Brigid head through the stacks. "Makes perfect sense that she would fall in with *that* family."

He means the Halsteds, but almost never actually says their name.

"I thought I saw some of those indecent items Roxanne used to sell in the window at her little magic shop. You should bring up the need to keep our town family-friendly during your speech next week."

I swear, a literal record scratch echoes through my head.

"Excuse me, what speech?"

"The speech at your official campaign fundraising dinner." He says this as if I have heard anything about it before. Trust me, a fundraising dinner has never been a topic of conversation. I would remember; the mere mention of public speaking makes my stomach turn. "We have thirty of my closest friends, with the deepest pockets in town, coming to the dinner. These signs don't pay for themselves you know."

"Burt, I told you I did not want to take donations for this. It is pointless, I have no opponent. There is no one to run against. No one to campaign against. I turned in the paperwork and no one else did, so unless the town suddenly learns how to spell a goose's name, I will be mayor."

Burt turns to me, and I can see immediately that fighting him on this dinner was the wrong move. Bringing up the goose that came a little too close to beating him last election doesn't help.

He folds his arms across his chest, trying to puff it out as if it will intimidate me if he looks a little bigger. "This is the way things are done. It is important to follow the traditions of those that have come before you. Now, I have already drafted a speech for you—"

Unable to talk about this anymore, I turn and leave Burt to talk to himself about the speech while I deposit the signs in the library supply closet. Maybe I'll get lucky and a big bottle of bleach will fall on them.

Chapter 7
Ten Years Ago

Delia

"Harley, you have to come with us to the library," I plead with my friend.

"Girl, I would if I could, but I have detention for like the tenth time this year and it's only the first marking period." Harley sips from a can of Red Bull. Should a teenager be drinking Red Bull like it is water? Probably not, but the girl is a freaking caffeine addict. Mom even tried hiring her at the cafe but had to fire her because she was drinking her profits.

"What did you do this time?" I love Harley just as much as my brothers. Actually, maybe more since she never put a bunch of frogs under the blankets of my bed while I slept.

"Told Mr. Casey that he would have made a truly fugly Juliet if he had played her back in Shakespeare's era."

I can't help but laugh; I don't even know where she comes up with this shit. "That doesn't even make sense."

Harley shrugs. "Doesn't need to make sense to be true."

"Whatever, just skip detention. You've done it before. Wes is going to think I'm trying to get him alone if you don't come." Harley is famous for skipping out on class or detention. I even found her in my brother's car once napping when she didn't show up to Geography.

"I can't. Mom is on one of her sober jags where she pretends she is actually a parent. If they call to let her know I skipped, I'll never hear the end of it." I don't know who is worse, Harley's mom or dad. Sure, her dad is a criminal who left them when they were little, but her mom is a drunk who barely even remembers to feed Harley. "Besides, that boy obviously has a hard-on for you. He literally couldn't keep his eyes off you at lunch and there was a book with huge boob illustrations right in front of him."

"Oh shit, here he comes—shut up right now."

"Oh, you want me to shut up!" Harley says even louder than she normally is. "You don't want me to talk about how you think Wes—"

I slap my hand over her loud mouth and she keeps talking into my palm. Thankfully, her words are totally muffled. Wes definitely thinks we're weird though.

"Uhhh hi there." He pushes his glasses up the bridge of his nose, something I've noticed he does a lot. "Ready to go?"

Harley licks my hand and I pull it away with a yelp. "Eww, you are so weird."

"Yup, and proud of it." She bounces on the balls of her feet, the caffeine surge of her Red Bull obviously starting. She's going to annoy the shit out of whatever underpaid teacher is covering detention today. "Well, I am off to serve my time. Like father, like daughter. You too have fun on your date."

And before I can beat her with her own bookbag for that comment, my best friend takes off running at full speed, full on cackling as she goes.

"Ignore her."

"You say that a lot."

I sigh. Yeah, I do. "She's great, just a lot."

"Better to be a lot and yourself than a little and hide yourself."

Whoa. Did this kid just get philosophical on a Tuesday afternoon? "Good point. So in the spirit of full transparency, how much trouble will you get in if you are seen with me?"

Wes winches. "Honestly, I'm not sure. Burt gripes about your family a lot. More than is probably normal for a full-grown man."

"Yeah, not much to do in this town. Holding grudges is like a hobby around here." I turn toward the exit of the parking lot and start walking, Wesley keeping in step with me as we go. "I'm going to take you the back way then. It is a little longer, but avoids Town Hall so he won't see us."

"Hey, Dee, where are you going?" Orion pulls up next to us in his shitty pick-up truck. "Dad's expecting us."

Shit, I totally forgot that we're supposed to help Dad with harvesting and braiding the garlic tonight. "Can you tell Dad I got detention and I'll be late?"

My brother's eyes dart behind me to Wes. "Delia..."

"Orrie, it's fine. We're just going to the library. I'll walk to the cafe and ride home with Mom, I promise." I give him my *please don't make me seem like a loser in front of a cute boy* eyes.

He looks doubtful, but after a second shakes his head and shifts the truck back into drive. "I hope you know what you're doing."

Yeah, me too.

* * *

Wesley

My parents were never very strict. To be fair, I was a boring-ass kid that never gave them a reason to need to crack down on me. So I'm not exactly sure how to navigate blatantly going against my uncle's wishes and hanging out with a Halsted.

But I also don't care what happens, because I just like being around Delia.

I know Harley was just stirring up trouble when she said we were going on a date. But I also really liked the idea of it. The only dates I went on at my old school were to formal dances with girls I never hung out with again after the event. I just never felt the push to pursue anyone like that.

Looking at Delia, walking two feet to my left, yeah, I feel the push. I've known her for two days and I desperately want to bridge the space between us and take her hand in mine. But I'm not sure if that is too soon.

I never asked my moms how to talk to girls or navigate these situations. They died six months ago, when I was still fifteen. I spent my sixteenth birthday in a foster home with people that were nice enough, but they weren't my people.

It took social services a long time to find Burt. Mom did a great job of erasing her time here in Amoresville from her history. She legally changed her last name as soon as she and Mama got married. She even got it changed on her birth certificate. Never talked to anyone from town, didn't mention it in any articles after she started getting notoriety in the theater scene. Finally, they got a hold of her original birth certificate from Pennsylvania, and with a name like Lickinbill, it wasn't long after that before they found Burt.

"So, is AHS a lot different from your old school?" Delia is wearing a pair of flare jeans with a graphic t-shirt that says *The Book Was Better*, which is a sentiment I wholeheartedly agree with. Her hands are down at her sides, and I wonder how she would react if I did try to interlace our fingers. Just the thought makes my heart race in a not totally uncomfortable way.

"Yeah, definitely. A lot less kids. The teachers are older and more strict. But the class sizes are a lot smaller, too. Believe it or not the food here is actually a lot better."

"Wow, that is sad. Do you miss living in the city? It must seem weirdly quiet here."

I shrug, but realize she probably doesn't see it since we are both staring at the sidewalk, with me sneaking glances every now and again. I should be paying attention to where we are going, Delia is taking quite a few turns down smaller side streets and even between houses. There is no way I'll ever be able to re-trace this route.

"Yeah, there is this omni-present background buzz in Brooklyn of just cars and sirens and people that only dims slightly at night. But here there are some loud-ass bugs, and Burt's neighbor has chickens, so the rooster wakes me up at the literal ass-crack of dawn every morning."

"Yeah, you get no sympathy from me on that front. My mom collects chickens like they are *Pokémon*. Someday she'll catch 'em all. One year she had really shitty luck with chicks and ended up with five roosters but didn't have the heart to cull any of them. We still have every. Single. One."

"Jesus, do you live on a farm or something?"

Delia finally looks over at me and gives me a dumbfound look. "I keep forgetting you know nothing about the town and everyone in it. I'm so used to everyone knowing everything about me already. Yeah, we have the big farm just on the edge of town. Like literally the town line runs through our back field. It's been in my dad's family pretty much forever. His family is like the fourth or fifth oldest in town. My mom's side were the first settlers. Your family were the founders of the town, the ones to set up the actual town. Let's just say there is a lot of history between our various ancestors. So much that I'm not sure how much of it is real and how much is just a really bad game of telephone where the details get distorted."

Huh. I had no idea it was like that. Burt just said the Halsteds were bad eggs and didn't elaborate. "Wow, I had no idea. Mom never talked about where she came from. Anytime I asked she just said she was from a small town full of small people."

"She wasn't wrong."

"I don't know, I've met at least one that seems pretty great." I notice we've drifted closer together on the sidewalk. No longer clinging to the opposite edges of the concrete, but side by side walking down the center. I shift toward her, pushing her slightly with my shoulder so she knows I am talking about her.

A furious blush darkens her cheeks and I wish I could reach out and touch the flushed skin, see if it is warm. "But seriously, other than the obvious, what do you miss most about New York?"

I don't dwell on the obvious, not wanting to bring down the moment. Instead, I think about what it is I wish I could pick up from my neighborhood and plop down here in Amoresville. "What I really miss is being able to walk in any one direction and find any type of food I can think of. There are like two restaurants in this entire town, it's weird."

"You have Burt to thank—"

We make another turn and like her saying his name summoned him, Burt appears about a block ahead of us, his back to us. I grab Delia's arm and drag her back around the corner we just came from. "Shit, it's my uncle."

I peek around the corner to check if he saw us, but thankfully he's walking away from us none the wiser.

When I look back at Delia, I realize in my rush to hide, I pressed her against the brick wall of the nearest building. My hands rest on either side of her shoulders, our bodies pressed together from chest to knees.

Our gazes meet but neither of us says a word. My heart slams against my ribs. We're so close. It would be so easy to just lean in and brush my lips against hers. Does she want that?

"Is he gone?" she whispers.

"Who?" Do people other than the two of us exist?

Red creeps up her cheeks. I can practically see the blood vessels in her skin dilating right before my eyes. It is fascinating.

"Burt. Is he still there?"

Oh, right. My uncle. I peek back out, trying to get myself under control. "No, he's gone now."

"Maybe I should go in first, just to be safe. Wait five minutes then meet me in the legal section."

I nod absently, still thinking about her pink cheeks. And lips. But then she ducks under my arm and speed walks into the library.

Wait, did she say the legal section?

Chapter 8

Delia

"Hey, did someone hack into your phone?"

Harley barges into my townhouse, no knocking, and drops her giant bag on the floor. Her shoes get kicked off and land where they may, to be left there until she leaves. She treats my place like an extension of her own house just down the street.

"No, why?" I click around on my laptop, trying to make a logo that is both eye-catching and not so over the top it will put off the more conservative members of our community.

"Because some psycho texted me from your number and said they are running for mayor." She plops down next to me in one of the wooden chairs surrounding my small dining room table.

I turn to her, sticking out my hand for her to shake. "Nice to meet you, I'm psycho and I am running to be your mayor." I plaster the biggest, fakest smile on my face.

She fakes a gag, holding her hand over her mouth. "Sorry, I think I just threw up a little in my mouth."

I flip her off, then turn back to my computer.

"You know the election is less than a month away, right?" She leans over the corner of the table, checking out the design I've been working on. "That has less genitalia than your normal designs."

"Well, I didn't want to alienate half the town right off the bat."

"Funny that never occurred to you when you offered to make the sign for your mom's cafe. And the grocery store. And—"

"Okay, okay, yes I might try to sneak in a little spice to the very free graphic design work I have done for our family and friends." I adjust the saturation on the blue shade I'm using for the background, taking it from navy closer to royal. "But this is important. We cannot have another fucking Linkinbill as mayor."

"Technically he will be Mayor Goldman. Not Lickinbill."

"A rose by any other name will still stab the fuck out of you with its thorns given the chance."

Harley leans back in her chair. The pressure of her eyes drilling into the side of my face is actually making my skin heat. "Why are you really doing this?"

Why am I doing this? I prod at the years'-old bruise that feels like it sits just below the surface of my entire existence. One of those bruises you can feel, but the rest of the world can't see yet. But pushing on that particular button immediately has me recoiling and shutting the door on the history that caused it.

"Because generations of his family have treated this town like their own personal puppet show and I'm tired of it." Is it one hundred percent the truth? No. Is it at least a part of it? Yes. "This town, the people in it, may have their faults, but they don't deserve another four years of someone from the Lickinbill family tree telling them how they can and can't run their businesses or how long their grass can be or what color they can paint their houses."

Yes, at some point every single one of those things have been written into town ordinances so that the whole town looks like a white/grey/beige/blue with exactly one-inch-long grass and shops that sell Burt approved goods. Well, except for Tiger's Boutique, owned by Brigid—who somehow managed to get it past Burt that she was opening a literal pagan metaphysical boutique. I still don't know how she managed to get away with that.

Harley's silence lets me know she does not buy my little tirade.

"Besides, I think I would be a good mayor. I own and run a very successful business—"

"—a den of sin according to most people in this town—"

"—I have done countless hours of community service by helping local businesses rebrand—"

"—sneaking penises and vaginas into their logos—"

"—half the town used my notary services—"

"—And you forgot to get your license renewed, so you no longer offer those services—"

"My family founded this town. We have a literal statue dedicated to my great, great, great infinity grandparents."

"A statue placed on the spot they first bumped uglies."

I slump back in my chair. "You don't think I can do this." Not a question. A statement of fact. The thing I love about Harley is she doesn't pull any punches. I always know whatever I get from her is what I need to hear.

Harley leans forward and picks my hand up from where it limply rests on my mouse. "I think you can do anything you set your mind to. As you have proved time and time again with each new adventure you undertake and ultimately succeed at. However, I do wonder if you *should* do this and if you are doing it for the right reasons."

"I just..." I take a deep breath, collecting all the frayed edges of my thoughts and emotions and trying to braid them back into some semblance of order. "I don't know if I can take seeing him all over town day in and day out for the next four years. Right now he pretty much keeps to himself. He's in the library when I'm in town and then I'm at the club when he isn't working, so we never have to interact. But as mayor, he'll be involved in so much. Events. Council meetings. Decisions that affect the people I love. Knowing he exists at all is rough enough. But to have to actually deal with his existence in a real way feels like—" I wave my hands around in wild circles "—like a lot."

The worst part is I honestly thought I was past this shit. It was a decade ago. It was two truly sucky years in high school then he went to college and I stayed home in Amoresville to take care of Mom and the cafe while she cared for my sick dad. I didn't have time in those years to even think about Wesley Goldman.

Except when his fucking uncle started a crusade to get The Bean shut down while Mom was distracted. I fought like hell to keep the cafe open without stressing Mom out more than she already was. All the while, I would curse the whole Lickinbill family line, including Wesley.

But that was years ago, and aside from one small insignificant blip right after Dad died, I've never looked back.

As a twenty-seven-year-old woman, I should not still be so focused on something that happened when I was sixteen. But here I am, getting ready to run a write-in campaign for mayor of a town that I love and loath in equal measure.

Harley wraps her arms around my shoulders and pulls me close. "That is a lot. And if you think running for and possibly winning the campaign is what is going to make you feel happy, I say go for it. I actually do think you would make a good mayor, but prepare yourself for the rest of the town not seeing it the same." She pulls back, leaving her hands on my shoulders as her dark brown eyes hold my gaze. "I hate to interrupt this touching moment of friendship, but the smell in here is about to make me spontaneously orgasm, so please tell me that you have been stress baking and not that I am having a weird symptom for a heart attack."

"Oh shit!" I leap up from the chair, nearly knocking over Harley in the process. But the woman has reflexes like a cat and always lands on her feet. "I almost forgot I have croissants in the oven."

"Bitch, if they aren't burnt there better be one on a plate with my name on it within the next ten seconds. Let's be real, I'll take a burnt one too."

Steam wafts from the oven the moment I pull the door open, clouding the glasses I only wear at home ever since investing in contacts. Thankfully, the flaky pastries are a perfect golden brown. Baking is my one true love in life. Cooking has always been a tradition in our family. But baking feels like it is just for me.

I discovered it while I was running the cafe for my mom in the years she had to nurse my dad though his battle with brain cancer. I still bake a lot of the sweets Mom sells at the cafe, but as the club has gotten more and more popular, time for baking has gotten harder and harder to find. The club, something I started ninety-nine percent out of spite, has quickly taken over my entire life.

"You want some tea, too?" I call out from the kitchen.

"Sure. Do you have some with less tea and more coffee?"

"You really need to cut back on the caffeine, girl. You are going to have a coronary." Despite my protests, I pull out the pitcher of cold brew that is always stocked and ready to go in my fridge.

"I would rather die than give up my bean water."

Grabbing two glasses, I lace the inside of the glass with my homemade vanilla salted caramel, add ice, and pour the cold brew. Some oat milk and more caramel for me, and nothing else for Harley's. She says cream and sugar are for the weak.

Two minutes later, I am placing a plate of croissants along with dishes of butter and jam on the table, followed up with the coffees.

"If you had any interest in vagina, I would ask you to marry me right now."

"Bullshit, the six months we lived together were literal hell. Between you bringing in strays until the whole place was covered in animal fur and me leaving my clumps of hair all over the bathroom, I'm surprised we are even still friends." Harley's penchant for picking up any hurt animal off the street and bringing it home became a real problem when she showed up after her shift at the club with a literal raccoon. "I love you, but we would kill each other within days if we tried it again." I tear one of the still hot croissants in half and swipe some butter and jam across the perfectly soft interior, taking in my friend's appearance for the first time since she walked in unannounced. "Um, what the hell are you wearing?"

Harley's sense of fashion is unique to say the least. But never, in the history of my friendship with her, has she ever worn plain black pants and a white t-shirt. Hell, the shirt isn't even tight enough to show off the new tits she is so proud of.

My best friend rolls her eyes as she chews a bite of the croissant. "I know, this outfit is giving me hives. But Rosie is hosting an event at the B&B tonight and she asked me to help out since apparently everyone on her staff is out with the flu." Rosie is Harley's younger half-sister, and they could not be more opposite. They share the same deadbeat dad, but while Rosie was raised by a loving mother and grandmother who doted on her at every turn, Harley was raised by a woman more concerned with where she was getting her next hit or drink than if Harley was fed.

Rosie is sweet and soft spoken. She owns the local B&B and the only decent place to stay within twenty miles. The only other place is the motel about a half mile down from the club and it is so disgusting even the dirtbags that get lap dances in sweatpants won't stay there.

"Wait, she asked *you* for help?"

"I know, she must be desperate. Plus, I owe her for taking that litter of kittens last month." It isn't that Harley and Rosie don't get along, they do. They just aren't as close as I am to my brothers. Everyone in town knows what Harley does for a living, and Rosie does her best to keep that away from the B&B. "It is some bullshit thing Burt is doing. She doesn't care enough about Burt to find someone else. And obviously can't ask you since that would cause a whole other host of problems."

"Wait, Burt is holding an event at the B&B?"

"Mmhmmm," Harley responds around a mouthful of croissant.

"What kind of event?"

"A dinner I think? It is like catered and everything. He hired someone from Wellsboro."

"Like, a fundraising dinner?"

Harley shrugs, swiping a dollop of jam from her finger with her tongue. "Want me to text and ask?"

"Duh!"

With an exaggerated eye roll, she plucks her phone from her pocket and types out a quick text. It doesn't take long before her phone dings with a response. Unlike my brothers, apparently Rosie actually responds to text in a timely manner.

"It is a fundraising dinner for Wesley," she reads off the screen. "Don't tell Delia. Oops, too late."

"Are you thinking what I'm thinking?" I stand from my chair, shoving the last of the croissant into my mouth and speed walking down the hallway to my bedroom.

"Unfortunately I do know what you're thinking," she shouts after me. "And you are going to owe me big time."

I pull clothes from my closet, dropping them as soon as I register what they are. Why are all my clothes so slutty? Do I not have a single responsible, respectable piece of clothing? Oh right, I own a strip club. Of course I don't own anything conservative enough for a political gathering.

Finally, I pull a black pencil skirt from the years I was obsessed with *Mad Men* followed by a white button-down shirt that I am fairly certain I stole from a hookup a few years ago and never returned.

When I turn, Harley is leaning against the doorway with a resigned look on her face. "I have a feeling this is going to result in my sister not talking to me for a week."

Chapter 9

Wesley

If I were to rank the top five most painful experiences in my life this dinner would rank as number three, only to be outdone by the day my parents died and the time Orion Halsted gave me a much-deserved black eye.

The sharp *tink* of a utensil hitting glass reverberates through the dining room filled with my uncle's closest and richest friends. Granted, in a town like Amoresville, we aren't talking millionaires. But they are rich enough that not a single one of the twenty or so people present balked at the one-hundred-dollar price tag per plate for tonight's dinner. The way too salty chicken is definitely not worth the price of entry. Neither is the cause if we are being honest. Where were all these people when I was asking for donations to replace the aging elevator in the library?

Once everyone quiets, Burt stands with his practiced politician's smile. Not too big, no teeth showing, just an upturn of thin lips that makes him seem patient and kind. Burt's age is showing more and more these days. His tall, thin frame is stooping just the slightest bit as he inches closer to seventy. He stopped bothering to cover his bald spot a few years ago and now cuts his nearly white hair short to his scalp. I have very complicated feelings about the uncle that finished raising me after his much younger sister died, but right now those feelings are leaning closer and closer to the resentment of my teenage years.

To the people in this room, the importance of this mayoral race in a town with a population of less than three thousand is equal to that of a national presidential race.

Which is literally insane.

"Thank you so much for joining us here tonight." His official voice always takes me a little by surprise. It is deeper, more robust than the thinly veiled disappointment he always regarded me with. "Wesley here may have been a little rough around the edges when he first joined us here in Amoresville—" he places one wrinkled hand on my shoulder and I have the irrational desire to shove it off "—but he has matured into a truly respectable, valuable member of our community. He took what can only be described as a painfully outdated library and brought it into modern times while holding onto the traditional, historical spirit of the area."

Man, my inner teenager is begging to be let loose right now. I have to fight the urge to roll my eyes. Librarian was not the career Burt saw for me. He wanted me to major in business and political sciences. When I broke the news I had declared English as my major with a minor in library sciences it had been an uncomfortable few days. Now here he is, eight years later, convincing a room full of people that he is proud of the road I've taken.

"When my dear Helen died nearly fifty years ago, I accepted that I would be the end of the Lickinbill legacy in this town. But twenty years later another tragedy brought this young man to my doorstep and my hope was reignited."

That is as close as I have ever heard Burt to acknowledging my mother and her death. He likes to pretend I materialized out of thin air as a surly teen who read books he deemed inappropriate and kept company with all the wrong people. Anytime I tried to talk about the sister ten years younger than him who left the town behind without a backward glance, I was shut down before I could finish a thought.

Shut down. That is the perfect way to describe Burt in general. I'm not sure if it is how he has always been or if losing his wife, a woman I have gathered through my research he truly loved, so early in their marriage hardened him. But either way, the man has never opened up to me in the decade I have known him.

"In just a few short weeks, Wesley here will carry on the Lickinbill tradition of serving and leading this community when he is sworn in as mayor of Amoresville."

While the room around us breaks out into a round of polite applause, I seethe on the inside that Burt has once again referred to me as a Lickinbill despite it never being my name. I am a Goldman. Despite his insistence, I will never change my name from the one my mother very precisely chose.

No matter what he says tonight, the Lickinbill legacy is ending with him. I am going to make sure of it.

As he drones on about the values of our town, I see a flash of strawberry blonde outside the window. Immediately my entire body perks up, straining to see outside with my glasses that could honestly use an upgrade in prescription. No way she would come close to Rose's B&B tonight.

The quick jab of adrenaline ebbs away, leaving me even more fed up with this night than I was before.

The door to the back of the room opens and Rosie and Harley emerge once again, this time carrying plates of crème brûlée and placing them in front of each guest. Burt was not happy that Rosie recruited her sister for tonight's event, but apparently everyone that would normally work an event came down with the flu and she had no choice. Burt went into full Karen mode and insisted on a discount for having to be reminded of the filth that went on just outside of town.

Harley turns to Rosie and whispers something in her ear before slipping back into the kitchen. I can tell by the tightness in his voice that my uncle does not appreciate the interruption in his speech.

"So, without further ado, I would like to invite the next mayor to stand and tell us about his version for the future of our proud town." Once again, everyone breaks out into polite applause.

Each muscle in my body goes rigid, on the verge of barging through the crowded dining room out into the fresh air. Everything seems to get dimmer, black creeping in around my eyes. I practiced the short speech ten times, each rehearsal twisting my gut tighter and tighter until I decided practicing was doing no good.

My breath comes faster as I push my chair back to stand.

But before I can say a word, a few things happen that if someone had asked me the probability of them happening I would have laughed in their face and said zero.

First the kitchen doors swing open to reveal not Harley with another tray of desserts, but someone I have not occupied the same room with in years.

Delia Halsted.

I freeze in my spot, ass halfway off the chair, mouth hanging open as she struts to the center of the room in a tight pencil skirt that accentuates every single curve I've been drooling over since she crashed into me in the hall outside Honors English. The blouse tucked into the waistband of the skirt is obviously a men's shirt, a little loose in the waist and slightly too tight as it stretches across her ample chest, leaving the buttons gaping just enough to see she is wearing a nude bra beneath.

I swear everything and everyone freezes. Even Uncle Burt, who must be so dumbfounded at not only any Halsted crashing his event but this particular Halsted that is his very least favorite of the clan.

"Thank you, Burp—" wait, did she say Burp not Burt, or am I losing my mind "—I appreciate the wonderful introduction. In addition, I am so incredibly proud to be running for mayor as a write-in candidate. I couldn't think of a better place to announce my candidacy than in this room with so many familiar faces." She looks pointedly at a few men in the room that we all know frequent her club but never mention in public.

Burt finally snaps out of his stupor, moving around our table and speaking at the same time. "Young lady, how dare—"

"Oh, Mayor—"

Someone interrupting him, especially Delia, is such a shock to my uncle's sensibilities that he once again freezes, two tables between him and the interloper.

"I know you're getting up there in years, Burg—" okay, now I know the name thing is on purpose and a small part of me wants to laugh so hard it's hard to contain "—but I am not a young lady. I am a grown woman. A business owner who donates to several charities and whose family has been in this town long before yours. One who is also running for mayor, and I look forward to a lively campaign leading up to election day."

Burt's mouth hangs open in shock. I'm not sure what is doing it more: Delia talking to him at all, especially in this tone, or the fact that for the first time in several decades it appears there will be an actual opponent for mayor.

Just as he appears to gather himself. Delia smiles around at the room. "Thank you, everyone. I look forward to seeing you all at the polls."

For some reason she bows, then turns and walks back out through the kitchen doors. My gaze follows her the entire way, glued to the way her body moves through the space, hips swinging around chairs in the tight dining area.

As soon as she disappears through the doors, the room erupts into confused chatter. Across the room I see Rosie glaring at Harley, who is trying her best to avoid her sister's gaze by placing more crème brûlée in front of people that could not give less of a shit.

Burt turns his furious gaze onto me, as if Delia's appearance were my fault.

Who knows, maybe it is.

Chapter 10
Ten Years Ago

Delia

Holy shit. Oh my fucking god. Did he almost kiss me? Why did I run away? What the hell is wrong with me?

I speed walk past Mrs. Thurston, the ancient librarian. I can't imagine her as a kid. It's too weird to think about, so instead I choose to believe she just materialized one day made of book dust and crumpled up pages.

"Slow down, Miss Halsted, the books aren't going anywhere," she says without looking up from scanning returned books.

"Sorry," I whisper back.

Without stopping, I make a beeline for the legal section, all the way in the back, down a dimly lit hallway in its own room at the back of the building. It's wedged behind where they had to retrofit an elevator so it could be accessible. No one ever goes back here, so when my brothers are being particularly over-bearing I like to come back here and read.

Making my way back to the last set of shelves, I plop down criss-cross applesauce style and pull out my phone, praying that whoever has detention duty today didn't make Harley hand over her phone.

Me: I think Wesley almost kissed me?

Harley: WTF?!?!? Details, whore!

I want to kick my feet and giggle like a maniac. I have had exactly two kisses so far. Once on the bus in seventh grade when stupid Bob McKee dared his brother to do it to see if my brother would punch him. He did. And once last year when Harley dragged me to a junior party and we played spin the bottle. I landed on Orion's best friend, Sam. It caused so much fucking drama I prefer not to think about it.

Me: Cliffnotes: Burt almost saw us. Wes pulled me around a corner and pushed me against the wall. He was starting to lean in and I bolted.

Harley: OMG, Y? YYYYYY?

Me: We were right behind the library. Anyone could have seen. Also, I freaked out! My other two kisses don't count. I don't know what I'm doing.

Harley: Woman, just stick your tongue in his mouth, you'll figure it out.

She follows that oh so helpful advice with a GIF of that gross pink Pokémon with the huge tongue waggling around.

Footsteps thud down the hall coming toward me.

Me: He's coming. Call you later.

I shove my phone back into my bookbag and try to smooth out my perpetually frizzy hair. My heart is racing so fast in my chest I'm a little afraid I might pass out. He probably won't even want to kiss me anymore. I mean, I did run away when he started to lean in.

"Delia?" His whisper is unsure, a little nervous maybe. For some reason that makes me feel a little better.

Leaning out from the edge of the aisle I'm in I whisper-yell *Marco* then duck back in fast.

He chuckles and quickly makes his way to my spot. "I'm pretty sure I'm supposed to be the one saying Marco."

"Okay, Polo then."

Wes drops down next to me on the floor, folding his long legs up and tossing his bag against the bookshelf across from us. "You studying for the bar or something?"

I toy with the edge of my backpack strap, picking at the weird hard plastic where they melt the nylon to keep it from fraying. "Oh yeah, I spend all my time reading the latest case law. I'm a regular Judge Judy."

"Okay, so if you aren't super into the law, why the legal section?"

I look around the small space I've always thought of as my spot. The carpet back here is still the old orange scratchy stuff, the shelves are beige metal, and there is a light bulb in the corner that has been burnt out as long as I've been escaping back here. "For the ambience, obviously."

He leans over just a few inches, knocking his shoulder against mine. "Seriously."

"When you grow up with two older brothers on a farm with a ton of animals, it's hard to find quiet. Plus the town is always talking about and watching my family." I lean my head back against the thick spines of the legal tomes. "Back here none of that exists. It's just me, the quiet, and whatever book I bring with me. Not even Harley knows about this spot. She's not big on quiet if you hadn't noticed."

He huffs out a little laugh. "Yeah, I could tell at lunch. Comfortable silences aren't a thing for her, huh?"

"No, not at all." I love Harley so much, but sometimes I need a break from her constant stream of conscious babbling.

"Well, thanks for showing it to me."

I roll my head to the side so I'm looking at Wes, and I'm surprised to see he is looking at me too. "I figured you could use a place to hide, too. The town might gossip about you more than they do my family until the novelty of your appearance wears off."

His eyes go hazy for a second, but he nods slowly. I don't want him to be sad.

"Hey—" I nudge his shoulder the same way he did mine, "—wanna trade glasses?"

My question seems to surprise him. "Um, why?"

"Yours look so thick, I want to see how they compare to mine."

"Yeah, I'm like three steps away from being legally blind," he jokes.

I take my glasses off and hand them out to him. With a shake of his head he does the same. "Don't blame me when these things ruin your eyesight for the rest of your life."

"They can't be that bad." But as soon as I slip them on, I know I am very, very wrong.

* * *

Wesley

The minute I take off my glasses, everything blurs. Delia, only a foot away, is still pretty clear, but anything beyond here is nothing but dark fuzz. I got my first pair of glasses at four years old. Ever since it has been a steady parade of stronger and stronger prescriptions. Thankfully, things have seemed to stabilize since hitting puberty.

"Holy shit, Wes, how do you, like, function?" Delia looks around at the things around us. "This is wild. It's like looking through a fisheye lens covered in Vaseline."

"I told you." I slip hers on my face and they make next to no difference.

"I have to take these off, I'm getting dizzy." She takes my glasses off and rubs her eyes.

"How do yours look on me?" Unlike my plain black frames, Delia has purple tortoiseshell frames with a cat eye shape.

She turns to me and immediately bursts out laughing, slapping her hands over her mouth to muffle the noise. I laugh too, happy to see my moment of horny teenager-dom outside hasn't made things weird.

"Those are definitely your look."

"Too bad I'd be walking into walls if I wore them." I slip them off and we trade back. Our fingers brush together on the exchange, little tingles from that small contact ricocheting across my entire body.

Delia blushes again, and even though it isn't quite as obvious in the darkened space, it still draws my eye. "So like how far back can you not see?"

"Everything behind you is a blur."

"Okay, wait, don't put your glasses back on yet." As she says it, she shoves her own pair back on her face, then turns over to crawl on her hands and knees to the very end of the aisle.

I try to be a gentleman. I am the son of two mothers who talked A LOT about consent from the time I was little. But when a girl crawls away from you with her ass almost in your face, yeah, I stared for a very brief moment before averting my eyes. Gaze firmly locked on the spines of the books directly across from me even though I can't make out a single letter on any of them.

"Okay, how many fingers am I holding up."

I swing my attention back to where Delia's voice is coming from at the very end of the aisle we've been sitting in. There is a general Delia-shaped blob there shifting around. "Um, do you have fingers?"

She laughs and I hear shuffling as the blob gets a little closer. "How about now?"

"I am just wondering why this blob has your voice."

More shuffling, more giggling. "Come on, I'm only like six feet away."

"Okay, blob Delia does now vaguely look human-shaped. But couldn't tell you how many fingers it has."

I can see now as she gets just a little closer that she is knee walking across the space, but the details of her face and her body are still distorted.

"Okay, three feet. You have to be able to see my fingers now."

I squint, the lighting in here is not helping things. "Ummm, are you the six-fingered man? Because I know a dude looking for you."

She laughs a little louder, but quiets it quickly, then knee walks closer.

There is some invisible line that she crosses and all of a sudden I can see she is holding up two fingers and is smiling this big goofy smile. "You have to be able to see it now or I am going to start worrying about your ability to someday get a driver's license."

She keeps getting closer and closer, and even though I can see clearly now, I don't say anything. I'm not sure I've ever seen something as beautiful as Delia Halsted laughing like this.

"Seriously? Much closer and I'll be in your lap."

Without thinking, I grab her around the waist and draw her close, draping her across my stretched out legs. "There. Now I can see you perfectly."

For a second I wonder if she will push me away, tell me off. But almost immediately she snuggles into me, arranging herself so she's comfortable in my arms. The smile on her face is huge, not hiding anything from me, showing me plain as day that she likes me the same way I like her. For someone whose life has been far too complicated for a teenager the past few months, the simplicity of liking a girl and having her like me back is almost soothing.

"Delia," I whisper her name, not wanting to break the spell we seem to be under back in this dusty corner of the library.

"Yeah?" She bites her lip and looks up at me from under her eyelashes.

"Can I kiss you?"

Her smile widens, popping that corner of her lip out from between her teeth, and pushing her cheeks high. She nods quickly.

Slowly, I lean down, not wanting to scare her when what I really want to do is rush in, to satisfy this sudden need I have to connect us, mark us as more than just friends.

She meets me halfway, our lips just barely brushing, a gentle pressure. We pull back just a little, excitement and joy rushing through me when I see her, pink cheeks and sparkling green eyes, smiling back at me.

We both move back in, one of her hands on my shoulder, the other moving up to my cheek as we start the kiss again. This time a little firmer, more pressure. One of my arms is supporting her across her back, the other at the curve of her waist. I tighten them both a little, pulling her tighter against me as the kiss deepens. Our lips bracket each other, hers on top then mine.

I'm trying so hard to keep this respectful. To not push anything further than she might be ready for. But then there is a tentative sweep of her tongue against my bottom lip, and I find myself opening for her at the same time she does for me.

I've kissed girls before, even made out, but never like this. Never has kissing someone made the whole world disappear. Nothing exists outside our little bubble of law books and ugly orange carpet.

When we finally pull apart, I lean my forehead against Delia's, breathing harder than I should be considering I'm a long-distance runner and we've only been kissing a few minutes.

"That was not like my other kisses," she whispers.

"No?" Please say it wasn't bad for her, because I don't know what I'll do if that kiss wasn't as transcendent for her as it was me.

"Not even close." Her thumb rubs across my cheek bone. "Now I'm realizing I might not have even been kissed before. Because what those were should not be in the same classification as this." Her thumb comes down to brush across my bottom lip that suddenly feels like a live wire.

Relief floods my system. She was in it with me.

"Same. If I had known this was what it was supposed to feel like I wouldn't have bothered doing that with anyone else."

Somewhere in the distance a muffled vibrating sound breaks through our little bubble.

"Oh shit!" Suddenly Delia is scrambling from my lap and grabbing her backpack. "Shit, shit, shit."

"What's wrong?" I stand ready to do whatever it is Delia needs in this minute while she frantically grabs her back and jacket.

"It's almost five. I have to go or Mom is going to leave without me and I'll have to bribe my brother to come pick me up."

"Okay, I'll see you tomorrow?"

With her bag back over her shoulders, she spins around, plants both her hands on my shoulders and presses up on her toes to give me another kiss that I desperately want to deepen but know I can't.

"Absolutely. I'm locker 364, wait for me in the morning?"

I nod and she kisses me once more.

"Damn, it's kind of addictive once you do it right." She laughs and turns to run out of the library.

As soon as she is gone I want her back. Can you become addicted to a person after just a couple days?

Chapter 11

Delia

Hours later and the exhilaration is still rushing through my veins.

For all the years of silent hatred, the Halsteds and the Lickinbills rarely ever confront each other face to face. Instead we just split the town into three groups: ours, theirs, and those that couldn't care less. I can count the actual real-life showdowns we've had on one hand. I wonder what it means that three of those involved me.

This time was different though. I'm not a scared, heartbroken teenager or an exhausted, worried daughter trying to hold everything together. I'm a grown-ass woman, just like I told Burt.

Being the topic of rumors around town is nothing new to me. I hear the whispers as I pass by the neighbors that don't love having someone in the sex industry sharing the same sidewalk. Hear what people say about the club and what must happen out there at night.

Sure, we have our supporters too, and not just the husbands that secretly slip out to catch the show. Harley gets a good dozen or so women out for her strip aerobics and pole dancing classes. But for every one person that doesn't treat me like they can catch the slut virus, there are two more in town that see what I do as a dirtiness that can rub off on them.

Being the one to stand up in a room full of people that hate me, that will be spreading the story like wildfire through town, there was something incredibly empowering about it. Taking the narrative into my own hands and shaping it instead of molding myself around what other people think and say, it's addictive.

The only downside had been my body's reaction seeing Wesley in his suit, hair rumpled like he couldn't bother to care enough to style it for the event. I avoid being in the same space as Wesley at all costs, and tonight is proof of why. My body reacts to him even as my head and heart scream to run. I can still feel the way his hands would feel on me, my body. How he would taste had we kissed. How many years have to go by before my muscle memory finally gets amnesia and forgets what it is like to be adored by Wesley Goldman?

"Hey boss, that guy from last week is back." Jack, one of the head bouncers and a mountain of a man, peeks his head into my office instead of using the communication system I bought specifically for things like this. I'm pretty sure he has a crush on me. Too bad for him he is the very opposite of my type, and I learned long ago not to get involved with anyone associated with the club.

"Jack, it is a Friday night. I can't have you leaving the floor to come give me messages. Your job is to protect the women working out there. Not to be my personal errand boy." I stand from the desk where I've been doing payroll for next week. "Use the intercom system, or we are going to have a deeper conversation about following orders."

For a man that could probably bench about ten of me, he does a really good impression of a kicked puppy. "Yes, ma'am."

I give him a nod. "I'll be out in a minute."

Running out every time there is a big wig trying to flash a bunch of money to impress the girls or me is never a good idea. I set the pace in this place, and I will greet Mr. Money-Bags when I am good and ready.

I take my time looking myself over in the mirror on the back of the office door. The pencil skirt from my impromptu campaign announcement is still molded to my body, but I replaced the button-down with a deep purple corset top that pushes my chest up to the point of it almost being obscene. This is not how I want to appear to the man who has shown up two weeks in a row apparently asking to see me. He probably already sees me as much less than his equal, men like him usually do.

Little does he know I run the most successful night club in the state. I have dancers lining up to try and work here thanks to my rejection of the normal business model where they have to pay for stage time. Instead, everyone from security to dancers to mixologists are paid employees who make a livable wage and keep all their tips. I make my money from the door, the up charge for VIP seating, and the bar, not off the backs of the women literally and figuratively bending over backward to get paid. As a result, we have the best talent, the best drinks, and a line out the door.

I grab the shirt I had been wearing earlier and throw it on, buttoning it up halfway so you can still see the corset, but the impact of my breasts is lessened. I tuck it in since it is a little too tight around my hips. Makeup and hair still look fantastic, so with a deep breath I steel my spine ready to kiss this douchebag's ass.

Crossing the floor, I see Harley has finally arrived for her shift, looking like she got the verbal smackdown from her sister for my little stunt. I make a mental note to bake my friend her favorite cookies tonight as a thank you-slash-apology.

Once again, Mr. Money-Bags is seated in the VIP lounge area, surrounded by sycophants. Word has gotten around to the girls that there is money to be made and everyone not currently on stage is milling around the outside of the VIP section hoping to get called in.

As I approach, Jack unlatches the velvet rope keeping the lounge separate from the rest of the club. He keeps his eyes glued to the floor, head on a swivel to make sure everyone is behaving themselves. Good, that should be what he is doing.

"Welcome back to Club Barely Over the Line." I reach out to shake the man's hand, not bothering to look around at his little minions all sipping their over-priced brown liquor. "Glad we made enough of an impression that you made the trip back."

Money-Bags takes my hand and settles on a shake this time, not bringing my knuckles to his lips like last time. "In more ways than one, I must admit." His eyes stay glued to my face, but I can tell he wants to take me in from head to toe. He's trying his best to be a gentleman, and I can tell it doesn't come naturally.

"Harley is certainly memorable." I give him my slightly bored smile as I drop his hand. My *you are no different from every other man that walks into this place* smile. Harley said he had been respectful. Kept his hands to himself, thanked and com- plimented her, then handed over ten crisp one-hundred-dollar bills. "Would you like me to have her pay another visit to your table?"

The man steeples his fingers together and taps them against his mouth before dropping them onto the arms of the club chair, crossing one ankle over the opposite knee. "Actually, I came to chat with you."

"My time is not available for purchase. But I have several performers that I am sure would provide you with great con- versation." I keep the smile perfectly in place, but let my eyes make a circuit of the room. It doesn't escape my notice that the men around us have stopped their talking and are not-so-subtly listening to our interaction.

Mr. Money-Bags looks to his companions and with a subtle nod they disperse, traipsing down the few steps to the floor and sitting along the edge of the main stage, wads of cash in hand.

"It isn't your time I wish to purchase, it's your club."

The words drop between us like an anvil. A gauntlet thrown.

"The club is also not available for purchase."

"You aren't even going to ask a price?" I intrigue him, I can tell by the way he tilts his head and inspects my face as if looking for the crack that will give him everything he needs to know. "You aren't curious?"

"Not even a little." I don't elaborate; this is where most people go wrong when it comes to business. They talk more than is needed and show their hand. I learned the lesson the hard way, through many mistakes.

Mr. Money-Bags' fingers curl around the arms of the chair, dimpling the leather under the pressure. "Three million dollars is far from a little."

I pull in a good amount from the club. Six figures good. Most of my dancers make close to that in just tips as well. Some days Harley makes more than I do. So I won't lie and say that multiple millions doesn't catch me off guard. But there is no doubt in my mind this man wouldn't undo everything I have built here. That means more to me than money.

"As I said, the club isn't for sale."

We stare at each other for the length of the entire next song. "Toxic" by Britney Spears, a favorite of one of our higher earning girls—Sheila, or Cherry on stage.

"I own a club in Atlantic City. I heard about this place all the way in New Jersey. You've even stolen a dancer or two right from under me."

"We don't poach talent. They seek us out."

I don't need to tell him why they do. I treat my employees better than any other club on the East Coast. I'm aware not all club owners are fans of how I run things. But there are others that have reached out hoping to learn more about my business model. Apparently, basic human decency is a business model now.

"Now, if you will excuse me, I was in the middle of some very important business. If you need anything Ginger will be happy to help you." Ginger is one of our bottle girls. She doesn't dance, but serves drinks and tonight is covering the VIP section.

The man's smile slips slightly from his face, not in an angry or threatening way, but in confusion. "Five million."

I don't bother to turn around. I won't sell this place and see the people I consider family sold down the river.

Jack lets me back through the rope, and just as I am heading back to the hallway leading to my office, I feel a hand grab my wrist. Mr. Money-Bags has gone too far, and I see my security staff react exactly as they should when one of our guests touches something they shouldn't. Within seconds three men tower over me.

"We need to talk." The voice that says the words against my ear is not the grating one of the man trying to buy my club.

It's a voice I wish I could forget but never will. Wesley.

Chapter 12

Wesley

My eyes stay glued to Delia's shocked face. I don't look around. Not out of curiosity. Not to sneak a peek at the half-naked women all around that are probably watching the mini-drama happening just feet from the stage. I have no interest in any of them. I'm here for one reason and one reason only.

Delia.

"What the hell are you doing here?"

Great question.

"We need to talk." Two very large sets of hands grab my arms, ready to drag me forcefully from the club. I won't resist. I have no desire to cause trouble, I just need to talk to Delia. As soon as the, admittedly intimidating, men start dragging me back, Delia raises her hand and they immediately freeze.

God damn, if that isn't the hottest fucking thing I have ever seen.

"Let him go." Both bouncers immediately drop their hands and take a step back. "I'm fine, he's no threat." She says the words with confidence, but I can see the doubt behind her eyes. The men don't move, so she swings her gaze to them, a hardness there I've never seen her use before. "Go back to your sections."

I feel as they move away from us, but don't bother looking. "Can we talk?"

After a brief hesitation, Delia nods and leads the way. The hall is painted black, with doors every few feet, all with numbers on them. I assume those are the VIP dance rooms given the many rumors I've heard about this place. At the end of the hall is a door with a digital lock that Delia waves a wristband in front of and then opens.

Delia's office is everything and nothing I expected.

Just like the hall, the room is painted a matte black, but it doesn't make the space look small; rather, it makes it seem cavernous. The ceiling is painted a sparkling silver with a chandelier hanging from the center. There are deep green velvet club chairs stationed before a large wooden desk that I am guessing her brother, Orion, made. The floor is a dark hardwood with a huge white shag carpet in the middle.

One wall features another velvet couch, but this one is a deep burgundy. The wall behind the desk is covered in monitors that look out at the club floor and each of the private rooms. The rest of the walls are covered in artistic photos featuring various parts of the female body. But one wall also displays watercolor paintings of scenic views. They aren't half-bad, but obviously not done by a professional. Perhaps by Delia herself?

Somewhere in the room is a speaker that plays the same music as out on the floor.

While I stand in the middle of the room gaping at finally seeing where Delia spends her days and nights, she walks to her desk and presses a button on a panel beneath the monitors. "I'm going offline for a bit, guys. Jack, you're in charge."

She doesn't wait for a response. Just presses another button and the music cuts out, leaving nothing but tense silence. This is the first time in six years we have been alone in a room together.

The last time isn't something I like to reflect on much.

"What are you doing here?"

She turns, and for the first time I take her in. She's wearing the same outfit as earlier when she crashed Burt's dinner. But under the white men's shirt she's wearing a purple corset that pushes her breasts up, the cleavage framed perfectly by the open lapels of the shirt.

I'm staring, I know I am, but I can't stop either.

"They're tits, Wesley, you just walked through a room of them out in the open. Get over it." Instead of covering herself like I think most women would, she places her hands on her hips, elbows jutting out in a pose so reminiscent of Wonder Woman it makes me smile a little.

Until I remember I'm pissed at her.

"What the hell was that tonight?"

"You're a smart guy, you know what that was. I believe they call it a campaign kick-off in the biz."

How can one person make me want to both pull her closer and throttle her in equal measure? "Do you have any idea what you've done?"

She scoffs a little, walking out from behind her desk to lean against the front of the solid piece of furniture. She crosses one ankle over the other, and grips the edge of the surface behind her with both hands. "Yeah, I let everyone know I am running for mayor. My guess is the entire town will know by sundown tomorrow."

More like they already knew hours ago. After Delia's declaration, the dinner broke up pretty fast, with everyone assuring me I had nothing to worry about. If only they knew.

Once everyone was gone, Burt went on the warpath, making plans alternating with berating me for not speaking up when she barged in. It took me two hours to shake him, and another hour to work up a head of steam so big I couldn't contain it and felt the need to do something I swore I never would. Walk through the front doors of Club Barely Over the Line.

"You're ruining my plans."

She rolls her eyes, something that makes me hot in multiple ways. "Poor baby is going to have to work a little harder to carry on his family legacy. Tough shit. It's about time this town had something more to choose from than the same old Lickinbill bullshit."

"I'm not a fucking Lickinbill!" The words roar from my mouth louder than I expected. Loud enough that I'm a little afraid the goons from before are going to knock down the door and drag me from the premises. Loud enough that Delia looks at me, really looks at me for maybe the first time in years. "My name is Wesley Goldman. That hasn't changed no matter what my uncle or you or the rest of the town likes to think. I. Am. A. Goldman. It is the last name I shared with my mother. The one my mom decided to replace Lickinbill with. I might be genetically a Lickinbill, but my mom made sure to strip the association with that name from our history. I am legally and in every other sense of the word a Goldman."

I'm embarrassed to feel the burning of tears building up in my tear ducts. I've been sitting quietly for so long just letting Burt say whatever he wants for the sake of this stupid fucking campaign, for the sake of my own sanity, and hearing Delia repeat his bullshit is the last straw.

She knows how I feel about my last name. It is the only thing I have left of my mother, the woman who might not have carried and birthed me, but was as equally a parent as Mom. We talked about it endlessly as teens. I know I did some truly unforgivable shit back then, but hearing Delia call me a Lickinbill feels like a betrayal as well.

"Wesley," she says my name so softly it almost makes me fall to my knees and ask her to say it again and again, "if you don't want to be a Lickinbill, then why are you running for mayor? As much as I try to block those old conversations, they are all still there in my memory. I know you never wanted to be your uncle. Never wanted to follow the path he saw for you. So why are you doing it?"

She is only the second person to ask me why I am running for mayor. The first was her mother.

"Because I need to make things right. Need to fix the harm my family has done. I have a plan." The anger and sadness and determination are swirling in my chest, mixing together into a concoction I can't stomach.

I pace the room. From wall to wall it is no more than a dozen feet, but standing still as I pour the truth out to the one person I both desperately want to know but never intended on telling is impossible. "When Burt first said it was time to start my campaign, I told him he was crazy. There was no way I would run for mayor. It is everything Mom *didn't* want for me. But he just kept bringing it up. All the things I could do to make the town better. It made me think. Maybe I *could* undo the harm he has caused over the last twelve years. Make the downtown thrive again. Take down the stupid fucking streetlights. Give business owners some protections from the bullshit ordinances he's put into place. Put money where it belongs, fixing roads and upgrading the school and the library. Once I accomplish all that, I will find someone that actually *wants* to be mayor for the *right* reasons. I thought if I could fix everything he has done it would make up for what I..."

For what I did to Delia.

I don't finish the thought. I don't need to. It hangs there in the air like a poltergeist rattling its chains to make itself known.

I've stopped my pacing only to realize Delia has come out to meet me in the center of the room. The light refracts off the crystals hanging from the chandelier, causing ribbons of light to spill across her face. She's so fucking beautiful it takes my breath away. Makes me wonder what could have been if I had been braver. Was willing to stand up to Burt as a teenager. I will never stop regretting the decisions I made back then. It is why I moved back to Amoresville after college. Or at least part of the reason.

"What are you going to do after you fix everything your family has done? Go back to being librarian? You expect me to believe you won't want to be like everyone else in your family and continue being town puppet master for another two terms?" The anger is evident in her stiff voice. But I also see the hope, and it lights something inside me. Some ember I had long ago thought was totally extinguished.

"I'm going to leave. When my first term comes to an end, I'm going to finally leave Amoresville. Maybe sooner if I find someone that wants to be mayor and can convince the council to instate them as interim mayor until there can be another election."

"So you are going to handpick the next mayor, make sure it is someone that will do what you think is right, then leave? How do you know *I'm* not the right person to be mayor?" She takes another step closer, her voice getting just the tiniest bit louder the closer she gets. "If you want to leave town so bad, just go! I'll be mayor and you won't have to think about this place or the people in it ever again."

She doesn't get it. Why would she? She has no idea what really happened all those years ago. Has no idea that it is *my* responsibility to make things right. If I don't, I'm not sure I can move on without the weight of guilt grinding me down every day. But I can't tell her any of that. It will all just sound like pathetic excuses from the man that didn't just break her heart, but crushed it.

"Never think about the people here again? *You* are all I think about."

Her eyes widen slightly, a change so minuscule it would be barely perceptible by anyone else. But I am so used to watching for the smallest glance from this woman that I clock it immediately.

"I *need* to fix things. And your declaration did not help. You think Burt is going to let you win even if I do leave?" I fling my hand out in the general direction of Amoresville. The town line is ten feet outside the front door of this place, and I swear its presence is so close it looms over our whole conversation. "You quite literally lit a fire under Burt's ass. Right now he's back at his house drawing up plans and strategies to bring you down. I've never seen him like this before. It's like he wants the challenge. If I leave, he will just insert one of his buddies from that stupid dinner in my place. Someone that won't stand up to him—"

"Oh, and you will?"

"Someone that doesn't see things the way they could be." My breaths come fast, my chest heaving up and down with every word. "I *have* to be mayor or the cycle is never going to end. It's just going to be Burt-clones until the town is run into the ground no matter how much the rest of us try to rescue it."

"God, you really do think you're some kind of town savior, don't you?" Delia shoves one finger straight into my chest, and despite having both an undershirt and a button-down on, I feel it as if she's touched bare flesh. The one point of contact seers through my already boiling blood. "You have some ego on you, Wes."

Wes.

She hasn't called me that since high school. Not even the one time after her dad died. It's only been dick, or asshole, or douchebag. Even said with so much venom I'm surprised I don't shrivel and die on the spot, the use of my nickname sends a sudden rush of pure joy through me it makes me dizzy trying to reconcile it with the frustration and anger.

My hands shake by my sides. We've somehow inched so close we're practically nose to nose, both breathing like bulls waiting to charge. Delia is tall, just like the rest of her family, but I'm taller by a good four inches, even with her heels. She has to tilt her head back to meet my eyes and I gaze down at her, trying not to let the love I still hold for her show through the cracks in my anger.

"Can you just—" touch me, kiss me "—trust me?"

Chapter 13
Ten Years Ago

Delia

It's like my life has been split between before Wesley Goldman moved to Amoresville and after.

Before things were good. Fine. I went to school, got good grades, worked at the cafe occasionally, hung out with my friends and family. But it was pretty much the same day after day.

Since Wes showed up, everything is just a little brighter. Good to great. Every day before school, he waits in the parking lot for me to pull up in Orion's shitty truck. It took a lot of begging and promising to muck stalls for my brother to get him to promise to keep my burgeoning relationship with a member of the Lickinbill family secret. But he agreed.

So now instead of five minutes at my locker before class, we get twenty as we walk hand-in-hand from the truck to his locker, then mine. But as soon as we turn down the hall to go to Honors English, we separate. We can't risk Mrs. Wheeler reporting back to Wesley's uncle that he's been canoodling with a Halsted.

It's like a much lower stakes version of Romeo and Juliet. At lunch I sit next to him, with Harley across from me, all of us talking about random shit while Wes and I eat our lunches with one hand while holding hands under the table.

"Ugh, you guys are so fucking cute it makes me want to puke." Harley fake gags and pushes her lunch tray away.

"Harley, it's not like we're sitting here making out." I roll my eyes and try to hide the smile.

"You might as well be with how much you guys eye fuck each other," she mumbles and pulls her half-eaten lunch back in front of her.

"We do not eye fuck each other." Okay, maybe I might look at Wes appreciatively occasionally, but eye fuck? Definitely not.

Harley points her fork in Wesley's direction. "Trust me, this one is thinking very dirty things while he's looking at you."

I roll my eyes again and look toward Wesley, waiting for him to deny it. But instead his eyes are supremely interested in studying the contents of the cafeteria's meatloaf surprise.

"Told you." Harley says proudly.

I can feel myself blushing furiously. Wes and I go to the library almost daily after school to hang out in our spot. Which is code for make out in our spot. I would be lying if I said I hadn't been getting more and more curious about things that can't be done when surrounded by legal briefs. But there aren't a ton of options for two teenagers who don't have cars and whose parents-slash-guardians are literally everywhere you look in town.

"Ugh, I need to go, the counselor wants to talk about how I'm wasting my potential again." Harley looms over Wes for a second, giving him her best bitchy face. "Listen, buster, I reserved her for after school today. You guys will just have to skip your regularly scheduled face sucking for today. Got it?"

Wes nods. "We can make a custody schedule if you want? I know I would be mad if someone suddenly said I got less time with Delia, too. Sorry I've been hoarding all her free time."

Harley softens for a second then stomps her foot, "Dammit, stop being so nice," and sulks off to what seems like her monthly meeting with the guidance counselor.

"Really, a custody schedule?" I glance over at him and indeed catch him looking at me with more than a little interest.

"You're in high demand." He shrugs like it is the most obvious thing in the world. "So, I got something for you by the way," he says shyly.

"You know it's not my birthday, right?"

"Yeah, I know. April 7th, got it committed to memory." He pulls a smallish box from his bookbag. I have absolutely no clue what it could be. "This is for our official one-month anniversary."

"Wait, we have an anniversary?" Seriously, I didn't realize that was a thing we settled on. "Don't we have to be like a couple to have an anniversary?"

His face loses all color. "We're not a couple? I just assumed with the hand holding and all the kissing."

I squeeze his hand under the table to reassure him. "I mean I was hoping, but didn't want to assume without there being like a conversation or something. I don't know how these things work."

"Right, yeah, I guess that makes sense." Wes looks at the box in his hand then slides it across the table between us. "Okay then, Crash, consider this my official proposal that you be my official girlfriend."

More blushing. More butterflies going absolutely crazy in my stomach. I remove my hand from his and gently lift the lid from the box. Inside, nestled among sheets of purple tissue paper, is a brand-new e-reader.

"I loaded a bunch of books on it and thought maybe we could pass it back and forth. I'll pick a book that you have to read then you can pick the next one that I have to read when you're done. You can put notes in the margins and everything. Since we can't text, I figured this would be the next best thing."

My eyes blur thanks to the tears starting to coat them at this kind gesture. We had exchanged numbers a couple weeks ago, but figured out pretty quickly that it would be impossible to keep us texting secret from Burt who insists on checking to make sure Wes isn't looking at anything inappropriate. Plus, the reception at the farm is shit, so it's a crap shoot if I would even get them. We decided it was too much risk for very little reward.

"This is amazing, but it had to cost so much."

Wesley smiles his wide, easy smile. Only easy with me, no one else. To everyone else, he is the sullen kid who never talks. "Nah,

I told my uncle it was for school and he gladly signed off on the expense from my account."

A teenager having his own money that hadn't been earned at one of the small businesses in town is still a foreign concept to me. But he'd inherited some money from his parents and also got monthly Social Security survivor benefits. As nice as it must be for him to have that money, I know he would give it all back if it meant his parents would come back.

"Besides, I can't keep trying to hide your bodice rippers under my mattress. Burt is going to find them eventually and that is one conversation I do not want to have."

Trading books back and forth has been something we started since our second visit to the library together. We had to at least try and pretend like we were there for something or Mrs. Thurston was going to get suspicious. So I found a copy of a book I liked and he checked it out, then he found one of his favorites and I did the same. Then we would sit in our spot and read them between bouts of making out.

I desperately want to kiss him. But besides holding hands, we haven't done any of the PDA stuff at school. Holding hands is enough of a risk when Burt has eyes everywhere.

* * *

Wesley

The smile on Delia's face is addicting. Every time I do or say something to put it there I get this little rush of endorphins. Life the past few months has been hard, but with Delia, all that just goes away. Life seems brighter, full of possibilities.

I hate having to go home at the end of the day. Burt is okay, stricter than my parents were, but he mostly just leaves me alone. His only rules are no inappropriate books or music, no staying out past ten, get good grades, and stay away from the Halsteds.

Three out of four isn't too bad.

Delia is giving me that look she does when she wants to be kissed. We're both worried about our families finding out, but more and more I don't care. It's been a month and all I want is to be able to take her on our first real date. I don't know what kids around here do for dates considering there isn't even a movie theater, but I could figure something out.

Quickly, I glance around making sure no teachers are paying attention to us, then lean in and give her a slow, tame kiss. It's no more than a brush of our lips, obviously no tongue, but doing it in the lunchroom feels like I've just stood in the middle of one or this weird little town's infamous town hall meetings and declared my love for Delia.

The second I end the kiss, Delia does the same quick glance around to see if anyone noticed. "We shouldn't do that here."

"I know, but it is incredibly hard not to when you look at me like that."

"Okay, I'll stop looking at you then."

I give her a playful, angry look. "Trying to turn me into one of those morally gray heroes you read about?" I lean a little closer, whispering in her ear. "Want me to say you're mine and I'll kiss you anytime I want?"

Delia squirms a little, her cheeks burning red at my comment. Unlike a month ago, I'm not shy about reaching up to brush the flushed skin to feel its warmth.

"Remind me not to let you read any more of the mafia books I found in Mom's collection. Harley was right, you are thinking far too many dirty thoughts."

I crack a goofy smile in her direction. Honestly, Harley isn't wrong. "I will neither confirm nor deny anything your friend said." Leaning back, trying to cool off some of the heat that has been working up between my girlfriend and I, I turn back to my lunch. "Speaking of whom, what do you two have planned for girls' night?"

Delia seems to shake herself out of a daze and turns back to her own lunch, a peanut butter and jelly today since apparently meatloaf gives her the ick. "Normal stuff. We'll probably color her hair again, she'll complain about her sister and mom, I'll complain about my brothers. I'll probably talk about you so much she tries to smother me."

That makes me smile. "You talk about me, huh?"

"So much sometimes it even nauseates me."

I wish I had someone in town I could talk to about Delia. I had lots of friends back in Brooklyn, but none of them knew how to act around me after my parents died. Since then it's just been a few awkward texts every now and again. Even those have petered out to a near standstill. Delia and Harley are the only people I've made real friendships with so far, and I doubt Harley wants us both gushing about each other to her.

Feeling suddenly untethered, I reach out, grab Delia's hand in my again.

"So no library tonight, but tomorrow?" I need to know I won't go the whole weekend without seeing her.

"I have debate team practice tomorrow. We're getting ready for sectionals and I need to make sure we crush and make it to divisionals." She squeezes my hand under the table. "But, we could meet at the library after practice. Maybe around three?"

Relief washes over me, I won't have to go two whole days without seeing her. Talking with her. Touching her.

Funny how someone I never knew existed just a few months ago has become so essential to my life.

Chapter 14

Delia

Trust Wesley Goldman. No. That is impossible.

So why is there a voice inside my heart practically screaming *YES!*

The goddamn pounding of my heart at his proximity has the bricks I've so carefully built up around the pesky organ crumbling, leaving gaps for teenage Delia and her foolish hope to peek through.

It has been so long. Years since I looked at him like this, without looking away or through the haze of hatred I pulled over my eyes. Since I listened, really listened, to something he had to say.

We're so close to touching, with each inhale my chest nearly brushes against his. There are many versions of Wesley I've seen over the years. The sad boy that first moved here. The sweet boy that used to hang on my every word. The nervous guy taking me on my first date, giving me my first kiss, all the other firsts we shared. The cruel boy that seemed to change overnight. The cold teenager that ignored me for the next two years. The earnest man that showed up after Dad's funeral and found a way to be the only one that could comfort me.

But this Wesley is one I've never seen before. Desperate.

"Delia, just, please, take back what you said tonight. I promise, I will make everything right, but I can only do that if I win."

There it is. This whole time he's been trying to convince me of his good intentions, but really, he is just like his uncle. He just wants to win. "You're scared. I could win this thing, and you know it."

The hands that have been hanging in fists by his sides come up and rake through both sides of his hair that always seems like it is in need of a trim, gripping the strands as if he might tear them out. We're standing so close I get a close-up of his biceps straining against the tailored shirt. Goddamn that sneaky fantastic fucking body of his.

"You are the most frustrating woman, has anyone ever told you that before?"

Yeah, several people have said the exact same words.

"It's true, you think I could win. And if I win, then you won't be able to carry on with your uncle's plans for the town."

"Have you listened to anything I said?" He spins in frustration, stalking away several feet before wheeling back around to stomp right back up to me. Despite towering several inches over me and the clear frustration on his face, I'm not scared. Wesley is many things, but he would never stoop to physically hurting me. Hell, he didn't even swing on Orion after he broke his nose. "I don't want to follow the blueprints laid out by Burt. How many ways do I have to say it before you believe me?"

"Words are easy. Actions speak volumes more, and from everything I've seen of you since coming back to town, you are more than willing to follow along with whatever Burt wants. Just like always."

My words hang there in the room, an accusation he can't deny.

"You have no idea what I'm willing to do." *For you.* The words might go unspoken, but he might as well have screamed them.

Something deep inside me pulls and twists, trying to get closer to this man that I have tried my best to ignore since he moved back to town. I sway in my spot, almost giving into this inexplicable need to climb him like one of the poles out in the club.

"I guess we'll see when I start winning this election."

"You're really going to do this?"

"God damn right I am." I straighten my spine, claiming every inch of my five-foot-ten height, six feet if you count my heels. "I am going to kick your ass all over this town."

"I'm not going to hold back."

"Good. Bring it on."

We stare each other down, heat and tension that has nothing to do with the election or our fight radiating between us. I swear, the air around us has gone wavy, like hot air rising off the pavement.

One moment we're glaring at each other and the next my lips are on his. I don't know who starts it or if we met somewhere in between. This isn't the tentative shy kisses of two teenagers in the dark stacks of a library. It holds the passion of our argument and years of pent-up need.

One of Wesley's hands slips into my hair, gripping it in his fist by the roots. The other goes to my ass, palming it to plaster our hips against each other.

He's hard already. God damn, that is hot.

I fist his starched shirt at his sides, pulling his body in tighter against mine. Everything inside me seems to light up, comes to life in a way it hasn't in years. The kiss is messy and aggressive. Each of us fighting for the upper hand. I bite his lip, he growls and pushes his tongue into my mouth, licking at me like a man starved.

I don't realize we're moving until my ass bumps into the edge of my desk. God, I forgot how good he is at this. Better now than we were fumbling teenagers learning everything for the first time. Better even than the night right after Dad died and the only place I found comfort was Wesley's arms.

There is a very real, very twisted, part of me that knew this was bound to happen again. As much as I swore to myself after that night it never would, here we are, holding onto each other like a life raft in the ocean during a storm.

He shoves my skirt up my thighs, giving me room to spread my legs, welcoming him between them. I roll my hips against his solid length, reveling in the drag of him against me. A low, needy moan slips out through my lips and into his mouth.

Just as fast as everything started, it comes to a screeching halt.

I wish I could say I'm the one that stops the inevitable path we are barreling down. But no, it is all Wesley.

"Delia, we can't."

He's right, I know he is. There are so many reasons anything happening between us is a bad idea. But all those reasons don't stop the ding my pride takes hearing him say it.

"I know." As discreetly as I can, I straighten my skirt until it is once again covering my legs, Wesley watching with a pained look the whole time.

"Fuck, you have no idea how much I want you. But—"

"Stop, Wesley, you don't have to explain. I'm a big girl. You haven't hurt my feelings." Maybe saying it out loud will make it true. As much as I like to think of myself as this badass bitch who turns down millions of dollars, then can make out with her teenage crush like it is nothing, the truth is that is very much not who I am. "And you won't hurt my feelings during the campaign either. This—" I wave my hand between us "—doesn't change anything."

"Yeah." Wesley turns toward the door, ready to leave, but stops before he gets to the door. "Just give me a second to get myself under control and I'll leave."

Something about that statement makes me laugh. "You think it will matter if you walk out into the club with a hard on? All the men out there that aren't on my payroll have a chubby. You'll just be one of many."

"Fuck. What was I thinking coming here?"

Okay, that rankles my nerves. "Oh, I see. The future mayor needs to keep his pristine reputation. God forbid it get back to Burt or his cronies that you were seen walking out of this room, hell, this building looking like he had something even close to a good time."

"That isn't what I meant—"

"Save it. You can go out the back entrance. No one will see you. I can open the parking lot gate from in here. I assume you parked up in your usual spot?"

He goes perfectly still, not even a breath slips out for a full thirty seconds. "You know."

"That you used to sit up on that hill and spy on me? That you started again a few weeks ago? Yeah, my security team is very good at what they do. Gathering information to take back to Burt?"

"No. Of course not."

"Sure." I slip around behind my desk, turning on the monitors and the speaker. Everything looks like it is running smoothly, no problems on the floor. Mr. Money-Bags is still holding court in the VIP area. Harley is on the main stage, halfway through her act. "Let me show you the door."

I strut past him without so much as a glance, despite my legs feeling like rubber. In silence, he follows me out of my office and down the last few feet of the hallway that leads out to the staff parking lot. This is also where the guys bring customers that have overstayed their welcome and need to sober up.

"I'm pretty sure you know where to go from here." I hold open the door, nodding at the bouncer posted there on the weekends.

Wesley hesitates for a moment. "Think about what I said. Burt isn't going to let anyone but me or one of his buddies win this election."

"Burt doesn't have as much sway over this town as he thinks he does." God, I hope I'm right. "I'll see you on the trail."

With a shake of his head, Wesley exits the club. I wish I could say watching him walk away once again doesn't sting. But it does. A lot.

Chapter 15

Wesley

I wonder if getting hard every time I think about that kiss is something I should be concerned about, medically.

Not that I can do a damn thing about it.

Twelve hours later and if I give myself so much as thirty seconds to stop and think about the feel of her legs wrapped around me, her hands gripping me, my tongue in her mouth, it all comes rushing back like a social media video that just keeps starting over as soon as it ends.

That moan, it was the thing that broke me out of my animalistic mindset. At the time all I could think was I wanted her to moan my name as I filled her with my dick. But instantly I knew that if I had that without everything being made right, then she would regret it. And I can't live with Delia Halsted regretting another thing that has to do with me.

So I put it to a stop. It was the right thing, but doesn't mean it wasn't also one of the hardest things I've ever done.

Damn it. My cock starts to swell once again as the images and sounds slam into me once again.

Deep breath in. Deep breath out.

000 is Computer Science, Information, and General Works

010 Bibliographies

020 Library and information sciences

030 Encyclopedia and books of facts...

By the time I get through the Dewey Decimal Classifications for social sciences the errant appendage in my pants has gone dormant once again.

Having a hard-on for the woman who hates me is not good form while one is organizing boxes of books for the upcoming annual book sale the library hosts every year on Black Friday.

I heft another book from the floor and drop it onto the folding table serving as my base of operations. Flipping open the lid to the plastic tote it becomes immediately obvious that it was mislabeled. The sticker on the front proclaims "Children's Board Books" but inside are stacks of self-help books that are either outdated or just damaged enough to not be on the shelves.

Oh good, maybe I can find something in here that will tell me how to cope with being in love with your opponent in the local town election. Or possibly this problem is a little too niche.

"Wesley, are you down here?" I'm not sure I can deal with Burt right now. If I just stay silent, what are the odds he'll give up and go look somewhere else?

Judging by his footsteps coming in my direction, not great.

"There you are. Why didn't you answer me?"

"Sorry, I was just focused on my work. What do you need?" I can't turn to look at him. With the mood I'm in right now I am honestly afraid he'll see the truth all over my face. He'll know in an instant that I made out with a Halsted in a strip club last night.

"What I need is for you to be upstairs shaking hands and charming the people of Amoresville."

"Lisa has it covered up there. I need to get things squared away for the book sale. It's only a few weeks away and this place is a mess." I rip off the label from the box, maybe a little more aggressively than necessary.

"Son, the book sale doesn't matter. You need to be focused on the election." Burt weaves around the precariously stacked boxes to stand on the opposite side of the table.

Physically, he's not an intimidating man. Shorter and significantly thinner than I am. But the way he carries himself, the unmitigated certainty he carries that he is the most important person in his world and everyone else can be damned, it's honestly a little scary.

"You need to be upstairs getting face time with the parents of our community here with their children for Story Hour. Sam and Paula Anderson are up there with all six of their kids. If you can get their vote, all the families and business owners in town will vote with them. They hold an enormous amount of sway in this town."

Honestly, I'm impressed Burt can admit to someone other than himself having an influence on the people of this town.

"Burt, the Andersons are best friends with Orion and Knox. There is no way they are voting for anyone but Delia." As true as that is, if all six of the Anderson kids showed up for Story Hour today, Lisa is definitely going to need more help.

"They are good, honest people. I have no doubt they will do the right thing when it comes time. I don't think they want a *sex worker* to be mayor of this town any more than the rest of us." The way he talks about Delia makes me want to lay him out. He talks about everyone in town as if they are just pawns to be moved around a chess board.

"She's not a sex worker. She is a business owner and a member of this community. Do not go around speaking like that about her. I will not run a campaign like that." A crack in the general area of the table makes us both look down at the box of books still on the table between us. I'm gripping the sides of the plastic tote so hard I've cracked the lip where the lid should rest.

Burt's dark eyes move back to my face, inspecting me just like he would when I first came to live here and he was trying to decide whether I was keeping something from him. I've given too much away, shown my hand when I should be bluffing.

"But you are right, I should be up there making an appearance." I replace the lid, hiding the broken plastic as if that will make a difference. "Let's go."

In silence, we walk up the ancient stairs in the historic building that has served as the Amoresville Area Library for more than a hundred and fifty years. The closer to the main floor we get, the louder things get. Just like most libraries, we try to keep a quiet atmosphere, but that all goes out the window during Story Hour.

Today's group is extra boisterous. I think every kid not currently enrolled in the local school must be here today. Right there in the middle of the fray are the Anderson kids running around playing keep-away from the second to youngest sibling. A skunk puppet goes flying over the small child's head as she reaches up on tippy toes trying to pluck it from the air.

"Mr. Goldman, thank god." Lisa comes hustling out from behind the circulation desk. She's a recent graduate from the community college a few towns over that I hired full-time last year. She's a sweet kid, is always on time and has great ideas for events and classes at the library, but the moment things get a little overwhelming she tends to shut down.

"They all just came out of nowhere. It was like a swarm of locusts just descended on the library ready to eat all the books in sight. I tried to corral them up to the children's section, but no one is listening."

She looks up at me with wide eyes, her hands wringing in front of her.

"No worries, Lisa, I'll take care of it from here. Why don't you stick to the desk and I'll take care of the Story Hour today."

She slumps against the front of the desk, her wild curls bouncing around her face. "Oh my gosh, thank you so much."

Burt trails behind me as I approach the mass of parents and kids of various ages. Walking between the two Anderson kids, I snatch the puppet midair and pass it down to the small girl nearly in tears with a wink in her direction.

"Okay kids, who wants to go on a bear hunt?" About twenty hands go up in the air, a few jumping up and down. "Line up!" I turn toward the stairs, snapping into a straight-backed posture.

"We're going on a bear hunt. We're going to catch a big one. What a beautiful day. We're not scared."

As I march along toward the stairs, reciting the lyrics to the song I could repeat in my sleep, the kids all join in behind me, following as I serpentine side to side up the stairs. Just as my mothers did when I was a kid, I make all the sound effects, using big, exaggerated movements for each obstacle mentioned in the book. If I had known we would be doing this particular song today, I would have set up props along the way as well. As the song winds up, we end up at the big round carpeted area used for Story Hour, me finishing in the chair at the front of the space, and the kids all laying down on the floor, pretending to hide in bed and declaring "We're not going on a bear hunt again!"

I'm a little out of breath as everyone settles in, but the smile on my face is worth the deviation from our normal Story Hour routine. I loved being the children's librarian when I first moved back to Amoresville. Something about seeing the same kids every week, watching as they grew over the years, as their interests and hyper fixations came and went, it made me feel part of something when I always felt as if I was looking in from the outside in this town. Speaking in front of a group of kids was never as much of a problem as adults. Maybe it's because they don't hide their judgment; they will flat out tell you when they think something is weird.

It's been hard trying to find my replacement since taking on the director position. None of the resumes I've gotten have seemed quite right. But maybe I'm just being too picky.

"Okay, should we read some more books about being scared?"

The kids all nod in near perfect unison, while in the back one skinny arm shoots into the air. One of the Anderson kids, I think this one is Robin. "Are you reading us scary books? Mommy says I can't watch or read anything that will give me nightmares because she needs her sleep to deal with all of us kids."

Paula Anderson steps forward, pulling Robin's arm down. "Okay, that's enough giving away Mommy's secrets, honey."

The rest of the parents all laugh quietly, probably sympathizing with Paula getting called out by her kid.

"Don't worry, Robin, these books aren't scary. They are actually all about how to work through being scared." This seems to satisfy the little girl and I pick up the first book and start reading.

An hour flies by faster than seems possible. By the time I lay the last book down my audience is a little smaller. Some kids have wandered away to play with blocks or puzzles, understandable considering an hour is a long time to ask a kid to sit still.

Others have fallen asleep in their parents' laps. But the kids that managed to hang in there all give me a polite round of applause.

Surprisingly, Burt is still sitting at the back of the group looking just as bored as the kids that wandered away. With a not-so-subtle nod toward where Paula and Sam are gathering their giant brood of kids, he gives me a death stare that seems to say *go convince them to vote for you.*

I do my best to suppress my sigh of absolute disdain for having to participate in small talk. But the other option is even worse: deal with whatever verbal tirade Burt will lay on me if I don't chat with them.

My palms turn a little sweaty as I approach the couple that I've only talked with in passing while buying something at the hardware store or here and there when they come into the library with the kids. Trying my best to keep it subtle, I rub my hands down the sides of my pants in an effort to dry them.

"Thanks for coming out, guys." I hold out a hand to Paula to shake and she takes it with a polite smile. "It's always a good day when I get the Anderson kids in here."

Maggie, the oldest, has wandered over to the Graphic Novel section. I think she might be teetering on teenager status. The next one in order I think is Max. He and his brother, whose name I can't recall, are sitting on the ground playing Jenga together. Robin, who I think might be around six, is adding more books to a pile already too big for her to carry. The two youngest are coloring at a nearby table.

"More like it is always a chaotic day when the Andersons show up." Paula laughs good naturedly as she drops my hand.

I hold out the same hand to her husband, Sam, who is nice enough if a little cold, probably out of solidarity with the Halsteds. "I gotta admit, you have a way with these kids."

My smile turns a little more genuine. "Thanks, kids are easy. Adults are the tough ones."

They both smile politely and nod awkwardly.

Behind me, Burt clears his throat, a sound that never fails to raise the hair on the back of my neck.

"Um, so I would really appreciate it if I could count on your vote in November." The words come out in a rush.

The couple exchange an uncomfortable, knowing glance before turning back to me. "Well, we're excited to see what you and Delia both have to say at the debate," Paula says

Um, excuse me, the what now? "Debate?"

"Yeah, honestly, the town is pretty excited about it." Sam bends down to snatch a block from his toddler's hand who was winding up to chuck it across the room. "It's been so long that we had two people running for mayor at the same time, so there hasn't been a debate in decades."

"I think I was ten during the last one," Paula chimes in.

Behind Paula I hear her daughter mumble, "Must have been in like the nineteen hundreds."

Paula gasps, and shoots her daughter a mocking dirty look. "Evil."

The girl tucks her head to hide her laugh as she wanders away again.

"I don't believe we are planning on having a debate." My hands are once again turning sweaty at just the thought.

"Oh, you have to." Sam seems to be getting some enjoyment from my obvious discomfort. "It's in the town charter. *All candidates for mayor must meet for a debate of the issues before the citizens of Amoresville can cast their votes.*"

"You know the town charter?"

"He has it memorized, so do I at this point. He recites it when he's trying not to c—"

"Darling, I don't think Wesley here needs to know that particular detail."

"Does Delia know about the debate?" Surely she won't want to do this either. Maybe we could just publish op-eds in the local paper and call it a day.

"Oh yeah, she's looking forward to it. You remember how much she loved mock-debate in high school." Sam locks eyes with me at the mention of our school days. "Weren't you in debate too?"

No, I wasn't. I just hung out after school hoping to hang out with my girlfriend after debate practice.

Delia, however, loved debate with a passion.

I'm screwed.

Chapter 16
Ten Years Ago

Delia

"In conclusion, the Amoresville School District should dissolve the football team and divert those funds to other more academically worthy programs. Thank you." I take a step back from the podium as the few people in the auditorium clap half-heartedly.

From the back, I hear one distinctly raucous set of applause. Shielding my eyes from the bright lights, I spot Wesley in the very last row, sitting ramrod straight in his seat and clapping as if I was just getting off the presidential debate stage, and not the practice session for the debate regional.

I try my best not to smile. We're not supposed to show overt emotion on stage during a debate. This is the first time Wes has ever come to one of my practices. Usually we just meet at the library or in the parking lot after practice.

After the debate coach gives us some pointers for the competition, we all say our goodbyes and I make my way to the back where Wes is still waiting.

Thankfully, no one here would care about the semi-secret relationship Wes and I have going. After three months of sneaking around, we started to get a little more lax around the school. Kissing by my locker, Wes walking me between each class, even the ones we don't share, are all totally normal and no one even bats an eye. If Mrs. Wheeler or any of the administration are around we keep our distance, but even that is getting harder these days.

"Holy shit, Delia, you were incredible." He wraps his arms around my waist and pulls me in for a tight hug, burying his face in my hair while I press mine into his shoulder, hiding the blush one of his compliments always produces. "No wonder I never win any of our arguments."

A giggle that I can't suppress bubbles up my throat. "What arguments? We've literally never fought about anything."

"Um excuse me, there was the great waffle versus curly fries debate. I was firmly waffle fries, but by the end I was practically trying to convince you that curly fries were better. I don't know how you manage to do that."

I roll my eyes. Sometimes I think he likes coming up with these silly *which is better* challenges just to see me work my magic. "That does not count as an argument."

"Okay, true, but still, what you do up on that stage is incredible. I got sick to my stomach just thinking about being up on that stage and I swear you came to life under the lights. It's like you photosynthesize the lights into grit and bravery." He tucks a piece of my hair that's fallen from my ponytail behind my ear.

"I'm pretty sure you would have even had the captain of the football team agreeing with you by the time you were done."

"Considering the captain of the football team is my brother, I can confidently say he would not have agreed with me. But thank you."

"How are you feeling about the competition this weekend?" He links his hand with mine and we make our way out the back doors of the auditorium, both automatically steering in the direction of the winding back route to the library.

"Good. The coach has been giving us wild topics lately to get us prepared for any scenarios they throw at us during our rounds. Since I specialize in extemporaneous debate I won't know the actual topics until right before the first round."

Wesley's face goes a little ashen. His dislike for public speaking became more than apparent when we had to memorize and perform the monologue from *Hamlet* as our first semester final in Honors English. I really thought he was going to puke that day. Actually, he might have and was just hiding from me. He didn't even eat lunch that day and it was like two hours after class.

"Getting up and talking in front of all those people is bad enough, but only having thirty minutes to prep is just insane." He visibly shudders next to me and I laugh.

"I love it. Even more when I have to take the position against what I actually believe. It makes me question things I normally wouldn't." I truly do love debate. Love being on stage even more. Too bad our theater program got cut before I even got to high school because of the budget being slashed yet again.

As we cross from Third Street to the corner of Elm, we automatically drop our hands and Wesley pauses at the stop sign. This is where we have to separate and go individually to the library. Any further and we run the risk of seeing Burt or his secretary.

"See you in a couple minutes." I wink at him and keep walking, feeling his eyes follow my movements down the two blocks to the turn onto Main Square where I will walk another two blocks back toward the library. Wes will double back four blocks and approach the library from the other side of the town square.

* * *

Wesley

I hate watching her walk away from me. Every cell in my body is telling me to screw my uncle and catch up with her. Take her hand in mine and walk through the sleepy town center like it is the most natural thing in the world, even if it would send ripples of rumors and innuendo through the town grapevine.

Five minutes later, I'm pushing through the library doors, something inside me settling that I hadn't even realized was turbulent. The library is in desperate need of an update. It's clean, but the paint is dingy, the front desk bows under the weight of piles of books waiting to be scanned and reshelved, and every single rolling cart squeaks like crazy.

Mrs. Thurston glances at me over the edge of her reading glasses, her gray and silver bob swaying slightly as she nods in my direction. "Mr. Goldman, I should put you on the payroll if you are going to be here every day."

She might be small, frail, and ancient, but the town librarian is not someone to be messed with. I've been coming to the library every day, even the days Delia can't make it because she has a shift at the cafe or debate or it is Harley's day with her. Some days I help Mrs. Thurston put books away on the shelves she can't reach. Sometimes I help her hang seasonal decorations. Most of the time I sit at a table and read.

"Pay me in free books and I'm good, Mrs. T."

"Hmp, you do know how a library works, correct?" I know she likes me, even though she has never once smiled at me.

"Indeed, I do. Speaking of which, any word on the next *One Piece Omnibus*?" I'm up to the fifteenth set. Each omnibus has three volumes of the long-running manga series. I still have ten more to go to make my goal to read all eighty volumes by my birthday in April. I think I'll be able to make it even though my reading speed has significantly reduced thanks to a certain girl.

Mrs. Thurston pulls out a stack of books from under the desk and slaps them on top of the worn wood. "I got the next three sets in the hopes that you will leave me alone for a while."

"Mrs. T, if you weren't a married woman, I would kiss you."

She waves her hand at me and turns away, though I get the feeling she is fighting a smile. "Take these and go find that girl."

I freeze in my spot, eyes going wide like a deer caught in head-lights. We've never acknowledged that Delia and I just happen to be at the library at the same time more often than not. And when she's here I don't sit at one of the tables reading, or do any of the tasks Mrs. T insists she doesn't need my help with.

"I don't—"

"Don't try lying to me, kid. I might be old, but my brain is still capable of adding one plus one. Your secret is safe with me, I don't participate in the rumor tree in this town." She looks around the mostly empty library and leans in closer. "I was always more a fan of your mother than your uncle. No offense to our mayor."

My jaw loses the ability to keep my mouth closed.

"Don't stand there like a fly trap, go on." With another wave of her hand, my newfound ally turns back to her computer and scans in books one by one.

I scoop up the stack of three thick books and walk back to the legal section in a daze, not bothering to pretend like I'm looking for another book on the way since apparently Delia and I were not nearly as sneaky as we thought we were.

In our spot, Delia sits cross-legged in the same black leggings and baggy sweater she'd been wearing all day. She's the most beautiful thing I've ever seen. "Hey." She smiles up at me and pats the spot next to her on the floor.

Now that I know Mrs. Thurston knows we're back here, I almost feel a little guilty about using the library as my makeout spot. Not bad enough to not immediately kiss Delia once I've taken my seat next to her though.

I could kiss Delia forever. Next to talking with her and holding her hand, kissing her is my favorite thing on the planet. I pull her long strawberry blonde hair from the ponytail she prefers, weaving it through my fingers as we twist to try and get the best angle on our kiss.

With the cutest frustrated growl I've ever heard, Delia backs up for just a split second before she throws one leg over my lap and settles against me.

This is new.

There has been some light petting, a little groping, but never her on top of me or vice versa. Not that the idea hadn't occurred to me, it has. A lot. More than is probably healthy.

Back to kissing, Delia moves against me, and my hands wander around her back and hips, slipping up under her sweater and the t-shirt beneath that. "Is this okay?" I whisper against her mouth.

She nods quickly, deepening the kiss. Something between us has finally snapped. All the shy restraint we've treated each other with up to now seems to have vanished.

A gentle moan fills my mouth and I realize we are dangerously close to going way further than is probably appropriate for the legal section in the local library.

Gently, I slip my hands out from under her shirt and grip her hips, keeping her still. "Delia, we have to stop."

With a little whimper she collapses against me, her forehead pressed to my shoulder. I wrap my arms around her in a tight hug.

"My parents are going away this weekend." She sits up, looking at me with a shy reluctance.

"Okay." I'm not going to assume anything, but holy hell am I hoping this is going somewhere.

"They have a friend getting married in Erie, so after my competition Friday night, they are going to spend the weekend there. Knox is coming to stay with us, but he's already said Orion could have some of the guys from the football team over. They won't notice if I sneak out."

She's talking fast, barely even taking in a breath.

"There is an apartment over the cafe. No one is living there right now. Do you want to, um, you know, meet me there?"

Holy shit. An entire night alone with Delia, no parents, no uncles, no nosy townspeople that we have to hide from.

"Yes, yeah, absolutely." I nod enthusiastically.

"Um, do you think you might be able to get something?"

"Yeah, I can bring whatever you want. Food? A movie? Like literally anything."

"Condoms?"

My heart stops; I go completely still.

"I'm not saying we will, you know, do *it*. But I figure we should be prepared just in case. Especially considering I was about ready to rip your shirt off about two minutes ago and we're in the library. It's just the responsible thing to do, right?"

I nod again, slowly this time. "Yeah, I can absolutely get some. But we don't have to do anything you aren't ready for."

We had a talk a few weeks ago about our limited histories. We're both virgins. I didn't realize she was there already.

Delia smiles sweetly at me and leans in for a gentle kiss. "I know you would never be the guy to pressure me. But I've been thinking about it, a lot. Like a lot a lot."

Okay, knowing the girl of my dreams is thinking about sex with me is going to go to my head. Both of them in fact.

"And I want it to happen with you eventually. I'm not sure Friday night will be the night, but in case it is, I just think we should be ready."

"Agreed." Something important that has been building inside me suddenly won't stay put any longer. Words that seem bigger than the eight letters that comprise them won't be held back another second. "I love you, Delia. I always will, even if we never have sex."

A huge, goofy grin spreads across her face, cheeks red and eyes a little misty. "I love you, too."

Chapter 17

Delia

Most people will never experience the distinct smell of a strip club the morning after a bachelor party.

They should count themselves lucky.

It is a combination of stale beer, Axe Body Spray, and cum-stained sweatpants. Thankfully, the guys last night were fairly well-behaved and no one puked on the floor.

I've become all too familiar with parfum de douchebag since opening Club Barely Over the Line. That smell is why I pay the cleaning crew their weight in gold.

Flipping on the lights, I take stock of the main room as I stretch out my sore muscles. The barback called in sick last night, so I found myself slinging drinks and pulling bottles of liquor until two in the morning when the state mandates we close. My body is paying for it today. Twenty-seven and complaining about aches and pains. Most women my age are still out partying on weekends, not working nearly every hour of the day.

The place doesn't look half bad. Trash needs to be gathered and taken out, but the cleaners will take care of that as well as disinfecting the whole place from top to bottom. As if summoned by my thoughts of them, the four women slip through the employee entrance sipping their personalized ceramic coffee mugs from The Bean.

Tomorrow morning, they will drop off these mugs to get cleaned and Mom will give them different ones, then the cycle continues every day for just about everyone in town. She finally broke down and started carrying actual paper to-go cups since we have seen a good deal more out-of-towners come through the past few years, and she was losing a crap ton of money on mugs that no one returned.

"Morning, Delia." Jenny is the oldest of the four sisters at thirty-five, though she looks about twenty years older thanks to a hard life. She's a no-nonsense, solid woman with premature silver hair and a semi-permanent scowl on her face. "Your mother sent along your usual."

I gratefully take the mug with flowers that vaguely resemble vaginas all over it. Some people might think my mom and I have a weird relationship, but I would not trade my sexually liberated, hippy mom for a June Cleaver type if given the choice. She's probably been to the club more than anyone else in town that doesn't work here. Plus, she takes every single one of Harley's classes, no matter how many times we tell her not to since she nearly broke her ankle last year.

"Thanks, Jenny!" I bring the drink to my nose and inhale deeply. Dirty chai latte with homemade raspberry syrup. On the menu, it's called Shark Week. I've been drinking them ever since I turned fourteen. "Do me a favor and give the stage an extra once over today. Misty added whipped cream to her set last night and the last thing I need is all my dancers getting a yeast infection."

Jenny, Jessie, and Julie all make matching faces of disgust while Joey fakes a gagging sound. J4 Cleaning has been in business as long as the club. Joey, the youngest, tried to get a job dancing here when I opened, but she kept falling over her own feet, so instead I offered her a position as a waitress. She cost me more money in spilled drinks than she brought in. Outright firing her was something I couldn't stomach. Instead, she took on the role of cleaning lady, which when we first opened both didn't pay well and was a truly disgusting job. She never once complained. As the club grew in popularity and cleanliness of its clientele, it became clear she would need more help. All of her sisters came on board as well. Now they clean for most of the businesses in town. Even the Mayor's office, which I forgive them for since they complain about Burt about as much as I do.

The tight-knit sisters went from barely being able to pay the rent on their trailer to having one of the most successful businesses in town. Last I heard they even bought a piece of property that they plan on building four small houses on as their own little family compound.

Once they get going, I retreat back to my office, already feeling the pressure of my seemingly endless to-do list. I pull open the bottom drawer of the desk and grab my backup laptop charger since I left my main one at home last night. Along with it come a bunch of papers I've just been shoving in the drawer. On top of the mess is the letter I've been doing an excellent job of ignoring thanks to my new quest to become mayor.

But there it is, surrounded by the endless junk mail that seems to never end, a stark white piece of paper among bright mailers for credit cards. I grab the trash can from under the desk and begin shoving the mess in until all that is left is the single piece of paper. Without thinking too much about it, I add it to the other discarded mail. I shouldn't give it any more thought than I give the semi-scammy offers for lines of credit.

Determined to get some work done, I plug in the laptop and set my alarm for noon. If I don't set alarms for myself I'll hyper fixate my way into skipping every meal until we open. I wake up the laptop and navigate my way to the document where I've been prepping for the upcoming debate.

Sam was practically giggling and kicking his feet when he swung by The Bean yesterday to fill me in on Wesley's reaction to finding out he would need to debate me. Apparently, my opponent nearly upchucked all over the kid's board bookshelf. Sam, Paula, and I ended up huddled together at one of the tables listing out arguments I needed to have prepared for the debate.

I dig in, going through the minutes from the past several months of council meetings that get posted online. I make notes on the few things Burt has gotten pushback on from the council. Start to form responses to possible questions the moderator will ask. There hasn't been any word yet on who the moderator will be. According to Sam it just has to be a citizen in good standing chosen by the outgoing town council, so I have to be ready for anything.

Three hours go by in the blink of an eye. "Living Dead Girl" starts blaring from my phone, the alarm for the start of my favorite part of the day.

Quickly, I change into my hot pink booty shorts and a sports bra so tight it pushes my Triple D breasts up under my chin. My stomach is nowhere near flat, bulging a little between the two pieces of clothing, but fuck it, I think I look hot as hell. The four-inch platform heels take a little work to strap onto my feet, but the instant they are secured and I stand to my now 6'2" height, a different part of me starts to awaken.

I grab the trash can and strut out to the club. Jenny and her sisters are just starting to pack up their equipment, and the stench from before has been completely replaced by the amazing scent of the homemade cleaning product line the J Sisters use.

"That for me?" Jenny reaches out for the can and takes it from my arms while Joey unties one of the many trash bags ready to go out to the dumpster.

I swear, everything fades into slow motion as I watch the girls start to dump the trash from my office into the bag with god knows what filth.

"Wait!"

All four of the sisters stop in their tracks and look at me.

I surge forward, snatching the letter from the top of the trash can before Jenny can upend it into the bag.

"I didn't mean to throw this one out."

"Oh, okay." They look at me like I might have lost my mind, which maybe I have. "We're going to hustle out before the brat pack shows up."

"Ha, yeah, make your escape while you can." Their activity seems to fade into the background as I smooth the now crinkled sheet of paper.

Dear Delia Halsted,

Congratulations! We are pleased to offer you a spot at...

"Okay, sluts, who's ready to shake their booty?" Harley struts into the club wearing a pair of baggy sweatpants perched precariously low on her hips, letting the top of her panties poke out above. She's wearing a matching sports bra and a coffee mug in one hand, an animal carrier that sways suspiciously in the other. Behind her is a line of women ranging in age from mid-thirties to well above seventy.

Quickly, I fold the letter in thirds, then in half again, trying to palm it so no one spots it. I should know better though, because almost immediately Harley's gaze zooms in on my guilty expression.

"What have you done?"

"Who, me?" I look around the room as if she might be talking to someone else.

"Bitch, you know exactly who I'm talking to. Why do you look like you're sniffing my panties behind my back?"

I roll my eyes and start backing away from Harley. I can lie to anyone on this planet with ease, but have never been able to pull the wool over Harley's eyes. "Please, you and I both know you would happily let me sniff your panties right out in the open."

"Damn straight." She snaps the elastic of her panties against her tan skin with her thumb. "Don't think I'm going to let you get away with whatever you think can hide from me. I will figure it out and you know it."

"But you'll let it go for now? I promise I'll fill you in eventually." And I will, once I can compartmentalize the contents of the letter in a neat little box to be stored away in the proper place in my head.

"For now." She points at me. "But you know I never forget."

I nod, because, yeah I do know. "Are you going to tell me what is hissing in that carrier and why you have it in my club?"

Harley smiles in her trademark trouble making way. "Remember how my sister stopped talking to me for two weeks when you crashed a dinner at her B&B?"

"How could I forget?" I've been waiting for Harley to get even for that night ever since.

"Well, this—" she holds up the carrier and something inside thrashes about and emits a low hiss "—is revenge. Also known as Sparkles the possum."

"A fucking possum? Are you kidding me? Come on, Har, that's too much."

"Two. Weeks. Not a word, and even now she only gives me one or two word responses. Trust me, it isn't too much." She holds the carrier out to me and I take it reluctantly, holding it as far from my body as I can. "I'll fill you in on his history and care instructions after class."

Harley spins back to the main stage where several women with hair in various stages of graying are all stripping out of their muumuus to reveal their own short shorts and sports bras. "Now, are my geriatric whores ready to shake it? Those old asses aren't going to twerk themselves."

Best friend effectively distracted, I turn and speed walk back to my office as best as I can in my heels, carrier held at arm's distance and letter clutched in the other hand.

Once in my office, I immediately place the carrier on the floor in the middle of the room, jumping back as Sparkles thrashes around some more inside. Spinning around I go to the closet and shove the letter into my purse to take home after tonight's shift. At least there Harley won't be able to find it.

Scratch that.

It will at least take her longer to find it. Harley is like a Jack Russell when it comes to information she wants. Once she gets her teeth into even a hint of a secret, she doesn't let go until whatever it is has been ripped apart and inspected to her satisfaction. Actually, that sounds similar to the literal wild animal she just hoisted onto my guilty ass.

I shut the closet door and lean back against the solid wood, my chest rising and falling dramatically.

Already out of breath and I haven't even started today's workout.

Chapter 18

Wesley

Feet slapping against the wet pavement in a rhythmic pattern usually helps to calm whatever anxiety plagues me.

Not today though.

Even after running six miles, twice the normal distance I shoot for on my running days, the thoughts keep swirling around in my head. The crisp, cold fall air seeping into my skin does nothing to ease the churning in my gut. Not even the crunch of newly fallen leaves under my feet brings the normal spark of joy.

Debate prep with Burt has been torture this week. The whole town seems to be buzzing with the excitement of two of its citizens getting on stage and trading barbs about how the town should be run. I hear about it at work, in the store, walking down the street. I can't fucking escape it.

For someone that was raised practically under the lights of a stage, by a fairly popular Broadway actress and a set-designer, the idea of getting up in front of an audience has always been one of my worst fears.

Story Hour with the kids doesn't count. Give them a good story and some voices, they are happy. If they don't like something, they will come out and say it directly to your face. And the occasional meltdown is expected from a preschooler. But adults are a whole other story. They judge. They whisper. They are rude on purpose.

And I am going to go in front of them and talk about what I want to do with the town.

Or what Burt wants me to do. I've tried telling Burt my ideas. How I think having a more diverse array of businesses would go a long way to attracting more traffic to our downtown. We need more restaurants, maybe even a brewery or specialty bar. We need to take down the fucking streetlights, or at least turn them to flashing stoplights after a certain time of day. And we need to stop making people jump through figurative, and sometimes literal, hoops to do anything in this town.

But he doesn't want to hear any of it. As far as Burt is concerned, change is the enemy of Amoresville.

My legs have gone past the point of pain and have hit the numbness that comes from a really long run. My lungs, however, are not as lucky.

A fuzzy figure appears on the path in front of me. Without my glasses it could be a person, a bear, or a poorly placed tree.

Running, sleeping, and showering are the only times my glasses come off my face. The jostling from a run makes them slowly descend down my nose, and constantly pushing them up annoys the living daylights out of me. The tradeoff is not being able to see anything more than three feet in front of me.

Despite the cool temperatures, my shirt is soaked through with sweat, sticking to every inch of my chest and stomach. I am deeply regretting my decision to wear sweatpants this morning. I should have stuck with my normal running shorts. Too late now.

A sharp twinge in my side that refuses to go away is my body's way of telling me it has had enough. My long-distance running days are far behind me in high school, no more marathons for me. Slowing my pace, I come to a walk, hands on my side as I suck in breaths. A familiar scent tinges the oxygen I desperately try to force into my lungs. Vanilla, sugar, and fall leaves.

Swinging my gaze up to the path ahead, the fuzzy figure has taken a little bit more shape, like a spirit becoming corporeal. A very curvy shape. A shape that haunts my dreams and fantasies.

Delia. I don't need my vision to know that the person standing in the path ahead of me, hand holding a leash, is the woman of my dreams. Or nightmares. Depends on the day.

I take the earbuds out, trading my running playlist for the hushed sounds of nature slowly going to sleep for the winter. But also Delia muttering to herself, "Please just finish shitting. I will be your best friend and feed you so many treats if you will please just finish shitting before he makes it to us."

A smile pulls at the corners of my mouth against my will. I couldn't hide my amusement any more than I can rid myself of the constant desire to just be near Delia.

"Hey."

She mutters something I don't quite hear and turns to face me. We're still far enough apart that I can't make out her expression, but I have no doubt it is pained at my appearance.

"Morning."

I take a couple steps closer, not liking that I can't see her features. "Kinda early for you, isn't it?"

Five a.m. is when I wake up every morning for either a run or strength training session, so it has to be at least six by now. That is pretty much the middle of the night for Delia.

Finally, I am close enough to see her tired eyes and scrubbed clean face. God, she is so fucking gorgeous like this. Of the millions of regrets I have where Delia is concerned, the fact that I never got to see her fresh faced first thing in the morning is one of the biggest.

"Yeah, well, Mr. Sparkles here hasn't quite gotten the hang of my schedule yet." She nods down to the creature hooked up to her lease.

"Do you have a cat on a leash in the park?"

"No, not a cat, look a little closer." Delia knows exactly how blind I am. She used to love to hold things far away and bring them closer until I could tell her what it was. She found my poor vision endlessly fascinating. Half the time I didn't know because I was watching her, not whatever was in her hands at the time.

Curious what she could be walking this early in the morning, I take another step closer and bend down to get a better look. The small gray blob starts to come into focus. "What the fuck kind of dog is this?"

The thing twists around, its long pink nose scrunching up as it hisses then flops over on its side.

I jump back, probably about as terrified as the animal. "Delia, why are you walking an opossum in the town park?"

For her part, Delia is laughing her ass off, leaning over, both hands on her knees, hiccupping between peals of laughter. "I'm sorry, oh God, that was too good."

"Is it okay?" The little guy is still curled up on its side, tongue lolling out the side of its mouth.

"Yeah, he does that whenever he meets someone new." She sucks in a deep breath and straightens, which is when I notice she's wearing a tight-fitting matching exercise outfit. One that is nothing more than a sports bra and leggings that fit like a second skin. The set is in her favorite color, a deep emerald green. Fuck, so gorgeous.

"As for why I'm walking him, Harley rescued him from some idiot that thought an opossum would make a great pet, then when it destroyed his house tried to sell it on Craigslist. She paid the guy fifty bucks then forced him on me at the club yesterday since her place is already full of animals that were stressing him out and I owed her a favor."

Delia goes suddenly and rather suspiciously quiet, staring down at the creature that should be out hanging in a tree somewhere.

"Why did you owe Harley a favor?"

She shifts her weight onto the other foot, looking uncomfortable for a minute before she seems to remember she's a badass and looks me dead in the eye.

"I got her in trouble with Rose when I crashed your little dinner the other night."

"Ah, yeah, that makes sense." I nod down at the little guy who seems to be rousing from his impromptu nap. "Well, I think this should definitely make up for it. Isn't this thing going to trash your house too?"

I've never been in Delia's place, obviously, but I pass by the cute townhouse almost daily when I drive to work.

"Nah, he's got the run of the garage. It's heated and we made it nice and comfy in there for him. Besides, he'll only be here a couple days. There is a zoo in Ohio that is going to take him."

I nod, happy to know Delia's house won't be overrun by a crazed marsupial. "So, about the other night—"

"So, Sam told you about the debate?" Delia practically shouts the words, so much so I glance at Mr. Sparkles, afraid he might play dead again, but he's happily sniffing around in the dewy grass.

The sweat dripping down my face seems to double with just the briefest mention of getting up on that stage. I grab the edge of my t-shirt and pull it up to wipe away the moisture from my face. And maybe give me a second to collect myself before having to face my opponent at the debate I'd do anything to get out of.

When I lower my shirt again, I catch Delia looking at my stomach, her mouth slightly open. Her eyes snap over to the feral animal, but the famous Halsted blush is already creeping up her face. Amazing that a woman that owns a strip club and must see any number of scandalous things on a daily basis can still blush.

"How many times have you puked just thinking about debating me?" I'm surprised she's bringing up something from our shared past. In high school, for Honors English we had to get up in front of the whole class and recite the tomorrow monologue from *Macbeth*. She rubbed my back for twenty minutes in the parking lot as I puked my breakfast up into the bushes.

"Not at all." I go to push up my glasses, only to realize they aren't there and immediately let my hand drop back down to my side. "Yet."

She smirks.

"Will you take it easy on me?"

Finally, she turns to look me in the eye. "Not a chance in hell."

Yeah, that is kinda what I figured.

Chapter 19
Ten Years Ago

Delia

I have never been so nervous in my entire life. Not earlier today when I was onstage debating everything from the death penalty to drilling in the arctic. I got second in regionals so I will move on to districts in a couple months, and then hopefully states.

But standing up on that stage with the judges in front of me and my opponents staring me down was nothing compared to preparing for my first ever boyfriend to come spend the night with me.

Looking around the small living-slash-dining room in the apartment above The Bean, I'm happy with what I've done. I didn't want to risk someone calling Mom and letting her know the lights were left on in the cafe, so I opted to squeeze a little card table and a couple folding tables into the vacant one-bedroom apartment.

The upstairs of the house that has been in my mom's side of the family for hundreds of years has two apartments and an office where Mom does all the business-y things for the cafe.

She rents out the apartments occasionally, but more often than not people are fleeing the town not moving in, so they mostly sit empty. Orion has plans to move into one of them when he graduates from college and moves back to help Dad run the farm. Eventually he'll take over the operation and Dad will retire, but I can't really picture that happening. Dad practically *is* the land, sometimes I think he sprouted up in the fields like the corn we grow instead of his mom giving birth to him.

But for now, the apartments are empty. This one at least has some furniture that Mom threw in here when she redid our house, and occasionally a family friend will stay here when they visit. In the main living area there is a small couch, a TV about five years past obsolescence, and now the card table and chairs I set up for tonight. The bedroom has a queen bed and dresser with one lamp on it. There is just barely enough room to walk around the furniture. I managed to sneak out some extra blankets, sheets, and pillows when my brothers were out working in the fields, and Harley swiped her mom's car and helped me haul everything to the cafe.

I thought about lighting candles, but that seemed like too much. So I settled for a lace tablecloth and some of the plates from the cafe. Other than lunch at school, Wes and I have never actually eaten together, so I wasn't sure what to make. I settled on a baked chicken recipe Mom makes for Dad when she wants to get on his good side and a salad.

My phone dings with a text from Harley. *Is your hymen still intact?*

OMG, why is my best friend such a bitch? *He's not even here yet, bitch, stop texting me.*

I'm not even positive I want to lose my virginity tonight. I mean, I think about it, and every time Wes and I make out it feels like too much and not enough all at once.

With one last look around, I go down to the cafe's kitchen to wait for Wesley. I don't know how he plans to sneak out of his uncle's house, but he promised he'd be here no later than seven, and I know he will do his best to keep that promise.

Nerves race through my veins like greyhounds chasing a rabbit around a track. I can't hold still, so I pace around the island in the small prep kitchen until my head feels dizzy and I start to wonder if he really will show.

A soft rap at the back door makes me jump even though I've been waiting for the sound. Without bothering to look through the gauzy curtains that block the window, I open the door to find Wesley standing on the back porch. He's wearing khakis and a button-down. It's the most dressed up I've ever seen him. Even on picture day at school he wore his usual jeans and graphic t-shirt.

"I brought these for you." He holds out a bouquet of flowers that I recognize from Dolly's Market on the other side of town.

He brought me flowers. My heart thumps wildly inside my chest as I take the paper-wrapped stems and our fingers brush against each other. This is not helping the dizziness from my laps around the island.

"Thanks," I whisper for some unknown reason. We don't have to whisper. No one is here. There is no Mrs. Thurston lurking around the corner just waiting to interrupt us tonight.

I step back, giving him enough room to walk through the door and close it behind him. His eyes track up and down my body and I'm suddenly so self-conscious of my decision to wear the twirly green dress I bought for Homecoming last year and never wore since Harley couldn't afford to buy one and we ditched the dance in favor of a girls' night.

"You look beautiful." He says it like he can't catch his breath.

"So do you, I mean you look good." We both laugh a little awkwardly, standing there in the middle of the kitchen where I've helped my mom experiment with new drink recipes. "Did you have any trouble getting away from Burt?"

He shakes his head and runs his fingers through his hair. "I told him there were some kids meeting to talk about student council and I was going to sit in to see if I wanted to run next year. He practically shoved me out the door he was so excited I showed interest in school politics."

"Haha, sounds good. Um, I made us some dinner. If you're hungry."

"Yeah, I could eat."

Tentatively, I take his hand and lead him up the back stairs to the top floor. Everything inside me is buzzing, like I drank all the cold brew concentrate Mom keeps in the fridge downstairs. The energy coursing through me is so strong I feel like I'm vibrating from my toes to the ends of my hair.

Once we're in the apartment, I put the flowers in a random glass left in a cabinet and dish up the plates, placing them at each of our chairs. Wes holds out my chair for me to sit before taking his own. It feels a little like we're playing dress-up. I suddenly feel very young sitting across from the boy I've fallen completely in love with and pretending we're grown-ups who cook dinners and bring flowers home from work.

But as we sit and the conversation starts flowing like it always does when we're together, the feeling goes away and more and more this just feels like how things are supposed to be for Wes and me. Maybe forever.

* * *

Wesley

As nervous as I was walking through the back door of Romancing the Bean, sitting across from Delia as we laugh about something Harley said at lunch that week feels just as comfortable.

The food she made is delicious, but then anything would be better than the sandwiches and pasta with jarred sauce Burt is prone to. He basically has three meals that he repeats over and over again. I tried offering to make dinner once, but he claimed food he didn't make gave him indigestion. This is the first time someone has put actual effort into a meal since I lost my mothers. Despite how happy I am to be sitting here with my girlfriend, a pang of longing for my parents echoes through my chest. I do my best to shove it down and focus on the moment.

As we finish the last bites of food, a little bit of the awkwardness from before sneaks back in. Together, we clear our dishes and wash them at the sink since Delia will need to return them to the cafe before we leave.

"Do you want to watch TV? This thing is so old I'm not sure it is actually hooked up to anything." Delia leans her hip against the counter, and I realize she must be wearing heels because she's almost at eye level with me. She's one of the tallest girls in our class, but I'm still at least three or four inches taller.

"Yeah, we could watch something." I step a little closer, she's so beautiful. There is a little bit of black lining her eyes, a shimmery gold eyeshadow on her lids that make her green eyes pop even more. The light pink lipstick she had been wearing when I got here has mostly rubbed off from eating and sipping from our drinks. I can't tell if the pink tinge to her cheeks is from makeup or her natural blush whenever she is nervous.

"Is it okay if I kiss you first? I've been thinking about kissing you since I got here and I just—" do I sound like a pushy jerk right now? "—Not that that is the only reason I came here, I just wanted to spend time with you where we didn't have to be sitting on a dingy orange carpet and—"

Before I can complete my word vomit, Delia leaps into me, wrapping her arms around my neck and pressing her lips against mine. I react immediately, wrapping my own arms around her waist and pulling her flush against me.

"I wanted to kiss you too but didn't know how to start outside the library," she mumbles against my lips.

"Is it weird that every time I walk into the library, I have to fight off a boner?"

Delia laughs, the little puffs of air percussing against my cheek. I love being this close to her. "I mean, Mrs. Thurston is quite the babe."

"Ugh." I screw my eyes shut trying to rid that thought from my mind. "Never say that again."

"I know what you mean though, I don't think I'll ever be able to walk into that library again without thinking about your mouth."

My luck has been pretty shit as far as teenagers go, no one can deny that. But having someone like Delia admit she thinks about my mouth at all makes it seem like not everything in my life has been bad.

I pull her tight against me once again, kissing her with every ounce of emotion I feel for her. I came to this town a lost kid who just missed his parents and wanted to be anywhere else. Then she literally collided with me in the hall and the clouds parted. The bad things are still there, no amount of loving Delia will erase the hole left by my parents, but it makes it seem manageable somehow.

Our hands are everywhere. The freedom of being able to kiss and touch without fear of someone walking in his heady stuff.

"Wes?"

"Yeah, Delia?" I kiss down the line of her neck, a weird urge coming over me to suck on the soft skin there, but I resist, not wanting to leave a mark that would make people talk poorly of her.

"Can we go to the bedroom?"

I back up, locking eyes with her to make sure I am getting exactly what she is saying. "Are you sure?"

She nods, biting her bottom lip, then releasing it to speak. "I don't know if I will want to go all the way, but I want to do a lot more than we've been able to in the library. I want to *see* you." Her eyes flick down to where our hips are pressed together and there is a very obvious situation pressing into her belly.

"Yeah." I swallow, because suddenly my mouth is dry and my nerves are going haywire. "I want to see you, too." It feels like a confession even though the statement should be as obvious as daylight. "But no matter what we do, you can tell me to stop at any time and I will. No questions. Okay?"

She nods solemnly. "I trust you."

We interlock our fingers and she leads me to a door on the other side of the dining area. Different parts of me seem to war with each other. My brain telling me to calm down, go slow, be careful with her. My heart trying to leap out of my chest and lay itself down for her to do what she wants with it. And, yeah, my dick definitely has some ideas, too. But I try to ignore him because he is the very last thing I care about listening to right now.

Number one is Delia, and always will be.

Chapter 20

Delia

Mr. Sparkles is tucked away safely in the garage, ready to sleep away the day. I, however, can't manage to fall asleep. Normally, after a long night at the club I will crash in bed and practically fall into a coma for a good nine hours, but this morning I just toss and turn, unable to turn off my brain.

The run-in with Wes.

The letter.

The campaign.

The guy who is relentlessly trying to buy my club.

They all fight for prominence in my brain. It's like my past, present, and future are all colliding. For so long I've just been marching from one moment to the next, never thinking about where my life is going or where I've been.

I never fooled myself into thinking I got past what happened in high school. So much of what happens in our teens acts as a foundation for our future. Wesley breaking my heart makes a hell of a shaky foundation. There is a reason I've yet to have a relationship that lasted more than a few months.

But the pain of those days was eventually over-shadowed by the death of my dreams when Pop got sick, then his death as well. A broken heart seemed small compared to losing the man you thought hung the moon and stars.

I spent exactly one week at college. I was so excited to be out on my own, away from Amoresville. I got into my dream school in New York City. I was going to be an actress. Or a writer. Or child psychologist. I hadn't really decided yet. But then, between classes, I got a call from Mom.

"Honey, Dad is sick."

Just like that, everything changed. I packed up the things that hadn't even had time to gather dust, grabbed the next train from Penn Station to State College where Knox picked me up. I've been here ever since.

Sometimes I wonder what my life would have been like if I had stayed at school. If a random cell in Dad's brain hadn't mutated and spread over the course of years until it started affecting who he was, would I still be in New York? Would I have finished college? Would I still be as close to my brothers?

I wouldn't have run the cafe for Mom. Wouldn't have opened the club to get back at Burt for trying to close my mother's business while she was at her most vulnerable. I definitely wouldn't be running for mayor.

With a huff, I roll over to my other side, trying to squeeze my eyes closed and turn my mind off. Wesley's smiling face appears out of nowhere. Sweat soaked with no glasses on. His abs, Jesus Christ, his fucking abs. Just a flash of them while he wiped away sweat and I wanted to run my hands over the firm muscles. A warm sensation trickles through my body, pooling between my thighs.

No.

I will not go there. After our misstep six years ago, I swore to myself I would stop getting myself off to memories of Wesley and the way he touched me.

"Fuck it." Throwing off my covers, I stumble out of bed. If I can't sleep I might as well do something useful. It's Monday, which means most of the businesses in town are closed, including the cafe and the club. If I know Mom, she'll be in her kitchen trying out recipes for drinks. Maybe she wants some company.

It doesn't take long before I'm dressed, just jeans and a t-shirt, throw my hair up into a ponytail and out the door. My townhouse is only a few blocks from The Bean. I bought it specifically for that reason, wanting to be close to Mom in case she needed me. While Dad was sick I became something of a caregiver to her. Reminded her to eat, sleep, and shower. It's been six years since he passed, and yet I can't seem to let go of the instinct to make sure Mom is doing okay. She's probably more emotionally stable than most of the town, but I still worry.

It's closing in on noon, but the town is quiet as ever. Kids are in school, people are at their jobs, the streets only have a light trickle of cars. It's a little overcast and chilly, with leaves scattered all over the sidewalks.

Any day now Burt will be sending out his annual end of October newsletter that reminds everyone to rake their yards or they will be fined. That man loves a good fine. I have a stack of them in my kitchen junk drawer to prove it. I even got the first one for failing to mow my lawn framed.

Oh boy was our mayor pissed when I had Knox come out and kill off my grass, replacing it entirely with native pollinator flowers and grasses. This time of year it is going dormant for the winter, but next spring it will once again be a riot of colors as high as my knees. Nothing makes me smile quite like pulling onto my street and seeing perfectly manicured lawns all lined up with my quarter acre piece of land sticking out like a big pink thumb.

I even had the Ag Extension from the local college come out and certify that my lawn is *pollinator-friendly* and should not be cut down.

Being petty is kind of a specialty of mine.

The bright pink of the Romancing the Bean Cafe sign is visible from a block away, and it might give me just as much joy as my garden front yard.

I will never forget the day that sign went up and Burt's reaction.

"You have to take that indecent sign down immediately." His face turned near purple with the outrage building up in his body.

"Burt, I don't know what you mean." I stood on the sidewalk out front watching as Sam and Knox secured the sign to the porch roof. Mom was at the hospital with Dad and I knew this would be a great surprise to raise her spirits when she stopped in later for her weekly check-in.

I tilted my head, looking confused. "I think it is quite charming."

For a second I think I might actually see smoke leaking out from Burt's tiny brain. "It is lewd. You can't fool me, you did that on purpose."

Scrunching up my nose, I gave him my best impression of a bobble-headed idiot. "Did what? Is there something you're seeing that I'm not?"

He would never say the words, I had no doubt in my mind. "I am bringing this up at the next town meeting. Mark my words, this will not stand."

The memory makes me giggle every time. I fucking love pissing that man off. To be fair, I did absolutely design that logo to look like a clitoris nestled between the folds of a woman's vulva. But if anyone asks, it is just a coffee bean stuck in the pages of a book. I used my very brief graphic design phase to absolutely terrorize the town with barely hidden sexual innuendo.

The Bean is quiet as expected and I let myself in through the kitchen expecting to see Mom at the stove working on some new syrup in preparation for her November specials. Instead, the place is spotless and totally empty.

"Mom, you here?" There are only a few other places she could be if she isn't bustling around in the kitchen. Out visiting Knox and his wife June on the farm, babysitting my brother's stepson, or maybe out to lunch with her best friend Dolly, owner of Dolly's Market, the only grocery store within thirty minutes of town.

Pushing out from the kitchen doors into the space behind the coffee bar, I stop in my tracks. The picture in front of me makes absolutely zero sense and I wonder briefly if I am still in bed thinking inappropriate thoughts about my nemesis.

At a small table in the corner of the room is Wesley Goldman, trying to stand from his chair while my mother pushes his shoulder down so he is trapped. There are piles of books on the table, some new and some old. Two empty mugs sitting in front of each of them. They've been here a while. Having coffee together. Talking about books.

As if a puzzle piece has just clicked into the last open space, the picture becomes clear.

"Holy shit, how did I not figure this out before? Are you friends with my mom?"

Wesley gently pushes Mom's hand off his shoulder and manages to stand. "I can explain."

"Oh, really?" I take another step forward, despite everything inside me recoiling at the idea of my mother hanging out with the guy who broke my heart in high school. "You're going to explain why *my* mom, of all people, is, what, book buddies with the guy who took my virginity and then crushed me the very next day?"

Maybe it is immature that I've held the actions of a teenage boy against the man he grew up to be, but what he did was inexcusable and I will never be able to get past it. *Never.*

I give into the instinct to run, turning on my heel, but before I can take a step, the voice of the woman I thought I could trust more than any in this world stops me in my tracks.

"Stop right there, Delia. It is long past time to air everything out. This mess between you two has festered so long it has cast its fetid odor over the whole town." Mom gets up from her chair and grabs another one from a table, moving it to just across from Wesley. "Sit your ass down."

The only reason I stay is because Wesley looks as terrified as I feel, and I kinda like the idea of getting to make him uncomfortable.

Chapter 21

Wesley

Oh fuck. This can't be happening.

I had one rule when Roxy and I started having coffee and books time on Monday mornings: no one can find out.

Last year Orion discovered our friendship when he walked in on me helping his now live-in partner with her business license application. He was livid. But Roxy talked him down and he got over it. He has even been somewhat civil to me since I helped The Tiger's Eye get up and running and tried my best to mitigate Burt's interference in the store.

But I held him and Brigid to the same promise, no telling anyone. The last thing I wanted was for Burt to find out I am friendly with anyone from the Halsted family and turn his ire on them once again.

"Is someone going to tell me what exactly is happening here?" Delia plops down in the chair opposite me, with Roxy taking her seat again as well.

Roxy looks at me expectantly, but my mouth has gone completely dry. I'm so used to never seeing or hearing from Delia, to suddenly have her very present in my life is disorienting.

With a sigh, Roxy turns to her daughter. "A year after your father died, Burt hatched a plan to try and get the state to pull my food license. Told Wes all about it. He tried to talk his uncle out of it, that The Bean is a staple in this town, and the people would be upset come reelection time. But he wouldn't be swayed."

I focus my eyes on the empty mug in front of me. It was an apple fritter latte that Roxy was planning to call the Arranged Marriage Latte.

"Wes came to the cafe early one morning, before I was open. He knocked on the back door." She pokes my arm with one finger. "About scared the shit out of me."

I give her a weak smile. She really did look terrified when she pulled back the little curtain covering the window and saw me standing on the back porch in my running clothes.

"At first I didn't want to hear anything he said. As far as I was concerned, he was no better than Burt. Maybe worse after how heartbroken you were in high school." Roxy puts her hand on Delia's arm, who is sitting ramrod straight in her chair as if ready to run at the smallest provocation, her gaze glued to her mother and absolutely refusing to look in my direction. That same sick feeling the memory always causes rolls through my gut and I stare down at the mug once again.

"He pleaded with me to listen. Told me all about Burt's plan to fake a mold report on the house." She looks around the room lovingly. "He was going to give the report to a friend in the Ag Department and get us shut down."

Despite keeping my gaze firmly downcast, I can feel the moment Delia's eyes slide over to look at me. Gathering every bit of strength I have, I glance up to meet her gaze. I can't read what she is thinking. There used to be a time I could tell her every emotion just by the way she looked at me. Those days are long gone now.

"The warning gave me time to contract two different companies to come out and do independent inspections, certifying The Bean was mold free. Not so much as a moldy strawberry in the fridge. So when the inspector came knocking, I had everything in order and it never went any further than that."

"And you two have been having coffee dates ever since?" Delia looks confused, like the story doesn't add up.

"No, not right away." Roxy stands from the table, gathering our cups and taking them behind the coffee bar. "Every now and then he would come by with information on something Burt was planning. Not just for The Bean, but the farm or even Sam and Paula's businesses. Burt wanted to make sure the people of Amoresville that were loyal to our family suffered."

Delia turns suddenly to look at her mother. "Wait, a year after Dad died? That's when this all started?"

She's put the pieces together.

"As in right around the time Harley and I were getting ready to open the club?"

"He couldn't do anything about it and it drove him nuts." Apparently I have finally found my voice. "You did everything by the book, right down to finding a location just outside his jurisdiction. Followed every rule the county and state have. Labor laws, age verification, liquor, everything was above board. There was nothing he could do except try to make everyone else miserable until you decided to close."

"And you stopped it all."

"No, not all. He blocked Sam and Paula from expanding the salon. Blocked Dolly from being able to sell alcohol at the market. Other things that I couldn't do anything about."

Those were some of the first items on the list of things I would be rectifying when I become mayor. *If* I become mayor. Right along with finally giving Roxy her official business license. Not that she needs it.

"So how did that turn into you sitting here gabbing about books and sipping coffee together?"

Roxy carries three glasses of another of her new concoctions, the Age Gap Cold Brew, bourbon flavored cold brew with a strawberry cold foam on top. "Well, when Mrs. Thurston retired and Wes took on the position of library director, he came to me with an idea. Mrs. Thurston wasn't a fan of Burt, but she also couldn't go against his decency laws and stock many romances without pissing him off. Wes wanted people to have free access to read whatever they wanted in this town. He proposed he would supply me with the titles Burt wouldn't approve of, and I would let people check them out essentially."

Delia gasps, "That's why you never charge for them? I thought you were just always being too nice."

"Oh, honey, you should know me better than that."

Delia picks up the book closest to her. "So these are all new books for, what, the library annex?"

"Exactly." Roxy smiles over at me and I appreciate her support, but I also know this won't change anything for Delia. No one holds a grudge like Delia. Except maybe Harley, who still occasionally leaves dead fish in my car. But I deserve their hatred, so I will bear it until I can make everything better in this town, and then I will leave and hope it is enough to allow me to move on.

"Wesley—" God, hearing Delia say my name after so many years of its absence on her lips is like the most potent drug. "Thank you for helping my mom. I appreciate it."

I don't move an inch, because there is absolutely a *but* coming.

"But, it doesn't change how much you hurt me all those years ago. It doesn't change that I truly think you shouldn't be mayor—"

"—Dee—"

"Mom, I understand why you have forgiven Wesley, sincerely, I do. I had to deal with Burt constantly trying to close this place when I was managing it. Dealing with his bullshit is something I wouldn't wish on anyone. I'm glad you had someone helping you."

"Wait! He was trying to close this place even when your dad was sick?"

My hands ball into fists so tight the knuckles go white. At the time, I was at college in New York City, I never visited, hardly talked to anyone besides monthly calls with my uncle who still held control of my trust. I had no idea what Delia was going through with her dad. Not until the last week of finals my senior year when Burt let it slip that there was going to be a memorial service for Gil Halsted that would be distracting the town.

I've known Burt isn't a good person for a very long time. But continuing to torture this family for no good reason while they dealt with a family tragedy is despicable and something I never would have imagined he would do. Especially when his own wife died of breast cancer when they were still newlyweds.

"Oh, he did that and more. He thought since Mom was pre-occupied and it was just an eighteen-year-old keeping this place running it would be easy." Delia smirks, her chin rising an inch in obvious pride. "He quickly learned the truth."

Roxy places her hand over Delia's on the table. "I don't think I ever thanked you and apologized for taking care of this place, and me, when your dad was sick. None of that should have been your responsibility and you never once complained."

Apparently there were a lot of truths that needed to come out today.

"It wasn't even a question, Mom. I love this place. It has my best and worst memories. I would rather burn the place down than let Burt be the reason it had to close."

Roxy and Delia lean around the table, gathering each other into an awkward hug from their seats. "I love you so much, my tough girl."

"Love you too, Mom."

A familiar pang echoes in my chest. I still feel the absence of my parents on a daily basis. It isn't something that ever truly goes away. It's like sound waves, always there hanging in the air, but sometimes they are quiet and sometimes louder. Right now, I miss them like I've been transported twelve years into the past, and I just lost them.

"Delia," Roxy backs up and takes her daughter's shoulder in a firm grip. "I want you to keep in mind that I love you more than anything else on this earth—"

"More than Orion and Knox?"

"—I'll deny it if you tell them. So keep that in mind when I tell you Wes has more to tell you and you need to listen. Really listen without that stubbornness that was obviously inherited from your father's side of the family."

Roxy turns to me, wiping tears from her eyes. "Wes, it is long past time you told her the truth. In a couple months, Burt can't do a damn thing to hurt anyone in this town ever again. It's time."

As soon as she drops that little bomb, Roxy stands from the table and sweeps out of the room, her long peasant skirt swishing around her ankles as she goes. I can't bring myself to look at Delia, so my eyes stay glued to the swinging kitchen door long after Roxy leaves the room.

Thick silence hangs in the air. Finally, Delia breaks the stand-off with a soft whispered, "What is she talking about, Wes?"

Chapter 22
Ten Years Ago

Delia

"Delia Jane Halsted." Normally, hearing my full name would make me freeze in my tracks and look around for my mom. But when it is said in the high-pitched voice of my best friend I just roll my eyes and close my locker, waiting for her to catch up. "I need details immediately."

I widen my eyes innocently and cock my head to the side. "I have no idea what you mean?"

"Bitch, if you do not spill this second I am going to literally scream in the middle of this hallway and you know good and well that I will do it." Harley sucks in a deep breath, expanding her chest in preparation for what will be a window rattling roar.

"Okay, okay, jeez, I'll tell you, but not here." Truth is, I had been ignoring her texts and calls all weekend because I just wanted to sit with everything that happened between Wes and me over the weekend.

Harley grabs my hand and drags me into the nearest girls' bathroom. She shoos out a few freshmen and even a senior that gives her a dirty look but doesn't argue, then locks the door behind them. "Okay, spill."

I take a deep breath, ready to tell her every single detail. Excited to have someone else know that I am a completely different person than I was the week before. Or at least that is what it feels like.

A huge smile breaks out across my face. "We had sex."

Harley's mouth drops open into a shocked express, a shrill squeal starting almost immediately. I can't help but laugh like a loon as she wraps her arms around me and we start jumping up and down together. "I seriously never thought you would be the first between us to get your cherry popped."

"I mean, same."

We laugh like maniacs for another minute before she pulls me down onto the floor criss-cross applesauce style. "Okay, tell me everything. Did it hurt? Was he nice to you? Did he pressure you at all? Do I need to beat his ass? Because I will."

"No beatings necessary. He was so sweet, checked in with me like every step of the way. Every time a piece of clothes came off he was like *'you good?'* or *'is this okay?'*" I try my best to mimic his deep voice. "It hurt a little, not as bad as I was expecting, but I think that was because we did, like, *a lot* before the actual deed."

"Did he go south—" Harley looks pointedly at my crotch then back up "—you know?" Then like the true lady she is, puts two fingers in front of her mouth and waggles her tongue between them.

I slap both hands over my face in absolute embarrassment, but nod between them. It was so weird at first, then weirdly good, then really good.

"Did you?" I watch from between my fingers as she pantomimes giving a blow job.

I nod again.

"Holy shit, girl! You didn't just round the bases, you fucking sprinted them." Harley plants her elbows on her knees and props her chin on one palm. "How do you feel today?"

"A little sore. Anxious to see him. We fell asleep together and then he had to rush out at like the ass crack of dawn to try and sneak back into Burt's house yesterday morning." I weave the hem of the skirt I'm wearing today between my fingers. "He wasn't waiting in the parking lot for me like usual. I'm afraid he might have gotten caught. And I can't even text him."

"He was probably just so exhausted from working you over that he overslept." Harley smiles wickedly at me. "Look at you all grown up."

The heat of a blush creeps up my face. "Honestly, I feel totally different, but not at all too. Like I can't stop thinking about it and when we can do it again. But I'm also still just me. You know?"

"No, because I'm still a virgin, you whore." Harley laughs and winks at me, her way of letting me know she doesn't mean the insult. If anything I think she considers it a compliment. She leans forward and hugs me again. "Congratulations, bestie.

I am both incredibly jealous and insanely happy for you. Wesley seems like he might actually not suck."

Just as I start to get weirdly emotional, the first bell rings and we both scramble to gather our things and rush to first period.

I expect Wes to be waiting for me outside Honors English, but he's not there. I wait right up until just before second bell and slip into the door just before Mrs. Wheeler can come out and berate me for being late. The second I sit in my desk, Wes slips in and gets a silent glare from our teacher. But he doesn't look back at me.

I can't stop looking at him through the whole period. He doesn't sneak even one glance at me. That is when the fear starts setting in. He has looked back at me from the front row every class since the first day we bumped into each other.

As soon as the bell rings, he's up out of his desk and practically running our classmates over to get out the door without ever saying a word to me. We don't have another class together until lunch, which means I have the next three periods to freak the fuck out.

Once lunch rolls around I am on the verge of a panic attack.

I walk into the cafeteria and look to our normal table, but it is empty. He's not in line either. There are only so many places he can be, this is a small-ass school. I'm not going into the afternoon wondering what the hell is going on, so I rush back out, searching the school library, the band room, the nurse's office. In a last-ditch effort I go out to the football field where some of the upperclassmen will eat lunch on the bleachers. I don't see him at first, but just as I'm about to turn and head back in, a dark shadow under the bleachers catches my eye.

Sitting in the same position he does in the library is Wes, knees pulled up with his arms wrapped around his shins and leaning back against one of the supports.

Despite my stomach being empty since I skipped lunch, I feel like I might throw up all over the gravel with every step closer I take to the boy I love. Because as soon as I see his face, I know. He doesn't love me anymore.

Wesley

What the fuck am I going to say to her?

I try my best to keep my face impassive as she draws closer and closer. Flashes of the night we shared mixing with the absolutely terrified expression on her face as she stands at my feet.

Slowly, I get up. I won't do this sitting on the ground, even though it feels like my legs are made of rubber and might just give out under the weight of my guilt.

"Wes, what's going on? Why are you avoiding me?"

Burt's angry face flashes through my mind along with his words.

"Young man, where were you all night?"

"Sorry, Uncle Burt, we were studying and I fell asleep on Kyle's couch."

His face turned redder and redder by the second until I was a little worried he might actually pop a vein in his neck. "Don't lie to me. Just like your mother sneaking around at all hours of the night."

"Don't talk about her. We agreed neither of us would mention her."

When I first got there, he gave me this whole speech about how he wouldn't put up with the antics his parents did from his sibling. I told him I wouldn't step a foot out of line as long as he never said her name again. She hated her brother almost as much as the town he lived in and it would have killed her all over again if she knew this is where I ended up.

"You think I'm blind? That I don't hear people talk? You've been flitting about with that Halsted girl." He pointed his finger directly in my face, shaking it up and down like I'm a bad dog he's berating. "That whole family is nothing but trouble, and that girl is just as bad as her mother. They think they are above the rules of this town. That they don't need to adhere to the rules of a proper society. And they are not going to drag the last bit of Lickinbill blood down with them."

"I am not a Lickinbill." My fists curled tight at my sides, my short nails pressing into the fleshy heel of my hand. "And Delia isn't trouble. She's brilliant and kind, and I love her."

"You might not have the Lickinbill name, but you are my blood and you will act like it or there will be consequences."

"What are you going to do? Lock me away like your parents tried to do with Mom?"

Burt smirked, his shoulders dropping from the agitated stance by his ears into a relaxed, confident pose that immediately set off warning bells in my head. "No, I'll ruin them."

I almost laughed. Burt might be the mayor of the town, but it's not like he has any real power. "Bullshit."

I swear, I could see the desire to slap me across my face for using foul language around him. But he restrained himself. Burt might not have many morals, but apparently hitting a minor is one of them. "I have very powerful friends. Senators, state troopers, business owners in this town listen when I speak. One word from me and they stop buying from the Halsted farm. They stop buying coffee at the cafe. The town survived without that thinly veiled den of sin for a long time before Roxanne opened her doors, and it will move on quickly once I shut it down. The superintendent of schools and I play bridge together. One word from me and suddenly your little girlfriend will be running into a lot of trouble with her grades.

"Give me six months and the whole family will be fleeing from this town on their hands and knees." God, he really did look like that idea excited him. "Or, you cut things off with that girl and we forget this happened. I let things lie with that family just like I have up to now."

I had no choice. We went around and around until we were screaming so loud I thought the neighbors might get concerned. But in the end, I couldn't risk that he can do everything he says he can.

"Wes? Did you hear me? Where have you been?" Delia's voice sounds so small, I hate it.

I can't tell her the truth. Delia is nothing if not stubborn. She loves a good fight, a challenge. If she knew the truth she would dig her heels in and stand her ground. If her parents found out things would be even worse. It would be like the war of the fucking roses in this little town. She would make everything so much worse.

"It was a mistake." The words taste like acid in my mouth. So bitter I'm afraid they will actually burn through my lying tongue.

"No." The tears start immediately. I don't blame her, I want to cry too, but I have to convince the girl I have fallen completely in love with that I think we should never see each other again. "You said it was the best night of your life."

"It was a lie. I think I just needed a distraction from my life, and you made it so easy." God, I fucking hate myself so much. Hate my uncle even more.

She sucks in a shocked gasp. So different from the gasps of pleasure we had shared just forty-eight hours ago. "How can you say that?"

"Burt just talked so much about how you were trouble. It made me curious, but once we did it, the interest kind of just went away." I give her a feeble shrug. "I didn't feel anything. I just pretended because I thought it was the right thing to do. But I can't pretend anymore. It was a mistake. It shouldn't have happened."

"I don't believe you. Something else has to be going on." She's full out crying now, her voice cracking with the pain I'm putting her through. I need to end it. Make it so she never wants to even hear my name again.

"I mean, don't get me wrong, it was good. You even said it felt good. It was just sex."

"You mother fucker." A familiar, deep voice booms behind me and I'm suddenly jerked around, a big, solid fist connecting with my nose. My glasses go flying, but I don't need them to see the raging red face of Delia's brother Orion screaming about how he's going to kill me.

I want him to. I don't bother to try and fight back as he fists my shirt in his hand and wails on me once more before the football coach and a few other teachers swarm us, pulling him off me. Everyone is yelling, Delia is sobbing behind me, Orion still fighting against several pairs of arms to try to get to me.

Everything is a blur after that. The three of us are marched to the principal's office. Delia's parents and my uncle are all called.

More screaming, mostly Mrs. Halsted at Burt, who in turn threatens to press charges. All I can do is sit there, everything numb except the churning in my stomach.

We're all sent home. Burt and I sit silently in the car for the short drive to his house. Suddenly nothing in this town feels anything like a home. It's a prison now. A place I have to survive until I can leave when I turn eighteen.

"You did the right thing, son." He says it with so much certainty it makes me sick.

Literally.

"Pull over," I yell just as he pulls into the driveway and jerks to a stop. I barely have time to wrench open the door before the contents of my stomach erupt from my mouth all over the too short grass of his front yard.

He doesn't check on me. Just walks into the house, leaving me alone on my hands and knees in the front yard.

Alone. That is truly what I am now.

Chapter 23

Delia

At some point during Wes's story I couldn't sit still anymore. I had to get up. Move. Preferably in the direction of fucking Burt Lickinbill's house that I plan on egging or throwing a Molotov cocktail through the window or something that is not at all an overreaction.

"So, all those things you said to me that day?"

"Lies. They made me physically sick. Burt wanted me to go get checked out for a concussion, thought it would strengthen the case against your brother. But I told him it wasn't a concussion, just a guilty conscience."

Wes looks completely exhausted. Like telling the truth has sapped him of every bit of energy in his body.

"But why wait until now to tell me all this? Surely you must have figured out at some point that Burt was full of shit. He's been trying to close this place down basically since it opened and hasn't even come close. Not even when a teenage me was the one in charge."

God, he tried so fucking hard. Sent cease and desist letters insisting we were in violation of town ordinances. But with the help of Sam and his dad, who are effectively the town historians, I was able to fight back and keep the place going. Then he tried spreading rumors that we had a rodent problem. Sent health inspectors. Even got a cop friend of his to come out and tell us there had been reports of drug activity. It was all insane and it all eventually went away thanks to people in town having my family's backs during the literal hardest time.

"Yeah, I figured it out eventually. It wasn't until I approached your mom with Burt's mold plan that it sunk in that I had grossly misjudged how much power Burt had." Wes pushes his glasses back up the bridge of his nose, unable to look up from the surface of the cafe table. I don't think he's looked at me once since we started talking. "I was a scared teenager who had been hearing stories of how horrible the Lickinbill family was since I was old enough to ask about why it was just the three of us on holidays and birthdays. Believe it or not, as much as you hate Burt, his sister hated him even more."

"I believe it. I can't imagine growing up in a house with him." Suddenly I can't take my eyes off the man slumped in defeat at the table across the room. "And you had to do it for two years before you went to college. I figured once you moved back to New York you would never come back here. Why did you?"

Silence swells and fills the room like a marshmallow expanding in the microwave. He doesn't answer, just looks at his hands resting on the table.

"Wes?" His name comes out in a whisper. "Why did you come back after college?"

Finally, he looks up and meets my gaze. "Because I would rather be close to you, even when you despise me, than anywhere else on the entire planet."

Everything slows to a stop. My lungs freeze in my chest. My fingers and toes go numb. Nothing makes sense anymore because it suddenly all falls into place.

"I thought once I got back to New York I would feel comfortable again. Those two years in high school were hell. This town loves your family. They love *you*. I had no one except Mrs. Thurston and the library." Wes is filleting himself before me, laying everything out on the table for me to inspect.

"New York had to be better. It *had* to be. But it wasn't. I made friends, went to my classes, dated, but it all felt like I was pretending. The whole time I was just pretending there wasn't a girl in a town five hours away that still held my entire heart in her hands. So, I made a plan. I would finish school. Move back, and I would put right everything my uncle has done to hurt this town. Your family. It's been harder than I thought it would be. God—" he chuffs out a humorless laugh "—I campaigned so hard for that damn goose during the last election."

"Wait, that was you that started the write-in campaign for CuGo?" I swear, of all the revelations of tonight, that might be the best. I always wondered who did that. The posters popped up on poles and walls around town seemingly overnight.

"First, I tried convincing people to run against him for real. Thought I almost had Sam's dad ready to go, but he decided against it when it came time to submit the official paperwork. I still think Burt might have done something to change his mind."

There aren't many times in my life I've been totally speechless. Hell, I pride myself on being able to come back with a witty retort when put on the spot. But in this moment, all words have escaped my shocked brain. This whole time, Wes has been trying to scheme against his uncle.

"I thought with this being Burt's last term, I'd be free finally. But then he started talking about his friends being interested in taking up the banner and I realized nothing would change unless I made it change. So a couple years ago, I started offering to help with things. Talked him into making some changes because it would contribute to his legacy. Convinced him *not* to try and make it so that he would be able to have a fourth term."

Oh god, even the thought of it makes my skin crawl.

"I convinced him everything from my teen years was forgotten. That he had been right. Each time I thought I would puke all over again."

"Then he asked you to run for mayor as the next in the Lickinbill line." I want to believe all of this so much. But after a decade of hating and distrusting this man, I can't wrap my mind around all this information.

"Yeah. Then you did something I really should have expected, but never saw coming. You fought back."

We stare at each other from across the room, a tension between us that verges on painful.

"I need you to know, I don't expect anything from you now that the truth is out. Revealing all of this doesn't erase the pain I caused you in high school." Wes breaks the eye contact, his gaze going back to his hands clasped together on the table. "At no point in any of my plans did I ever have the delusion that I would ever be able to earn your forgiveness. I won't try. The scars of what I said to you back then—" He swallows hard, stuffing down some emotion I've never seen from him before. Revulsion, I think. "—what they must have done to you, I can't imagine."

He's right. The words he said that day, after giving my innocence to a boy I thought would never hurt me, have caused damage. I've had boyfriends, but they were always the complete opposite of Wes. Dark, rough guys that I knew not to rely on too much. Men I was never in any danger of falling in love with. Instead, I've devoted myself to the club, my family, my friends. Accepted that I will be the cool aunt, but never the mother.

"I'm not doing any of this to try and win you back. I'm doing it because it is the right thing to do."

I nod even though he isn't looking at me. It's good that he doesn't want to win me over. Because that isn't going to happen.

...Right?

"I'm not going to drop out of the campaign." The words come out before I think about them.

"You can't."

He's right. If I suddenly stopped campaigning against Wes, it would look weird. Suspicious.

"Actually, I kind of hope you win. I've never actually wanted to be mayor, it just seemed like the only option to do what I need to."

Do I actually want to be mayor? Harley asked me that same question all those weeks ago when I jumped with both feet into the campaign. But I never slowed down enough to truly consider it.

I do truly love this town. Take pride in my family's history here. Cherish the people that rallied around my family when we needed them most. But until Wes announced his candidacy and my family all seemed so ambivalent about the idea, the thought had never even crossed my mind.

If I win, I would be tied to this town in a real, tangible way for the next four years. The folded piece of paper still shoved in the bottom of my purse pushes through the confusion of this day and practically plops itself in front of me. I hadn't even been considering it anyway. I have the club to think about, too.

"Since we're telling the truth, I'm not sure if I wanted to be mayor or if I just didn't want you to be."

Wes laughs a little and leans back in his chair. "I swear, only this town could manage to have two people running for mayor that actually have no interest in the job."

That is so incredibly true.

"But there's nothing we can do about it now. Right?" I slump down in my chair, a wave of exhaustion sweeping over me.

"I don't think so. We just need to keep going. You'll kick my ass at the debate. Burt will pull all of his strings. And we'll just have to see what the outcome is."

I nod along with Wes, because yeah, I couldn't drop out now even if I wanted to. Not only would it look weird to Burt and his cronies, but it would be embarrassing as hell to just drop the election like one of my side hustles that have come and gone over the years.

"I really am going to kick your ass at the debate."

Wes laughs again, dropping his head back between his shoulder blades to look up at the ceiling. "Trust me, I know. I was secretly so happy you crashed that stupid campaign dinner because I was pretty sure I was going to puke if Burt actually made me speak."

"What were you planning on doing during town council meetings? Meetings are always packed."

"Honestly? I was going to try and scale back how involved the mayoral role is in the meetings. The mayor should just be a tiebreaker and then the person that makes sure the town is running day-to-day. Trash, road maintenance, paperwork, that type of stuff. It isn't supposed to be this all-powerful person that Burt and the couple mayors before him have turned it into." He shrugs. "But if that fails, pretend like the audience is a room full of six-year-olds there for Story Time."

Dammit, I'm not ready for him to make me laugh. But he does. "Sounds like a plan."

We lapse into silence, and despite all that we've said, there still seems like so much left to say. I'm just not ready yet. For any of it. I'm not sure I can truly let go of what happened in high school and forgive him.

"I should go." Wes stands from the table, grabbing our glasses and putting them in the sink behind the counter. "It's almost time for Burt to wrap things up in his office and head home. Don't want to risk him seeing me here."

"Right." I hadn't even thought about Wes needing to sneak out of here.

"It must seem so pathetic to you, a grown-ass man needing to tiptoe around his uncle." Wes pushes his glasses up again, and that familiar pang of affection I used to get every time he did that back in high school shakes off the dust of the years I've ignored all the good things about our time together. "But, it's only a few more weeks. Once the election is over and he officially can't do a damn thing about the outcome, the first thing I'm going to do is walk through the front door of this place and order a coffee and sit in the window reading the filthiest book I can find."

I don't say it, but the first thought that pops in my mind is, *Maybe I'll join you.*

* * *

After Wes and I say goodbye, I don't know what to do with myself. Trying to sleep is futile. I putter around the house, baking about every recipe I have ingredients in the pantry for. But after my third batch of cookies, I realize I need to get out of the house or I'm going to slip into a diabetic coma.

After peeking in on Mr. Sparkles, I hop in my car and point it in the direction of Club Barely Over the Line.

I love being in the club when it is empty, already cleaned from the busy weekend. The stage, bar, and poles all gleam. No music. No whispered shifting of money as men throw dollar bills at the feet of the dancers. No girls bickering back in the locker room arguing over who gets to dance to "Pour Some Sugar on Me" tonight.

Just me and the business Harley and I grew from the ground up. I might have been the one to put up all the money for the club, the remnants of the meager college fund my parents had stashed away and I never used, but this place is just as much Harley as it is me. That first year, we both worked the poles like our lives depended on it. But I quickly moved into a more administrative role while Harley kept dancing and managed the rest of the girls.

I consider catching up on paperwork, but my mind is so overflowing with everything I learned today, I would probably end up staring at my computer monitor like a zombie. Instead,

I slip into one of many sets of booty shorts I keep on hand for when I join in on one of Harley's classes.

With the lights low, I put on "Dangerous Woman" by Ariana Grande and take my place at the pole. There isn't a particular routine I have in mind, I just groove along to the heavy, sensual beats of the song. Back when I was a dancer, I never got excited dancing, unlike Harley. It was a job, not something I did for my own enjoyment. But tonight, I'm giving myself permission to picture how I would move for Wesley. The way his gaze would follow my every move. The way his long legs would stretch out in front of him while he watched from one of the chairs at the edge of the stage. Each roll of my body, sway of my hips, and slide of my hands up my body is a show for the phantom of Wesley. For the first time, working the pole is causing a heavy weight to settle low in my belly. A warmth spreading through my body, the space between my thighs aching for his touch.

Knowing the truth has freed something in me. Brushed away the guilt I've felt each time he popped into my mind. The truth is, over the years there have been more than a few instances where I pictured us together to get off. When the scorching hot books I love to read weren't quite getting me there, and the toys I've come to rely for pleasure took too long for a desperately needed orgasm, I would pull the long-buried memories of our first time together, then later the one frantic night we spent together after Dad's funeral. Each time I would be disgusted with myself and swear it would never happen again.

But now, that is all gone. I know the truth; Wes did love me. Our night together had been as magical as I built it up in my mind. The knowledge is the key to unlock the mental block I build brick-by-brick around my continued attraction to him. If he were here right now, watching me writhing against the pole, my hands drifting closer and closer to my pussy, I'm not totally sure I wouldn't climb into his lap and do all the things I've dreamed about over the years.

Just as the song winds to a close, a slow clap starts from the direction of the bar. "Damn girl, maybe we should put you back in the rotation. The bills would be raining after that performance." Harley lets out a wolf whistle waggling her eyebrows suggestively.

It takes me a second to fully come out of the weird, sexy headspace my little dance put me in. But once I do, I jump down from the stage and head over to my friend. "Yeah, I don't think so. I can barely catch my breath and I don't even have the heels on."

"Meh," she says and waves her hand dismissively. "They like it when you're all breathy." She adopts the voice she's referring to, a babyish almost hyperventilating tone that I have seen her use to extricate more and more cash from a man's wallet. "Oh, all this money for me—" she presses her arms together on either side of her chest, plumping up her tits so much even I can't help but stare down at them as they nearly fall from her black tank top "—thank you so much, sir."

Yeah, there is a reason Harley rakes in the tips hand over fist. The woman is absolutely ruthless when it comes to working a man. She might be bisexual, but she deeply resents the side of herself that still likes men.

"Oh my god, stop or I'm going to get my wallet and start shoving dollars in your pants." We both laugh as Harley grabs a couple bottles of water from behind the bar, handing me one as I take a seat on one of the bar stools.

"So, what's with the solo dancing? Did you bake everything in your house?"

"Ha, yeah, actually, I did."

"Bitch, there better be cookies in here tomorrow or I am going to riot." She takes a sip of her water, her elbows planted on the other side of the bar and her eyes inspecting me like she can discover my secrets just by staring at me hard enough. "What's going on, Dee?"

"I caught Wes and my mom together tonight."

Harley's eyes go wide and she slaps her hand over her mouth to prevent a spray of water from her mouth.

"No, not like that eww. Jesus, you are filthy."

"Come on, you know how that sounded," she says in defense.

I glare at her for a second before filling her in on everything. Their secret book club. The truth about what happened in high school. Our tentative truce.

"Holy shit. That is a lot." She cocks her head to one side, almost touching her ear to her shoulder, her eyes going hazy as she considers my words. "That all makes a lot of sense. I always wondered why after he broke your heart he never moved onto any other girls. He was hot enough to pull just about anyone back then. Being the mayor's nephew would have worked in his favor, too. But there was never even a rumor about him with another girl. He just studied, ran track, and volunteered at the library."

I honestly hadn't thought about that. "Yeah."

"And he actually said he'd rather be near you even when you hated him than anywhere else in the world."

I nod, picking at the paper label with our logo wrapped around the bottle.

"Fuck." I can feel Harley's eyes on me. "No offense, honey, but if anyone said that to me my panties would be on the floor faster than you could say *fuck me now*. Why on earth are you here instead of boning his brains out?"

"Because, it's all so complicated still. There is his uncle and the election. Plus, knowing why he said what he did back then doesn't erase it."

Harley nods along with each of my words, but as soon as I stop talking she shakes her head slowly back and forth. "Fuck that shit. Even when you hated him, a little part of you always loved Wesley. You hid it well, but after he came back I could see it in the spaces between you remembering to hate him. He was a scared, traumatized sixteen-year-old boy that did the wrong thing for the right reasons. Stupid reasons that a simple conversation with any other adult probably could have fixed, but still. Can you really still hold it against him?"

No. I can't. I try to grasp the dying wisps of resentment and hatred, but they are so thin at this point they might as well not exist.

"Plus, I know you fucked him the night we never talk about."

Yeah, I figured she knew what was up that night. But for once she didn't push. Just drove me to Wellsboro to sit in the parking lot of a drug store waiting for it to open so I could get the morning after pill. I sat in the car sobbing, her arms wrapped around me and whispering it would be okay.

"Do you really think it was a coincidence that the night you needed comfort you turned to him?"

No. I don't.

"So what do I do? Just forget everything and go bone his brains out?" It's too simple. Too easy. After so many years of hate, that can't be how this ends.

"Hell yes. Then you talk. Then you keep fucking and talking for the rest of your lives." Harley slides our waters to the side and grips my hands in hers over the bar. "If there is anyone in this town that deserves a happy ending it is you. And I mean that in both the purest and dirtiest way."

Chapter 24

Wesley

It's almost midnight and I can't sleep.

After unloading all those truths on Delia today, I thought for sure I'd sleep like a baby tonight. But I keep thinking about all the things I didn't say.

That I love her. I always will. That the two nights we shared together were some of the best of my entire life. That I would take a million more of them, even if it meant I would have to endure the same pain I did after each encounter.

But telling her those things would be purely selfish.

With a frustrated groan, I throw the blankets off and stalk down the hall to my living room. My apartment is small, just a one bedroom with a living area and a kitchen. I thought about buying a place in town, but it seemed too permanent. I need to stick to the plan. Fix what Burt broke, then leave and find a way to live a happy life. It is what my parents would want for me.

The problem is, when I picture that happy life, all I see is Delia.

I need to get her out of my head. With a huff, I drop to the floor and start in on some push-ups. Sometimes the only way to get my brain under control is to just physically exhaust myself until everything shuts down. It's too late to go on a run. So push-ups will have to do.

Somewhere around fifty, sweat dripping off my skin, the ding of my doorbell echoes through the whole apartment. My place is on the second floor, with an exterior staircase leading up along the side of the building from the sidewalk to my door, so it's not like someone accidentally rang my bell instead of someone else in the building. It's just me and my downstairs neighbor who I've honestly never seen. They are a bit of a mystery.

The only person that ever comes to my place is Burt, and even that is a rare occurrence. Everything is about appearances to Burt, and my apartment says sad bachelor, not leader of a community.

Popping up to my feet, I grab a sweatshirt from where I threw it on the back of a chair and wipe off my sweat with it.

Unlocking the door, I swing it open and my entire world comes to a halt. Because right in front of me is Delia, wearing the shortest booty shorts I have ever seen. They shouldn't even be classified as shorts, but underwear. They look like old school gym shorts with the white trim around the edges and I'm fuck-ing hypnotized by the way they hug her curves.

Once I rip my eyes from the shorts, they track up the rest of her body. A tight t-shirt with our high school logo on it. Her thick hair pulled up into a messy ponytail. Not a speck of makeup on her face, just the freckles I used to love to trace with my fingers. *Fuck.* How can one person be so fucking beautiful?

"Delia?"

"I want you to try," she says the words like we're in the middle of a conversation I haven't been privy to.

"What?"

"You said you don't expect anything from me. That you know I can't forgive you and you won't even try. But I want you to try. I think, maybe, I *could* forgive you."

My heart beats so hard, filled with so much traitorous hope, that I'm sure she'll be able to hear it from just the other side of the threshold.

"I might already be halfway to forgiving you. I think I've ac-tually had to actively work at hating you for a long time." Delia sucks in a breath that verges on a sob. "I remember how much pain you were in back then. The conversations we had where you held back tears talking about your moms. The ones where you couldn't hold them back and I held you on the floor of the library. I know what it feels like now to lose a parent."

Full streams of tears streak down her cheeks. Without hes-itating or thinking better of it, I take a step forward, cupping her face in my hands and wiping away the moisture with my thumbs.

"It was the worst pain at twenty-one. At sixteen? I can't imagine it. And then to have that asshole threaten the only person you still had. I don't know what I would have done in your place—"

"Yes, you do. You would have fought tooth and nail against him."

"Maybe. But the truth is we'll never know. Those decisions are behind us." She pulls in a stuttering breath, but steels her spine, gaining another inch in height. "What I want is to find out who you are now. I want to know the man you've grown into. I want you to learn about me as I am now. I'm not the same person I was a decade ago."

"I know. But there are still threads of that girl that I see every day. Even from afar." I bring my forehead to hers before realizing I'm a sweaty mess and take it away, dropping my hands from where I've been cradling her face. "Sorry."

Her hands grip my waist, just above where my flannel pajama pants hang on my hips. "Don't be." She steps forward until we are pressed together, skin on skin since I have no shirt on. She keeps walking forward, pushing me back into my own apartment. "I think you've tortured yourself enough for a while. I think *I've* tortured you enough."

"Delia—" I'm not sure if I'm going to beg her to touch me more, kiss me, or to stop. This isn't a good idea. It's been less than twelve hours since she learned the whole truth behind my actions when we were kids. Starting something now isn't smart.

"Wes." She pushes the door closed with her foot. "I need to tell you some truths, too. The truth is part of the reason I avoid you is because every time I see you my heart speeds up for just a second. Before I could register our past, I saw your face and I felt happy. I hated that split second so much. But I couldn't ignore it. So I went out of my way to not see you. But it was there. Every. Time."

Words are my safe place, but her confession has stolen every single one, leaving me floundering.

"I don't know what our future holds or where we go next. There is still so much we need to work through and we'll get there. But what I do know is since that night at the club, after I crashed your dinner and you came to yell at me, my vibrators have been getting a workout every fucking night."

Every man has his limits; Delia telling me our too brief make out session from a few weeks ago has been fueling her orgasms is mine. Like something inside me has been let loose, I grip her thick thighs and lift her up, her legs automatically wrapping around me.

"I am going to put your toys to fucking shame."

With a surge, I press her back against the door, our lips meeting in a frantic kiss. A kiss full of ten years of longing denied. My tongue delves into her mouth, licking at her like a man starved. I move to her neck, kissing along the long line.

"Oh honey, you might be overpromising. I never finish a session with my vibrator without coming at least three times. I'm not sure you can match that." A playfulness has replaced the sadness in her voice.

"Fucking watch me." Gripping her wrists, I pull her arms up over her head and pin them there while I ravage her mouth. Her body twists and undulates against me, my dick feeling every slide of her through the thin pajama pants that have seen better days.

I've dreamed of dozens of ways to fuck Delia Halsted. They scroll through my mind like pictures in a slideshow. Here against the door. Bent over the edge of the couch. Her perched on the kitchen counter. They go on and on, an endless buffet of filthy possibilities.

Without question, one stands out among the rest. In my bed. I want her thrashing around in my sheets. Want them to smell like her for days.

Goal decided on, I release her wrists and wrap my arms around her once again. Turning, I carry her down the short hallway to my bedroom. Where just minutes ago I was complaining about the tiny footprint of this place, I am suddenly very happy it won't take long for me to reach my destination.

I climb onto the bed with her still clinging to me, lay us down so that I'm on top of her, her soft body conforming to each hard plane of my own. Finally, my hands are free to roam as I please. I could touch her for a lifetime and never get tired of the soft skin under my fingers.

Her legs and arms are bare in the tiny pieces of clothes she calls an outfit, but I want more. Want to see her all. Which is when I realize the lights are off and that will not fucking do. I leap from the bed, Delia squealing as I pull myself away to flip the switch by the door, flooding the room in light.

Delia blinks for a second, then smirks. "Good idea. Those—" she nods at my abdomen, "—should be admired."

Fuck, I want to preen and pose like those fucking douchebags in the gym trying to find their best angles in the mirrors with their phones set up on tripods capturing every flex.

"I want to see you." Slowly, I stalk back to the side of the bed. "Get those sinful fucking shorts off."

She arches one eyebrow and comes up onto her knees, then climbs to her feet in the center of the mattress. With two thumbs hooked into the waistband of the shorts, she bends at the waist, keeping her legs and back straight as she pulls them down over her legs. Then stands back up in only the t-shirt and a thong. Teenage me would have come on the spot if he could see her now. Adult me might too.

I have to tip my head back to see her face, and it's just on that edge of my vision between clear and blurry, which won't do. I climb onto the bed, knee walking until I'm kneeling in front of her, ready to beg to see the rest of her curvy body if I have to. But she doesn't make me; she crosses her arms in front of her, taking the hem of her shirt and lifting it up and over her head, ponytail swinging behind her like a pendulum when it is freed from the fabric.

Her feet are bare and I'm honestly not sure if she showed up like that or if she lost her shoes somewhere along the way. I love the thought of her things scattered across my floors, evidence she was here.

She stands before me in a black strapless bra and black lace thong, my face even with her soft belly. She reaches behind her back, arching to unhook the bra and tossing it somewhere on the other side of the room.

Fucking hell.

I've seen Delia naked exactly twice in my life.

Once as a teenager when we spent one perfectly awkward night learning each other's bodies through giggles and fumbling touches.

Once as adults, after her father's funeral when she needed a distraction and I happened to be there. That night was frantic, it all happened so fast then turned to shit before I could even appreciate the moment.

This time, I plan to commit each moment to memory. I will give her the greatest pleasure she can imagine, memorize her body and her sounds so if I never get a fourth shot at this I will have a highlight reel to fall back on for those nights I can't resist and take my dick in hand with thoughts of her in my mind.

"You are remarkable, Delia." Slowly, I slide my hands up from her ankles up over her legs, gripping her lush hips and burying my face at the apex of her thighs. She sighs, grips my hair, her hips pulsing toward me as I pepper kisses against her lace-covered pussy. "I need to taste you. Need to know if you're as sweet as I remember."

Delia slides down onto her knees in front of me, ghosting her lips over mine without deepening into a kiss. "Let me spoil it for you." She kisses my bottom lip. "I'm not. I'm much saltier now."

Chapter 25

Delia

With a deep growl, Wes bands his arms tight around me and spins us so I'm trapped beneath him once again, my knees bracketing his hips. He's hard, long, and pressed directly against my center.

His body is all hard muscle under hot skin and I can't stop touching him. My fingers slide up and down his spine, into the waistband of his pajamas where I find he's not wearing any underwear.

"Wow, Wesley Goldman going commando, what would the town rumor mill think?"

He chuckles against my lips, kissing across my jaw to my neck. "They should be happy it was a cold night. Otherwise, I would have been butt naked."

The warm wash of his breath against my neck as he speaks sends a wave of goosebumps along my body. "Where is global warming when you need it?"

"To be fair, I would have put pants on before answering the door."

"Mmmm, too bad. The least you could do is get naked for me now." I grip both his ass cheeks, pulling him tighter against my core as I grind my lace covered clit against his shaft covered in flannel.

"Fuck, Delia, goddamn you keep doing that and I'm not going to last." He rests his forehead on my shoulder taking measured breaths in through his nose and out through his mouth in a steady rhythm. "It has been too fucking long. The pants need to stay on or this is going to be over before I can enjoy it."

My chuckle has a little edge of mischief to it; something about driving Wes to the edge far faster than he wants excites me. "Afraid you won't be able to live up to my vibrators?"

He picks up his head, his eyes locking and holding my gaze. "You think just because I might blow my load early I won't give you so many orgasms you beg me to stop? Just because the party ends early for me doesn't mean it does for you."

Wow. Okay then. Let's be so honest: nine times out of ten if a man comes the evening is over for everyone.

A detail breaks through the lust fog weighing down my thought process. "Wait, how long exactly has it been for you?"

He freezes on top of me, I swear even his breath stalls in his lungs, it happens so fast I wonder for a moment if I imagined it. He goes back to kissing down my neck, gradually making his way to my chest and patently ignoring my question.

Yeah, no, I'm curious now. I grip his hair and pull until he is looking directly at me, a little wince of pain pinching his face. "How long, Wes?"

He tries to free himself, closes his eyes and rubs his cheek against my forearm. "It's not important."

"I think it is."

He sighs with defeat and looks at me. "Six years. It's been six years."

I think I knew before he said the words. Why else would he have hesitated to tell me. "Was I the last person you had sex with?"

He nods once, avoiding my eyes. "It isn't a big deal. It's not like the Amoresville dating scene is lush with possibilities."

Okay, true, but still. Not one single trip to a dive bar in Wellsboro or Erie or any of the other half-decent sized towns that are within driving distance of our town just to pick up a girl and fuck her in the bathroom?

As much as I am shocked that he hasn't had sex once since our mind-blowing disaster of a night, it also doesn't surprise me at all. Wes isn't the one-night stand kind of guy.

"Wes—"

"No, don't say anything." He runs his hand up my arm to entwine with my fingers in his hair, then brings it down to kiss my wrist. "Our situations and mind frames have been radically different. All I need to know is that you are one hundred precent here with me now."

I nod, my cheek brushing against his soft wavy hair as he makes his way to my neck. Yeah, I can't even recall the name of a single guy I've dated over the last six years. Everything before the last twenty-four hours feels like a distant memory. Something so far in the rear mirror it is nothing more than a speckle on the horizon.

All I want to do is make the man pressed on top of me feel so fucking good it makes up for the years we haven't been right here, entwined together. I find his lips, trying to communicate through a deep, soul-filled kiss exactly how here I am right now. He groans into my mouth, his hips thrusting against me.

"Wes?" I kiss the corner of his mouth.

"Yeah?" He's breathing heavily as my hand makes its way back down to delve beneath his pajama pants.

"Hold on."

"Wha—"

I plant my feet on the mattress, drive my hips and flip our position so I'm on top and he's pinned beneath me.

"Holy shit." His brown eyes are wide with unmistakable awe.

"You can thank Harley for making everyone at the club take self-defense and grappling lessons last year."

"I've always liked Harley," he says, breathless beneath me.

I start kissing him in the middle of us both laughing and it reminds me of our first time. God, we laughed so much that night. There were lots of awkward moments where neither of us knew exactly what we were doing and had to fumble and laugh our way through it.

A stinging pang contracts in my chest for those two innocent kids that had no clue what they were in for.

Slowly, I kiss down his chest, brushing my lips across every one of his defined abs. It will never fail to blow my mind that when he's clothed you could never guess this body is what lies beneath.

As I make it to his belly button, then lower, Wes sits up, leaning back on his elbows. "I'm serious, Delia, if you go where I think you're going this is going to be very embarrassing for me."

"Oh ye of little faith." I smirk up at him just as I pull down the obviously well-loved pajama pants, revealing the dick I have very fond memories of. "Hello, stranger."

"Oh god—" I glance up to see he has his eyes screwed shut "—just you talking to it has me close."

"This is going to be so much fun." I need one full taste, more for my own curiosity than for his enjoyment. Gripping the base of him, I plunge him into my mouth, all the way to the back of my throat, then back off, taking him from my mouth with a wet pop.

He's sitting straight up now as I lay flat between his spread legs. Both his hands are fisting the sheets on either side of his hips, holding on for dear life.

"Tell me when you think you're about to come."

He nods quickly, his body relaxing in increments as I lazily shuffle my hand up and down his length with a loose grip. Every now and then I kiss and suck a line up the underside of his cock, then back off when I see his body tensing again. I repeat this over and over again until he starts to get used to the pattern.

Then I change everything. Take him into my mouth once, twice before he says he's getting close. I take my mouth and hands off him completely, scratching my nails up and down his quads, kissing along the deep grooves around his hips.

Once his breathing evens out again, I suck him in deep. Only once, not taking him to the edge, just getting him used to my mouth.

I can feel him watching me as I pepper kisses down his shaft and cup his balls in one hand. He leans forward and to the side, running one hand across my ribs, down to my hip. "I'm supposed to be giving you so many orgasms I put your vibrators to shame, remember?"

"Oh, I remember. The truth is, it will be embarrassingly easy to get me off, too."

"Is that right?"

I nod as I cover him with my mouth again. He sucks in a breath, but doesn't tense up. Instead, he caresses my ass, running his hand down to trace the path of my thong between my legs, pushing a finger beneath the expensive fabric and into my folds.

"Fucking hell, Delia. You are so fucking wet."

Folding my legs beneath me, I kneel in a wide stance so he has free rein to explore my pussy as I continue to work his cock in my hand.

As much as I have been teasing him, he gives it right back. Circling my clit, then plunging one finger into my pussy, riling me up until I'm panting against his thigh while I jack him. It's like we've silently started a game of who can last longer.

I am famously competitive.

Not messing around anymore, I take him into my mouth, swirling my tongue along the straining vein that runs the length of his shaft. Pulling up with a long suck until only his head is resting on my tongue, then plunging back down followed by several fast bobs.

His fingers are still between my thighs and above me he mumbles something under his breath.

"Three hundred social sciences. Three hundred and one sociology & anthropology. Three hundred and two social interaction. Three hundred and three social processes. Three hundred and four..."

Oh my god, he's reciting the Dewey Decimal System to stop from coming.

"Fuck." The world turns upside down and in a flash Wes has me beneath him. "Fucking siren trying to lure me to my death."

I pout my bottom lip out and look up at him with my best doe eyes. "I almost had you."

"Yeah, you did. But so help me I am not coming in your mouth tonight." He kisses me before I can protest, the words dying in my throat as his cock, still wet from my working over, slides against me. "Condom."

He yells the word, leaping from the bed and rifling through the top drawer of his dresser. While he searches, I ditch the thong he had been working around to bring me to the edge. He holds an unopened box up victoriously and jogs back, diving back on top of me.

I can't help but laugh as his mouth returns to mine, his own smile curling against my lips. A thought occurs to me and I push him away to voice it. "Wait, when did you buy those? You know condoms have an expiration, right?"

His eyes go wide. Frantically, he bobbles the box, looking for the label with the date on it. "Goddamn, why do they make the type on these things so fucking small?"

I love how he starts dropping the F bomb every other word when he gets worked up. "Let me see, old man."

"I'm a whole six months older than you."

"True, but you have the eyesight of an octogenarian." I take the box from him and read the label. "Wes, these expired two years ago."

He collapses on top of me. "That's okay, I will make you come so hard with my mouth and then in the morning I'll run to Dolly's"

This makes me laugh even harder. "Oh my God, are you trying to hand me the election? *Future mayor buys condoms at local store* will be on the front page of the Amoresville paper and I'll be a shoo-in. Don't worry. I have some in my purse, Harley stuffed them in there as I was running out the door of the club."

"Did you have a purse with you? All I saw was your ass in those shorts"

I roll my eyes and nod. "I dropped it by the door."

Before I even have the words out, Wes is up and sprinting down into the hall, leaving me laughing naked on his bed.

Chapter 26

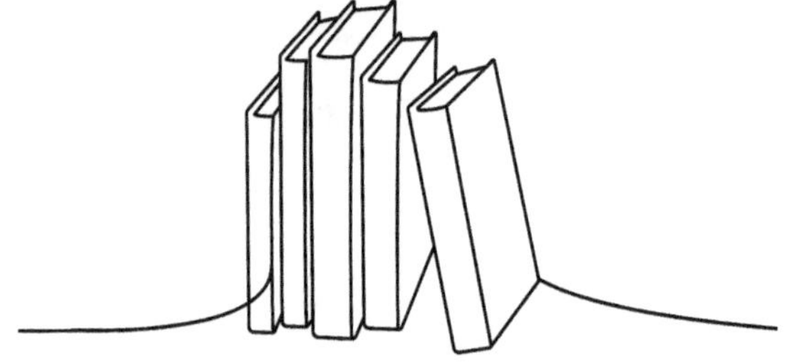

Wesley

I find the black bag tipped on its side next to my door. I'm only a little ashamed when I pick it up and dump all the contents out onto the floor. Listen, I have about two functioning brain cells at this point and they are both screaming to find a condom and fuck Delia. Everything else doesn't matter. Besides, I'll clean it up in the morning.

A chorus of angels practically starts singing when I see the strip of black label Trojans. I snatch them from the floor and run back to my room where Delia is still laughing her ass off on my bed.

For a moment, the sight of her there takes my breath away. Yes, she is fucking gorgeous naked in the middle of my bed. But I think I would be just as hypnotized by this sight if she were clothed head to toe in sweats and gym socks. Just seeing her here, in my space, happy and smiling at me for the first time in a decade is enough to make me want to fall to my knees and start praying in thanks for the first time in my life. Or shove a ring on her finger before she can reconsider her decision to forgive me.

"Are you going to stand there and stare at me... or are you going to fuck me?"

With a growl I surge forward, ripping one square off the strip. But I don't open it yet. Delia needs to come at least once before we start because I still have a goal to meet and I am nothing if not goal oriented.

I throw the condom onto the bed by her hip and quickly settle my shoulders between her thighs, licking up her slit before she can protest. Flavor explodes on my tongue. I need more.

My hands spread her thighs wider, thumbs parting her folds so I have unfettered access to all the parts that will make her scream herself hoarse. She's so fucking wet and I want to lap up every single drop.

Her hands fist in my hair as I lick around her clit, teasing it a little before sucking on it lightly. "Holy shit, Wes." Her hips writhe beneath me, her grip pulling me tighter against her very center. "I need you inside, Wes."

As she moans the words I have to remind myself I can-*not* come yet. Releasing one thigh, I fill her with two fingers, pressing them in and out as I search for that little patch in-side that I know will make her detonate. When I find it, she tugs even harder on my hair and screams, her back arching and head thrown back.

Goddamn my shitty-ass eyesight, I can't make out the details of her face as she comes all over my fingers and mouth. I keep going, not letting the orgasm ebb away, but working her higher and higher into a frenzy. I recall every bit of advice I read when I was a teenager, preparing to have his first night alone with a girl. Studying is my love language. I studied for hours on how to pleasure, how to make sure she had a good time that night we were together as teenagers.

Then when I put it into action, I studied Delia, her reactions and what made her moan and scream. Thankfully, I remember every single second of our first time together.

The leg I still have a hold on breaks free, her knees closing around my head as she grinds her pussy against my face while I continue to lick her clit and fuck her with my fingers. After tonight my hearing might be just as bad as my vision, but I don't give a shit. I would give it all up to make Delia happy.

Frantically, Delia pushes my head away and I relent. "Are you okay?"

She nods and grabs the condom from the edge of the bed and rips it open. "Get this thing on right now and I will be even better."

Coming up onto my knees, I take the condom from her and roll it securely down my shaft to the base of my cock. As soon as it is in place, Delia pushes me onto my back, straddling my hips and notching the tip of me at her opening.

Slowly, painfully slowly, she takes every throbbing inch of me into her until I'm enclosed in her wet heat.

A tingling at the base of my spine foreshadows an absolute disaster if she tries to move right now. I squeeze my eyes shut, afraid that even the sight of her sitting on my cock is going to make me blow. Just as she starts to lift up again, my eyes fly open and I grip her hips and hold her tight against me. "Don't. Move."

She smiles wide, then bites her lip to try and hide her amusement. But she does as I ask. "Three hundred and one was sociology, right?"

"What, how did you know?"

"You were mumbling it under your breath earlier."

"Well, now you know, I'm a big nerd."

"Oh, honey, I already knew that." She skates her hands up over her stomach, palming her tits, squeezing them, pushing them together, twisting at her nipples, her breathing increasing with her ministrations. "Three hundred and two social interaction, right?"

"Fuck, now I'm going to get hard at work every time I shelf something in the social sciences section."

Her smile widens.

"Keep going, Crash." She looks down at me, a little smile on her face when I use my nickname for her from school. "Keep playing with those tits." I place my thumb over her clit, pressing down slightly and then moving in a deliberate circle so I'm not touching it directly.

She gasps, moans, tries to move on top of me, but I squeeze her hip. "Don't move. Just sit on my cock while I make you come. I need to feel you come on me at least once."

"Oh my God, Wes." She plays with her nipples, tweaking and twisting them as her pussy pulses around me. "I'm so close."

"You like using me as your toy? Taking all your pleasure while I lay here waiting my turn."

She nods frantically, her touch on her breasts getting more harsh, deeper. I take my cues from her, giving her clit direct contact now, dipping down briefly to gather some of the moisture leaking out around my cock and spreading out over the bundle of nerves.

"You come first every time. In all things. Your needs come before everything else. You understand?"

She opens her eyes, gazing down at me with unadulterated pleasure and joy. Pride swells through my whole body that I did this to her.

"Come on, Dee, come all over my cock. Use me to get off."

"I need to move," she whines and moans as her hips try to rock back and forth.

I can't deny her anything. I release my grip on her hip, give it a little slap. "If that's what you need, then ride me, Crash."

Now that she has the freedom to move she wastes no time, plants her hands on my stomach and starts bouncing on my cock while I do my best to keep my thumb working her clit. Within seconds, she's screaming, squeezing my cock over and over, daring me to spill inside her.

I tense every muscle, will myself to not come. Try to recite the Dewey Decimal classifications again, but now that trick is ruined because it's tied to her sexy voice repeating it back to me.

Her orgasm crests and she collapses on me, still writhing on top of me, my hand trapped between our bodies still working at her clit, softer now, but not letting her completely come down.

We reverse positions again, I roll her over gently, settle between her thighs. We've made a circuit of the whole bed; I don't think there is an inch of the surface that we haven't used in this marathon of pleasure.

Slowly, I thrust into her once, amazed I managed to hold on through her orgasm. "Fuck, Delia, you feel so fucking good around my cock."

"Wes, fuck me, please. Oh god, don't hold back anymore, please."

I let go, pounding into her exactly three times before I feel the orgasm I've been denying myself barreling down on me. I'm shocked when she starts screaming again, too, her hot cunt pulsing around me as I empty myself into the condom. Pressed together like this, I finally get a clear view as she comes for the third time tonight.

Take that, battery powered boyfriends everywhere. Consider yourselves shelved. Until I decide to use them for my benefit, that is.

I allow myself a few deep breaths after the climax is done ravaging my system. But before Delia is totally recovered, I pull myself from her center, then sit back on my heels kneeling between her legs, and fill her once again with my fingers.

"Wha—what are you doing?" she pants, brow furrowed in confusion.

"How quickly you forget. Just because I'm tapped doesn't mean the party ends for you."

Her mouth drops open as I begin working her back up. It doesn't take long, she's so sensitive after three orgasms. Within seconds she is moaning and screaming again, her hands gripping the sheets over her head.

After two more orgasms she's pushing me away, clamping her legs together as little aftershocks rack through her body. "No more, holy shit, please no more."

I turn us both on our sides, her back pressed to my chest, and wrap her in my arms. Whispering praise in her ear and gently petting her hair and down her body, helping her float back down to earth.

"Motherfucker, where did you learn to do all that?" She laughs the question out, snuggling back into me.

"Hey, I've read every single one of those books in the Den of Sin."

"Yay reading." She says it all sleepy and I bury my face in her hair, most of which has fallen out of her ponytail at this point.

A warm glow flows through my chest and into my limbs. I'm so fucking gone for this woman. Holding her in my arms after bringing her as much pleasure as she could stand is the very definition of the perfect way to end a day.

I plan to do it many times over, every day for the rest of our lives if I can help it.

Chapter 27

Delia

"Wes, wake up." I shake his shoulder, almost regretful that I have to wake him up when he looks so peaceful, a small smile curling the edges of his mouth even in his sleep. "Wakey, wakey, sex god."

He has me trapped against him, both his muscled arms holding me firmly against his chest. I turned over at some point in my sleep so we are chest to chest, one of his legs thrown over my hip as if to make sure I can't get away. I reach down between us and grip his half-hard morning wood, giving it a tentative stroke.

"Mmmmm, okay, if this is how I always woke up I wouldn't need coffee ever again." His hips push forward as he grows to his full, impressive size. "Need more, Crash?"

God, that nickname in that husky, sleep filled voice is going to be the end of me. "I mean yes, but that isn't why I woke you up."

His eyes fly open. "Are you okay?"

His sudden awareness and panic make me chuckle. "Yes, except I have to pee so bad I might cry, plus I'm starving after you fucked away every calorie I ate yesterday, and you are doing your best impression of a Venus fly trap right now, so I can't do anything about either of those facts."

"Sorry, damn. I haven't slept that hard in ages." Slowly he releases me from his death grip.

As relieved as I am to be able to move again, I also hate the loss of his warmth.

"Bathroom is right there." He nods to a door on the other side of the small room and rubs his hooded eyes.

Sprinting for the bathroom, I take care of business, then take a second to poke around his cabinets. I've never been in his space before. In high school I obviously couldn't make an appearance at his and Burt's house. Everything is neatly lined up on each shelf. Basic medications and first aid supplies under the sink. Shaving cream, face wash, moisturizer, and cologne in the small cabinet hidden behind the mirror.

I sniff the cologne and nearly spontaneously orgasm at an undiluted whiff of his scent. It's not one of those overpowering things like Axe or Old Bay. It's a subtle thing with a label I recognize from a local woman that has a booth at the farmers' market a couple towns over. The label says the scent is leather tome. God, that makes so much sense for Wes.

Plain black towels, bathmat, and shower curtain. His sheets are black too. This man needs to bring some color into his life. Good thing I'm here.

Satisfied with my inspection of his bathroom, I make my way out only to find Wesley is no longer in bed. "Wes?"

I may have come a long way with Wes, but I'm not quite to walking around his apartment butt naked level of comfort yet. Grabbing my shirt and shorts from the floor, I slip them back on and pad out to the living room.

"Do eggs still skeeve you out?" Wes is standing in front of the stove, flipping pancakes in nothing but some mesh gym shorts and an apron that says *This Is How I Roll* with a picture of a library rolling cart filled with books beneath.

"Yeah, I'm fine with them in things, but I can't eat just plain eggs." A shiver of revulsion rolls through me.

"So weird."

"Listen, you try growing up on a farm where the chickens lay eggs literally everywhere, usually in a pile of poop if they have the opportunity. I don't care that we washed them before eating them, it still skeeved me out. I promise you it changes how you feel about them. Chickens are one of the filthiest animals to exist."

Wes chuckles and flips another pancake. "But you still eat them."

"That is beside the point." His kitchen is small but functional. No room for an island, all the cabinets and countertops are along one wall with the sink right in the middle and the stove at one end. The fridge is tucked back into a little alcove on a perpendicular wall. He has a small table with two chairs floating in the middle of the space, but I don't want to be that far away. Instead I pad up behind him and wrap my arms around his waist, pressing my cheek against his shoulder blade as he cooks. "Wesley Goldman is making me breakfast after sexing me into a coma. Up is down. The sky is green. Grass is purple."

"Delia Halsted is standing in my kitchen." He says it with a wistfulness that makes my heart feel like it's been filled with helium. "I would say I'm dreaming, but you're wearing far too many clothes for it to be one of my dreams."

"You dream about me?"

He puts the spatula down after another flip and turns in my arms, banding his around my waist too so his arms are trapping mine. "Damn near every night since I met you. The reality is a thousand times better."

He stoops down to give me a sweet, gentle peck on the lips. Seriously, my heart might be leaking helium into my entire body because I think my entire being might float away in happiness. Something so mundane as standing in his kitchen and kissing like teenagers makes everything seem lighter.

"Go sit down, breakfast is almost ready." He nudges me away. "Seriously, get away from me before you distract me into burning everything."

For once, I listen to directions and sit at his tiny, little table. Hanging on the back of it is my purse which I dropped by the door when I pushed my way inside last night. My cheeks heat as I recall the moment everything snapped for me and I knew I had to touch him immediately.

"Okay, what dirty thoughts are you thinking to earn that blush?" He pushes a plate in front of me loaded with a stack of pancakes, sausage, and cut up banana. His plate matches mine, only it also has a mound of scrambled eggs and cheese.

"You know, after owning a strip club for over five years you would think I'd be past blushing over anything. I thought I was at least. I've seen things you wouldn't believe and met it all with a stony-faced seriousness. But I think about shoving my way into your apartment and throwing myself at you and suddenly my whole face is red." I take a bite of one of the pieces of sausage and mumble around the food. "It's not fair."

"I bet you have lots of stories from running the club."

"You have no idea. The early days especially when we were still figuring things out were rough. I probably shouldn't be telling the potential future mayor this, but that first year my biggest problem was making sure the girls weren't being coerced into prostitution by assholes who came into the place thinking they could pay for more than a dance."

"Wow."

"Yeah, most of the women that work in clubs don't do it because they love taking their clothes off for money. Except Harley. I think she'll be taking shifts on the pole until she physically can't climb it anymore." I drown the pancakes in syrup then cut off a piece and stuff it in my mouth before continuing. I'm so fucking hungry. "I mean, they enjoy it to some degree, but the money is the biggest motivator and the temptation to suck a dick was definitely hard to overcome for a lot of them."

I look up to find Wes staring at me with his fork halfway to his mouth.

About right now is when I realize while he might know logically that I am the owner of a strip club, the reality of what that means is a lot different.

"Sorry, I forget not everyone is comfortable talking about the perils of the sex industry over pancakes."

Wes shakes his head and puts his fork down. "It's not that I'm not comfortable with it, just that you continually impress and amaze me."

There goes that damn blush again. At just a fucking compliment. "I mean, when it comes down to it I'm just a business owner. Every small business has its pitfalls."

"I'm fairly certain Sam and Paula don't need full-time security details at their shops to make sure everyone is safe."

"Well, with all those chains and ropes Sam stocks, he should seriously look into it."

"Ha, true. He's practically begging for a serial killer to come stock up at The Nail and Bail." Wes pushes his glasses up and glances down at the floor. "Oh man, you are going think I'm a filthy bachelor. I got shit hiding under my couch."

He stands from the table, and bends to grab something from under the couch. It's a folded piece of paper that looks all too familiar. As if in slow motion, he carefully unfolds the letter that has been buried in the bottom of my purse for days. Honestly, I had almost forgotten about it with all the excitement.

"Oh, no, you're off the hook. That's actually mine." I reach for it just a moment too late. Wes has it open and is reading the first few lines.

"Delia," he says as his jaw falls open while he reads the words on the paper.

"It's no big deal." I stand and snatch the paper from his hands, a buzzing in my ear making me a little dizzy. "How did this even end up on the floor? It was like at the very bottom of my purse."

Wes runs his hand through his hair, pushing it back out of his eyes as he looks at me like I have three heads. "I dumped your purse out to find the condoms last night. It must have slid over there while I was rifling through things."

"You were going through my stuff?"

He levels me with a look that says, *are we really doing this?* "First of all, you told me to. Second of all, I know you just looked through my entire bathroom while I was out here cooking."

I shrug, because fair.

"Are we going to talk about what that letter says?"

"Nope." I fold it back up, giving it a couple extra creases, trying to make it as small as possible.

"Delia. You got into law school."

Fuck. He said the words I have been avoiding for weeks.

"It's not a big deal."

He grips my shoulders, squaring my body to his and ducking down so he can look directly in my eyes since I am avoiding looking at him at all costs. "Delia Halsted, you got into law school at the University of fucking Pennsylvania. One of the top universities in the country. A fucking Ivy League. I know Elle Woods said it isn't hard, but it really fucking is. I didn't even know you got a bachelor's."

Dear god, I *do not* want to talk about this. "Yeah, well, you can do a lot online these days. Higher education is struggling as an institution, they will take just about anyone."

"What do you have a degree in?"

The paper won't fold anymore, the edges thick from how many times I creased them. It's no bigger than a postage stamp now, stiff because of course they use some fancy heavy weight paper and not the crappy printer stuff you can get at any store.

"Delia. What do you have a degree in?"

He's not going to drop this. "Associates in social work. Bachelors in business administration." I list them off fast, in one breathe, mumbling the final one. "MBA."

"You have three fucking degrees? When did you have time? How does no one in this town know about any of this?"

I slump back into the chair, discarding the mutilated acceptance letter in the middle of the table. "I got the associates while Dad was sick. We were in and out of hospitals and I had lots of downtime at the cafe. I ended up finishing it in like a year and a half. Then we opened the club, and I realized I had no clue what I was doing. So, I started taking classes here and there, not with a degree in mind necessarily. But the community college let me know I was only a few credits shy of being able to get a bachelor's degree and that the credits would all transfer to Penn State. So I finished that up a couple years ago. I took an accelerated MBA program and basically didn't sleep for a year. Harley knows because she had to step up a lot when I was doing the MBA."

I look up at Wes, who is still standing in the middle of the kitchen, his jaw hinged open wide-mouth bass style.

With a shrug, I pick my fork back up and start cutting my pile of pancakes into pieces. "Seriously, it's not a big deal. It's like all the hobbies I pick up and put down. Or the side hustles that I rush into then get bored with after a while. I get bored and antsy, so every couple years I start taking classes again."

"Are you seriously telling me getting an MBA is no different from the three months you spent knitting all over town?"

"Yeah, only it didn't result in some bomb-ass gloves for my whole family."

"Delia, I need you to take this as the compliment I intend it as." Wes crouches down beside me, his big hand cupping my chin and forcing me to look at him. "I think you might legitimately be insane."

Chapter 28

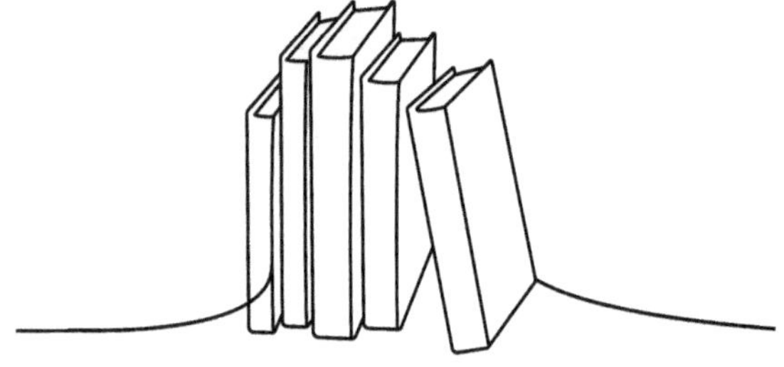

Wesley

Delia rolls her eyes and shoves my shoulder hard enough that I fall on my ass. Which is fine, because honestly, I need a second to gather my thoughts.

"Okay, so if it isn't a big deal then why are you hiding all of this? You don't hide the hobbies or the side hustles. Everyone in town has supported you with every single move you've made. Hell, half the retirees in this town take stripping classes at the club because they want to support you and Harley. Is there anyone in this town that hasn't either used your notary services or bought something you were selling at the market?" I reconsider my words. "Okay, is there anyone that isn't my uncle?"

"That's different."

"You literally just said the hobbies and being a fucking perennial student are no different."

"I mean to me they are no different. But if I tell people then they will have all these—" she waves her hands in the air in front of her, but I have no idea what she is trying to say, "—expectations. Failing at knitting or candle making or even forgetting to renew my notary licenses are no big deal. It doesn't sting when people nod and say there goes Delia with *another* obsession. It doesn't annoy me when my brothers exchange a look they think I don't see. But this—" she flicks the folded piece of paper so it skitters across the table and goes flying off the opposite side of the table to rest in the corner, "—if I fail at this it will be so much worse."

I stand from the floor and sit across from the table, reaching over to take her hand in mine. "Delia, you have never failed at a single thing you have done in your life."

She gives me an exasperated look. "Did you not listen to the knitting and candle making and notary stories? Then there is the resin and the macramé and the sourdough starter that sits on my counter neglected half the time."

"You didn't fail at any of those things." I squeeze her fingers. "They just didn't serve you anymore so you moved on. Look at the club. That place is fucking amazing. You employ, what, fifty people? The only business in town that employs more people is the school district. You kept the cafe going for your mom when she needed it most, apparently while being attacked by my uncle the whole fucking time. You finished three degrees while juggling more shit than most people have to deal with in a lifetime. And more than all of that, you are an amazing person that deserves to do whatever the fuck she wants without judgment from the people in this town."

Avoiding my eyes, Delia stares at her plate. The words I just threw at her are probably swirling in that complicated brain, trying to find a way to poke a hole in my statements. Let her try.

"Okay, tell me this. Why did you apply to law school in the first place?" I don't need to know the why, but I am curious. It makes complete sense to me. Delia loves nothing more than a fight, a challenge. A scene plays out in my imagination as if it is a movie on a screen. Delia standing before a judge defending those that can't defend themselves. Backing up each word with evidence and passion in equal measure.

She separates our hands, bringing both of hers to fidget with my fingers, crossing them and uncrossing them as she talks. It's something that she used to do back in high school, too. We'd be sitting side by side on the floor of the library and it was like she had to do something with her hands to get her thoughts straight, so she would play with my fingers. The fact that she still does it makes my chest tighten.

"A year and a half ago there was a girl that we hired as a dancer. She was beautiful, graceful, not the best at pole tricks at first, but eventually got the hang of it with help from Harley."

I move my other hand onto the table and lay it flat on the surface, knowing she'll pick that one up and start folding my fingers together, moving them to steeple against each oth-

er then nestling them between each other in different configu-
rations.

"She was quiet, kept to herself. We found out she was sleeping
in her car in the back parking lot, so Harley got Rosie to let her
stay at the B&B since it was the slow season."

"Wait, I remember her, Tina, right? She used to come into the
library but seemed nervous about giving me her ID, so I used to
let her just sit and read without checking anything out." I think
back to the girl that always looked on edge. "She was a fan of
autobiographies, I think."

"Yup, that's her. Said she liked reading about people that overcame the worst to be successful." Delia swallows
hard. "One day she just stopped showing up to work. It turned
out she was on the run from her ex. Had tried to get a restraining order against him, but the police said there wasn't enough
evidence of abuse. So she ran instead. Tried to cover her trail by
only using cash."

Delia lays my hand flat on the table, then places hers on top,
so I put my other hand on top of hers, and she completes the
tower by putting hers on the very top. Slowly we slide our hands
out and alternate being the one with the upper hand.

"Despite everything, he found her. I still don't know how. He
beat the shit out of her when she went to Wellsboro to get her
monthly check-up we require of all the girls. Put her in intensive
care. Eventually the police found him, but he barely got any jail
time. He didn't have priors, so they went easy on him. I think
he has like six more months on his sentence."

"Jesus, Delia, that is fucking awful."

She nods, her eyes going glassy. "Yeah. Harley and I sent her across the country to live with some friends in Seattle. Last I heard, she was teaching ballet and dating a sweet single dad of one of her students. But that is just one of a million stories I've heard from the girls that have come through the club. Not all of them have tragic stories, but more than there should. I just kept thinking I wish I could do more. For all of them. I've done what I can to make the club a good place to work. But for every woman that gets hired, we have to turn away just as many because we just don't have room for everyone. I thought maybe, if I knew more about the law, maybe I could do something more. So I took a few online classes and loved them. Not like I loved knitting or even the club. It felt like I had found something that had been missing. So I applied and didn't really think more of it."

"Until you got the letter."

She nods.

We stop our game of stacking hands and I entwine them together. "You have to do this, Delia. I'm guessing you haven't accepted yet."

"It's totally impractical. This isn't like my other degrees, I can't do it all online. I have to actually move to Philadelphia for a while. I can't leave the club, my family, and you know." She squeezes my hands and I think she is saying she can't leave me. Silly, brilliant woman, as if four hours means anything when it comes to what I would do for her.

"You said Harley covered for you when you were getting your MBA, couldn't she do that again?"

"It's not her responsibility, though. When we opened the club, she made it clear she didn't want to deal with the financial bullshit. She only wanted to dance, I had to convince her to become the talent manager." Delia sighs. "If I ask her, she'll say yes, but she'll be miserable."

"Then your mom can handle the financial stuff. Or hell, June's mom can help. She ran a whole national bank for most of her career, I'm pretty sure she could handle the club for a while. Tell me what to do and I will help. But, Delia, this is huge. You deserve this."

One tear falls down her cheek, then another on the other side. I've pushed enough; she's got to take the rest of the leap herself.

"Come here, Crash." We both stand from the table and I pull her into me, wrapping my arms around her shoulders while hers go around my waist. "One last thing and then I'll drop it."

I press our foreheads together, tucking her hair behind her ears. "I know we've only just started to resolve our history together, but make no mistake, you are my future. Four hours or four days, I will drive as far and as long as I have to make sure that we keep growing and healing together. So I am a non-factor in this decision. You are stuck with me no matter what."

"Wes," she whispers my name just before arching up onto her toes to kiss me slow and deep. "Take me back to bed."

I do, and for the first time since starting at the library, I call in sick. We make love, talk endlessly, eat all our meals in bed, ignore every text and phone call that flashes across our phones.

Then we fall asleep together for the second night in a row.

Chapter 29

Delia

The fire hall is packed. Standing room only with several people complaining that they come to every town council meeting and it isn't fair that they don't get seats just because everyone wants to see the debate fireworks.

"Hey," Wes whispers but I can't see him. They have us holed up backstage, which is really just down a hall that leads to the bathroom. "Crash, over here."

I turn around to see Wes's face peeking out in the crack of the door to the utility closet. "What are you doing?" Glancing behind me to make sure no one is coming, I jog the few feet separating us and Wes pulls me into the door, shutting it quietly behind himself.

"I missed you last night." He nuzzles his face into my neck, pressing me back against the only wall that doesn't have a mop or broom hanging from it.

Dating in secret was tricky as teenagers, as adults it's even worse. Wes and I agreed that until after the election we need to keep our truce-turned-romance quiet. We can't let Burt know anything is different with us. The man is absolutely diabolical and I would not put it past him to try something.

So our dates are either in the cafe after closing, his apartment, or my house. Harley and Mom are the only ones in on the secret and help as much as they can. My life is nocturnal and his is diurnal—which he let me know means active during the day. But it works for us. I sneak into his apartment after I get out of the club at three in the morning. I wake him by slipping into bed naked and we make love in the dark.

When he closes up the library for the night he goes to his house, then runs to mine where we shower together, eat dinner, and I go to the club. It works, and to be honest I'm relieved there is no pressure from the town watching us as we embark on these first steps into what I am starting to believe might actually be the rest of our lives.

Except last night when Burt insisted they needed to prepare late into the night for the debate. I told Wes to inform Burt that we had the debate prep covered thanks to our practice sessions together. In bed. Naked. But he didn't think Burt would accept that.

I joked that on debate day his body will be a war of trying not to puke from nerves and not getting a boner remembering our practice session.

The fire of the election has dimmed for both of us. With the truth out, and Mom and I reassuring Wes over and over again that he is not responsible for cleaning up Burt's messes, we both agree to be good with whatever happens. I decided to put off my decision about law school until after we get the election results. If I am elected, the decision will be made for me. If I lose, well, I'm not ready to think that far ahead yet.

"How's your stomach?"

"Let's not talk about it." There is an edge to his voice, a barely contained panic.

I give him a mock pout in the dim closet light and rub my palm over the hard plane of his abdomen. "Want me to kiss it and make it better?"

"Don't start. Going out there with a boner is not going to help things."

"I don't know, when the ladies of Amoresville see what you're packing I think your female voter base will double."

"Just promise me tonight we meet at your place and get to spend the whole night together and I'll be happy. The rest of the Amoresville female population be damned." He kisses me sweetly, keeping it very PG to avoid a boner situation.

"Deal." I seal the promise with another kiss, mine not nearly as innocent. The need to deepen things, get my hands on his bare skin, grows inside me. But he's right, we can't do this right now, so I pull away with a groan of regret. "Okay, I'll see you out there."

I slip back out into the hall just in time for the town council president, Tim Hadler, a retired dentist who has lived here since marrying his wife forty years ago, to stride down the hall. "Ms. Halsted," he says in his snobby-ass way. "We are ready to get started. Have you seen Mr. Goldman?"

"I think I heard him throwing up into a bucket in there." I point a thumb to the door I just came out of before walking past Tim to stand to the side of the small stage. It is no more than two feet off the ground with one stair up to the platform.

Normally there are two long folding tables set up where the council and mayor sit each month for the town meeting, but the tables have been removed and replaced with two podiums that look like they might fall over if I breathe on them wrong. Just in front of the little stage is a small table with a folder and microphone, not that we really need to use the PA system for this; the room is small enough that no one will have trouble hearing every word.

I take my place at the podium with my name on it and a moment later Wes takes his place at the other. I don't look at him. If I do, I'm not sure the entire audience, which is basically the whole town, won't see that I am falling hard and fast for my opponent.

"Woooo, go, Delia! Knock him on his ass!" Harley shouts from the back of the room. Glancing in that direction I see she and a handful of our employees from the club are standing against the back wall. We have half a dozen girls that have worked at the club since that first year, and they are all there clapping for me before we've even started.

"That's enough of that." Tim steps between the two podiums, glaring back at Harley, who silently raises an eyebrow at him. "This will be a civil debate with no uproars from the audience. In my role as council president, I will be moderating the debate asking questions of both candidates. Each will have ninety seconds to answer their question, with a minute for the opponent to respond and ask follow-up questions and another minute of response. There will be no cheering." He looks pointedly back at the group of girls against the wall, then down at my mother, brothers, and their partners, who all sit in the front row of folded metal chairs. Mom flips him the bird and I suppress a laugh, trying to give the aura of taking this very seriously.

"Okay, let's gets started." Tim goes down to the small table and takes a seat, flipping open the folder and clearing his throat. "Now, I flipped a coin before we started and Mr. Goldman won to introduce himself first. You have two minutes, young man."

I swear I can feel the anxiety wafting off Wes from across the stage. "Um hi." He leans a little too close to the microphone in front of him and the room fills with shrill feedback. He flinches and backs up again. "Hi. I'm Wesley Goldman, as you all know. I am the director of the library. Which you also all know."

Oh god, he is so adorably bad. I have to resist the urge to jump in and save him.

"I have lived in the town since I was sixteen. But you all know that too." He takes a deep breath, his hand going to his stomach and for a second, I think he is going to puke. But he keeps going, a little steadier now.

"What you might not know is that this town saved my life. I lived in a foster home for six months before moving here, and while the people who cared for me were perfectly nice, I was completely bereft after losing my parents and everything I knew in the world. But when I moved to Amoresville I discovered a town that welcomed me and accepted me as one of their own."

He shifts on his feet and even though I can't really read his mind, some part of me knows that he is thinking about me. "When Burt first approached me about running for mayor, I was reluctant. As you can tell, I'm not great in front of a group that doesn't consist of five-year-olds at Story Hour. But this town has given me so much, I think it is time I gave back in a tangible way. Thank you."

"Is that it, Mr. Goldman? You still have a minute left in your introduction."

"I'm good." His shoulders have relaxed slightly. He might not look at ease, but he certainly doesn't look like he's going to lose the contents of his stomach either.

"Okay then, Miss Halsted, you have two minutes."

"Hi everyone, as my opponent said, you all know me already. I think I have served all of you at the cafe at one point or another.

I know your orders as well as I know your families and the problems you have faced." I smile down at my family sitting in the front row. "My family is as much a part of this town as the soil we plant our crops in and the mountains that surround us. This town was founded on the love of my ancestors, and that love continues to grow through the families my brothers are building."

Knox and Orion look at their women, soft smiles on their faces.

"Much like Wesley said, this town has been there for my family through thick and thin. You have celebrated our successes and mourned our losses." *I will not get choked up, I will not get choked up.* "Whether you show your support through purchases at our businesses, or covered dishes handed over with a hug, this community is great because of the people that live and work here."

I look over at Wesley and do my best to keep my smile neutral. "I know it caused quite the stir in town when I decided to start this campaign. But I thought it was important that all of you are given a choice on who you should vote for. We haven't had a lot of choices over the last few elections. In fact, since I turned eighteen, I have never had more than one name in the mayoral slot on the ballot." I shift my focus out across the audience. There are a lot of people nodding in agreement with what I am saying. I'm not sure I have ever felt more connected to this community than I do right now. "We should be able to decide the direction our town takes. All of you are active participants in our town, but very few of you have had the ability to truly choose who leads the town. In fact, this is the first time a candidate has been required to get up in front of all of you and share their vision for the future of Amoresville. I hope you all listen to what both Mr. Goldman and I have to say tonight, and cast a vote for who you think will best achieve the future this town so richly deserves. Thank you."

There is a soft round of polite applause, a little louder in the very front and very back of the room where my fan club is stationed.

"I said no cheering," Tim spits out.

"Oh, no one is cheering, you old grump." Mrs. Thurston, who is looking especially ancient today, interjects. "Get on with it."

Looking positively livid, Tim turns back around and consults the papers in front of him. He looks back up making eye contact with me, obvious hatred plain as day on his face. "Fine. Miss Halsted, I noticed you did not mention in your introduction the business you own just outside of town. Why should voters trust you with the future of this town when you are running a sex club within spitting distance of town lines?"

"Hey!" I hear the exclamation from my mom, brothers, several other people in the audience including Sam and Paula, but above them all is Wesley right into the microphone.

"Watch it, Tim. You know very well Delia does not run a sex club."

I can't help but look over at Wes, whose face is crimson, his hands gripping the sides of the podium as he leans close to the microphone.

"It's okay, everyone." I say the words to the audience, but I mean them for the man I have been with every night this week.

Once the outrage dies down a little I lean into my own microphone. "Tim, you are right, I failed to mention my business in my introduction. I believe everyone here knows I am the owner of Club Barely Over the Line. Here today are several of my employees and my business partner Harley." I nod back at the girls and they all wave happily at me. "I believe all will tell you that I have been a fair and generous boss."

"Damn right."

"Best boss ever."

"She doesn't even try to get with us."

"I run the club completely above board. The first year we were open there were no doubt some growing pains. But in the last five years there has never been a need to call state police unless it was to escort someone who had overindulged at home. In fact, with the increased security I have put into place, our club has made the surrounding area even safer. Several of our community members have frequented the club either for dance classes or as patrons to the entertainment." I pointedly look at several townspeople in the audience who I know for a fact have come into the club to get a lap dance. Tim among them.

"But aside from all of that, because the club is indeed just over the town line, I have never had a tax liability to this town. Despite this, I have consistently donated ten percent of our profits to local non-profits. The food bank has never had bare shelves, the library has never lacked funding, and the high school drama, speech, and debate teams have all been the recipients of our generosity."

I turn to a spot in the room I've been avoiding looking at. Burt, who sits front and center on Wes's half of the stage.

"While some in this town consider it a hobby to look down their noses at me and my business, they never seem to let their disdain for the club get in the way when it comes to accepting checks."

"You're ninety seconds are up, Miss Halsted," Tim interrupts me.

"Let her finish talking," someone shouts from the back. I can't tell who because I am still having a staring contest with our current mayor.

"Yeah, these rules are dumb, just let them talk," another town person pipes up.

Sam stands in the middle of the audience. "Tim, nothing in the town charter says we have to follow a certain format. Just that any candidate looking to run for office must have an open airing of issues for the town to hear."

"These are the rules we have agreed—"

"I'm fine with her finishing her answer." Wesley's voice is no longer shaky. Just the opposite; he is solid as stone now.

I look away from his uncle and meet Wes's gaze across the stage. Big mistake. The fire lying behind his dark brown eyes has nothing to do with the campaign or debate and everything to do with how much he wants to drag me off the stage and rip my clothes off. Quickly, I glance down at his groin and back up to his eyes. He catches it and I see the corners of his mouth twitch. It all happens in a fraction of a second but it goes miles to ease the tension.

"Fine, you have thirty seconds to finish your thought, Miss Halsted."

I look back at the audience. "I just have one more thing to say on this topic. If anyone has real concerns about the club, I invite you to come talk with me. I will answer any questions, even give a tour of the club to anyone curious about what happens there and the measures we have taken to ensure everyone's safety. I promise you, it is not nearly as scandalous as some make it out to be."

"Mr. Goldman, follow up?"

"I'm good," Wes clips the words out.

"You have no response or follow up questions?" Tim seems to be trying to bore holes into Wesley's head with the power of his stare.

"Miss Halsted's career is not a factor in my campaign." Wes smiles slightly at Tim. "As someone who has recently visited Club Barely Over the Line, I have no concerns on that front."

Well, that gets the audience murmuring.

Chapter 30

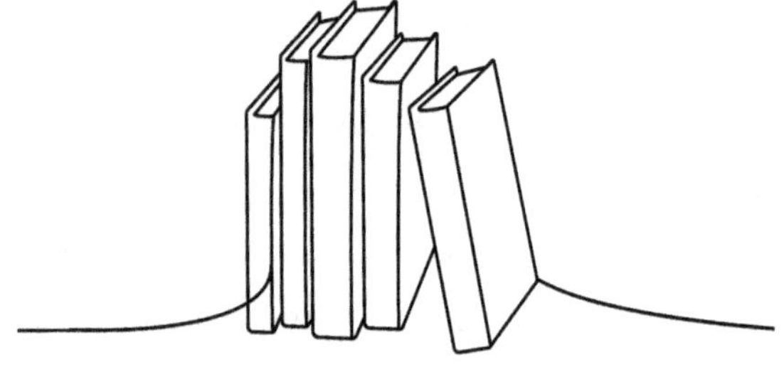

Wesley

Burt looks like he's about to leap on the stage and throttle me. Part of me wants him to try. Not only did I not attack Delia for her involvement in the club, as he coached me to do nonstop last night during his prep session, but I have now openly admitted to going to Club Barely Over the Line.

It's none of anyone's business that I went there to talk to Delia, not get a lap dance. Though I will happily tell them about the hot as hell make out session we had in her office if they are curious. I am finding I care less and less about what these people think of me. The only thing that matters is Delia and what she wants and needs.

Tim's mouth opens and shuts a few times. He looks back over his shoulder at Burt, but my uncle is far too focused on trying to strangle me Darth Vader style than to notice. But it has me curious. Was I the only one Burt prepped for the debate?

"Okay, next question." Tim clears his throat and searches down his list of bullshit questions. "Mr. Goldman, Amoresville has seen a recent upswing in tourism thanks the work of June Ammar—"

"June Halsted, my name is Halsted now," the woman in question shouts from the audience.

Tim ignores her and keeps going. "What is your plan for encouraging more tourism?"

Jesus Christ, this is such a fucking softball question. Burt seems to settle back into his chair, confident that I will go with the answer we rehearsed. I should. That would be the smart thing to do. Talk about adding social media and updating our website, regurgitate the things June has been telling him to do for ages.

But I suddenly have no desire to keep playing along with this game of carrying on the legacy.

"I think tourism could be a real asset to this town and that we could do a lot more to draw people in who are visiting the state parks that we are so lucky to have so close to our town."

Burt smiles, happy that I am starting off exactly how we discussed.

"But the truth is, I don't think we can take full advantage of the expertise of June Halsted until we solve the problems Amoresville is facing by not attracting new businesses."

Burt stiffens and I turn away from my side of the audience, instead focusing across the room to block him out.

"As a town, we have made it far too difficult for new businesses to set up shop within the town lines. Too difficult for our existing businesses to expand and grow. Walking through the town square, anyone wandering into town would think this is a dying town because there are only three storefronts currently occupied. The only reason we have that many is because the deli and hair salon have been here for generations, and through the tenacity of Brigid Wolke to fight through the endless red tape to open the Tiger's Eye. We should be adding incentives to draw businesses into town rather than making it harder for them. We can't promote our town as a destination without first tackling the lack of reasons for them to make the trek."

Tim seems to know that I have gone off Burt's script because he looks at me as if I am morphing into a pile of slime right here on stage. He also isn't turning it over to Delia to respond.

"What do you think, Miss Halsted, any response?" I lean on the podium with an elbow— it wabbles beneath me slightly, so I try not to rest too much of my weight on it— and angle myself toward Delia.

I can tell she is fighting to keep a smile off her face. "Actually, I don't. I think you are absolutely right, Mr. Goldman."

I wonder if she would call me Mr. Goldman in bed?

"Um." Tim flips one page back and forth in his pile. "Right. So let's move on."

"Hey, are you two going to debate anything at any point or just keep agreeing?" a man from the back of the room I recognize as a ranger for the Pine Creek Gorge that moved into town a handful of years ago grumbles.

I smirk because the truth is, Delia and I pretty much agree on everything when it comes to how the town should be run, as we discovered while she helped me practice in bed the other night. Which I should definitely not be thinking about right now, or there will be a far bigger problem than how much I am pissing off Burt right now.

"Okay, Miss Halsted—" Tim suddenly seems more confident than just a moment ago which has my hackles on edge "—as someone who also already opened a business that encourages drinking in excess, would you support allowing businesses to serve alcohol within town limits?"

My head whips over to look at Burt. That question is almost verbatim how Burt worded a question that might be asked of Delia. He has his arms crossed over his slight frame, looking very satisfied with himself from his front row seat.

"I think it is definitely something that we should look into." Delia smiles down at Tim, giving him this look that makes it seem like she is explaining something to a small child that is trying to horn in on an adult's conversation. "As the operator of an establishment that serves alcohol, I know that it comes with several benefits and penalties. Higher insurance and liability issues is one, but also just the difficulty of getting a liquor license in our state. What we need to consider is how to deal with people who do overindulge and need help safely getting home. Since we have no public transportation to speak of in town, that is especially tricky."

A few people in the audience murmur in tones so hushed I can't decipher how they are taking Delia's answer. Burt looks like he is about to start spitting nails.

"On the benefits side, being able to sell alcohol means greater profit margins and attracts more patrons. We would need to balance the good of our community with the good of business owners. I would not make a unilateral decision on something like this; it would need to be discussed and possibly even voted on through a ballot question by all of you."

I want to pump my fist in the air and shout, *fuck yeah*, in response to her answer. Instead, I simply lean into the micro-phone and say, "I agree," then lean back again.

"A brewery in this town would be amazing," the same ranger shouts from the back of the room, which is when I remember he has checked out a few books on home brewing.

"If we weren't a dry town maybe an actual restaurateur would open a location in town," Roxy pipes up in the front row. "No offense to Brian and his deli, but someplace where people will sit and stay for a while. Take their significant others on dates. It is something we are lacking in town."

"This town has always been a dry community, and it always will be," Burt explodes to his feet from the front row. "If you all elect this heathen, she will have motorcycle bars and drug addicts overrunning the town within a year of taking office."

Several people start yelling at once, including me, screaming at my uncle to not call Delia a heathen. With everyone talking over each other, no one is being heard.

A loud whistle brings the chaos to a halt. Sam's hulking presence in the center of the audience becomes the focus of attention, his fingers still in his mouth. "Settle down, everyone. First of all, Burt, this town has *not* always been a dry town. It became a dry town during prohibition, but before that it was common practice for farmers to distill their own grain liquors with the crops they couldn't sell and then trade it for other goods. Second of all, I highly doubt a motorcycle bar would succeed here. Third, let's not have any name calling, my kids know better—" he points a stern finger in Burt's direction, "—and so should a room full of grown adults." He shoots Burt a disappointed dad look and I swear for the first time in my life I see Burt look slightly regretful. "Now, Tim, do you have more questions that are fair and balanced or just the drivel that everyone in this room can tell Burt fed you?"

Tim's eyes go wide and he opens his mouth to respond, but Sam cuts him off before he can. "Before you try to deny that, I think you should remember that you are up for reelection in two years and this town has a long memory."

The council president's mouth clamps shut and he seems to consider his options before turning back around to face Delia and me. "Let's continue."

The rest of the debate is pretty uneventful. Tim's questions are a little more balanced, both Delia and I answer easily and

more or less in agreement. At one point we ignore Tim completely and start just talking with people in the audience about
what they want from the town's government.

The excitement at the beginning of the event somehow eases
my nerves. Apparently, I just need an adrenaline rush to get over
my fear of public speaking.

The evening winds down with Delia's family gathered
around her smiling and hugging and telling her how wonder-
fully she did while Burt berates me for wandering so far off
script. I ignore him, not able to take his empty threats seriously.
It has taken me far too long to realize it, but Burt no longer has
any power over me. He might be the last blood relative I have,
but as it turns out, I don't need a genetic connection to have a
family.

I just need Delia.

Chapter 31

Delia

The debate last night was about as much of a shit show as I thought it would be. The town council president insinuating several times that I am no better than a low-level pimp was the icing on the cake. But even if it was a disaster, it was also very interesting.

The election is in exactly four days. Wes and I are just barely managing to keep our relationship to ourselves. I don't want to hide it anymore, which is why I invite him to my favorite night of the month, family dinner night.

When I was a kid my family had dinner together every single night, all five Halsteds around one table each and every night. The nights dwindled as we got older and added in activities and friends to the mix, but even then once a week Mom insisted we all sit down at the table together. Then we all became adults,

Knox running the farm, Orion in the Marines, Mom and I taking care of Dad, and the cafe and dinners together became a thing of the past.

Until right before Dad died. Orion was finally home for good. Dad was barely conscious most of the time. But Mom insisted the whole family get together for dinner to celebrate the whole family being together again. A week later, Dad passed. Mom moved out of the farmhouse to live above the cafe, claiming it was too painful to be there without Dad. Really, I think she was trying to give Knox the space he needed to make the place his own.

Without ever discussing it, we started meeting up on the farm once a month to have dinner and remember Dad. Sometimes it is more than once a month, but never any less.

So inviting someone to dinner is a big deal in our family. June came to her first family dinner the very first night she was in town, and I knew she would be a permanent fixture even if Knox didn't yet. Brigid and her son made their appearance a month after moving to town, for Thanksgiving. At that point Orion and Brigid were already solid in their relationship, diving in feet first after knowing each other only a few weeks.

By bringing Wes, I am giving him and the family a clear message: this is real, and I want it to be permanent.

By bringing him on a night when the Andersons are also going to be at dinner I might be testing Wes just a little.

Sam, Paula, and their kids all join us from time to time as well, because they are an extension of our family and Sam's parents moved to Florida after passing the hardware store onto him to run. We decided tonight would be one of those nights as a sign of solidarity for my impending election.

By the looks on everyone's faces when Wes and I walk through the front door, his presence was not expected. All fifteen people that are spread throughout Knox's first floor freeze at our appearance. I half expect to hear a record scratch somewhere in the distance. The best thing about these people is their ability to accept and move on.

"Hey, you two, watch out, I'm pretty sure there are toddlers somewhere around here testing whose new sneakers are the fastest," Paula calls to us from her position at the long table coloring with Robin, their five-year-old.

Right on cue, Mica and Maggie come zooming from behind the stairs at the far end of the house where there is a sunroom on the back of the house. They sprint right for us and I brace for collision.

"Auntie DeeDee!" Mica takes a flying leap and I catch him in midair, stumbling back a few steps because he is getting way too big at almost three years old.

Not to be out done, Maggie, who is six months older than my nephew, flies at Wesley yelling, "Mr. Book Guy!"

To his credit Wes doesn't hesitate, just opens his arms and catches the girl with ripped holes in the knees of both legs of her pants and one pigtail falling from the ribbon it was tied up in. "Hey there, Maggie. This is quite the welcome wagon."

"Did you bring books?" She pushes his glasses up the bridge of his nose, which slipped when he caught her.

"As a matter of fact, I do have some books in my trunk. Want a story later?"

"Nah, I just figured you would need some since you like books more than anything else." She wriggles and pushes at him until both feet are back on the floor. "Look, my sneakers light up." She stomps one foot on the floor and they do indeed light up in the most obnoxious flashing neon pink I can imagine.

"Wow, that is super cool."

She shrugs. "I know." Apparently done with show-and-tell, she tugs at Mica's foot since I am still holding him. "Come on not brother, I'll race you back."

"Down, please," he says to me. I kiss him on the cheek and do as he asks.

"Welcome to family dinner!" Mom sweeps up to us in her favorite yellow and green maxi dress swishing around her ankles. She leans in giving me a hug and I take a second to enjoy the warm embrace of both her arms and the scent of sugar, vanilla, and coffee that follows her everywhere. She releases me and gives Wes the same treatment. "You ready for the chaos?"

"As ready as I'll ever be." He smiles at her as they release each other.

I take his hand in mine as we walk the rest of the way into the huge space that is the first floor of the farmhouse. Knox and June are in the kitchen putting the finishing touches on dinner, which really means that June is handing her husband things while he does his best to keep her away from sharp objects. The woman is useless in the kitchen, even after three years of us trying to teach her.

Brigid and Orion are on the couch with Sam, who is holding his one-year-old, Erica. The oldest three of the Anderson kids, Molly, Max, and Henry, are all gathered around a smaller table set up to the side of the living room playing Jenga and yelling at the toddlers to not bump the table as they run by.

June's mom is even here tonight. She doesn't come to every family dinner, but most. She and June didn't have the best relationship, but after a few years of therapy and working on it they are in a good place. I don't think they will ever be as close as Mom and me, but not everyone needs their mother to be a best friend.

The next hour is a whirlwind of small talk and getting the table set up for our big crew. I never thought the enormous live edge dining table Orion made for the house would be too small for family dinner night. It used to be comically empty with just the four of us.

It takes some work, but finally we are all seated at the table, with the youngest kids set up next to their parents and the older four eating at their own table.

"So, Delia, Wes, how are you feeling about the election this week?" My mom asks the question, I think because she knows there is a reason I asked Wes to be here tonight. The truth is, as much as I did want to make it clear to the people most important to me that Wes and I are a *we*, I had ulterior motives as well.

"Funny you should mention that." I look over at Wes. He has no clue what is coming and I'm not sure exactly how he will feel about it. But my idea is a little on the crazy side and I wanted to run it by everyone that I would need to make it work before going forward. "The truth is, neither of us want to be mayor for ourselves."

There goes that record scratch moment again. With the exception of the kids in the room, all eyes turn to Wes and I sandwiched in the middle of the table. But I ignore them all and turn to look at Wes.

"Part of me wonders if either of us would do the town we love so much justice as its mayor. Do we have ideas on how to move everything forward? Sure. And I honestly believe that we would perform the job well." I look around the table to make sure they are listening, not just hearing but absorbing my words.

"Say what you want about Burt, he was dedicated to the role and he did it because he wanted it. Neither Wes nor I can say that." I turn back to Wes, trying to tell him with my eyes that this is a safe space and it is okay to tell the truth. "Right?"

He nods. "I agreed to it because I wanted to earn the ability to be here with the woman next to me. No matter how much I might have denied it, even to myself, this was always what I truly wanted. I just thought cleaning up what Burt has done was the best way to that goal."

At the end of the table I hear Paula whisper, "Oh my god, that is so sweet."

"And I got into it because I was angry and wanted revenge." I squeeze Wes' hand under the table. "But that isn't a motivator for me anymore."

"So, what, are you going to drop out?" Knox interjects from the head of the table to my left. His words rankle a little, that same old joke between my brothers that I pick something up just as soon as I put the thing it was before down. But that isn't what this is.

"Technically, I can't drop out since I'm not on the ballot."

"And neither can I, because the ballots are already printed and ready to go."

"So why are you telling us this, honey?" Mom knows why I'm doing it, but she's tee-ing me up to knock this home.

"Well, I'd like to give the town of Amoresville one more option and see who they think should really be the mayor." Everyone looks around the table confused. "I think Sam should run as a write-in, too. And I want Wes and I to campaign for him the day of the election."

Everyone turns to look at Sam, who is seated on the corner of the table between Paula and Mom. His eyes are wide, a forkful of salad halfway to his mouth. "Wait, what? You want *me* to run?"

"Finally!" Paula fist pumps the air, then plants her hands on the table and leans her entire torso over the surface so she can see us all clearly. Her curly black hair bounces where it is pulled back into a ponytail as she swings her head between both ends of the crowd. "I have been telling him for *years,* he should run for something. But he always brushes me off."

"Honey, come on. We have six kids and two stores. I don't have the time to take on something else," Sam immediately puts in.

Paula gesticulates wildly at him while looking at us all as if to say *see, I told you so.*

"Plus, who would even vote for me other than the people sitting at this table?"

Orion scoffs from the other end of the table where he, Brigid, and Mica are set up. "You have to be kidding, dude. People love you in this town. How many people have you helped with projects at a moment's notice? I think you've patched holes in half the roofs in this town. I know because half the time you make me help."

"Plus, you go to every single town meeting," June speaks up, and all our heads whip in her direction. "I only go to the ones that have something up for vote I'm involved in, and you are always there making sure the council isn't going against something in the town charter."

"Thank you!" Paula elbows her husband in the side. "You go to every meeting anyway, why not actually be a part of it?"

"But I wasn't part of the debate. The town charter says all candidates need to be heard before election day."

"Okay, you are proving my point, you know that, right?" His wife playfully glares at him.

Before he can contradict her I interject with my own point. "You did participate in the debate. I think you talked more at the debate than either Wes or I did. Plus, you kept Tim and Burt in line. The whole town was going nuts in there and you brought them all to heel with just a few words. Not even Burt can do that."

This seems to make Sam think and he lapses into silence.

"Not to be the naysayer here, especially since I am an outsider who thinks the local politics in this town are insane and that is coming from someone that spent most of their adult life in Philadelphia, but how would this even work?" The last person I expected to weigh in on the topic is June's mom, but I actually love that she is contributing her two cents. She's a smart woman who hasn't lived under the dynasty of Lickinbill mayors. "There are, what, three days until the election. How would we even run a campaign in that time?"

This is where I will need all their help. "We would run a one-day blitz campaign. I've already started designing some signs and leaflets talking about his qualifications—"

"—No hidden dicks in those designs, right?" Paula gives me a mom look that would put my *actual* mother to shame.

"I promise, they are completely innocent." I look around at the ten adults. "We would need to all spread the word. Everyone you can think of, go talk to them in person. Let them know that while any of the three of us would do well as mayor, Sam is the one that loves the town, its past, present, and future so completely, so purely that he could be a true impartial leader.

He isn't weighed down by the legacy of two families that have warred for so long most of us don't even know where it started."

I have everyone's attention, I even notice the older kids at the separate table have stopped their chatter and are listening in. "Then on election day we are a united front. We can't be any closer than ten feet from the front of the firehouse where voting happens, so we all stand at least a foot outside that line to make sure Burt doesn't call foul, and we tell everyone as they walk in that both Wes and I are throwing our support behind Sam as they walk in to vote."

Finally, I look down the table at Sam, because it all comes down to him. "What do you think, Sam? Give this town the fresh start it needs?"

He looks up from his plate, locks eyes with his wife, then looks at me. "I've always wanted to use that gavel at meetings."

Chapter 32

Wesley

The second Sam agrees to Delia's plan the room erupts in activity. Paula is hugging her husband, quickly followed by the four oldest Anderson kids who were following along with the adult's conversation. Molly, the oldest, assures her dad she is going to tell all her friends to tell their parents to vote for him.

Knox and Orion have pulled a town map from a desk in another room and have spread it out on the kitchen island, divvying up where everyone is going to canvas.

June, her mother, and Delia are talking specifics about printing and where they can get t-shirts last minute. Brigid gathers the younger kids and gets them set up with an episode of *Bluey*, then takes the one-year-old and straps her into one of the weird baby wraps she used to carry Mica around in before he got too big.

Roxy is brewing coffee, because of course she is. I just sit and watch them all. I've never seen a group of people so connected. And it isn't just tonight, in this moment. They are like this all the time. Just there for each other without question.

I had that with my parents, but it was just the three of us. They only had a few friends and it was nothing like this. This is a web of love and trust that seems to blanket and envelope anyone that comes near. Including me.

Emotion clogs my throat. I'm so fucking thankful I get to be part of this. But I also miss my parents fiercely. I'm sad that when Mom left the family that didn't understand her behind, she didn't know that this was a possibility.

As if sensing my turmoil, Delia breaks off from the group and turns back to me. "Are you okay?"

I nod. "Just caught in the moment."

She looks around at the renewed chaos. "Yeah, it's something. Are you upset I didn't tell you the plan before we got here?"

"Not even a little. Honestly, I'm not sure why it didn't occur to me before."

"He's perfect, right?" Delia's smile is as wide as the world and twice as beautiful.

"He really is. I don't even think Burt could object to him too much. I mean, he will, but not much."

"You know between this—" she waves her hands between our chests, "—and this—" she waves her hands to indict the planning happening all around us "—Burt is more than likely not going to speak to you ever again. He might not be the best person on the planet, but he is the only family you have left. I'd understand if you wanted to try to preserve that."

I'm shaking my head before she can finish the thought. "No, he's not the only family I have left. I have you. And with you comes this."

She looks around the table once again before turning back to lean in and kiss me right there in front of everyone.

"Okay, that is going to take some getting used to," Knox grumbles from the kitchen.

We break apart and realize everyone is looking at us with huge grins.

Delia leans in and whispers in my ear, "You're the one blushing now."

* * *

It's nearly midnight when everyone disperses from the Halsted farmstead. The Anderson kids are all in various states of sleep or near sleep and Sam and Paula need Delia, Knox, and me to help carry them out to their huge van.

After handing the kids off safely to their parents, Delia and I climb into her car, but instead of driving away, she turns to me with a mischievous smile on her face. That is a smile that spells trouble for me.

"What are you planning now, Crash?"

"Remember that night you barged into the club to tell me off and instead we made out?"

"Oh, you mean the night your security almost dragged me out back and broke my kneecaps?"

She scoffs. "They have never broken anyone's kneecaps. But yes, that night. I've been thinking, maybe we should finish what we started that night."

"I hate to tell you, but we've finished several times since that night. Several times in a single night in fact."

She rolls her eyes and spells out exactly what she means. "I mean, I want to take you back to the club, bring you to my office, and have my way with you right there on my desk." She leans in close, her hand skating down my quad then over to caress the appendage quickly tenting my pants. "I've played it out in my head so many times. Let's see if the reality lives up to the fantasy."

I grip her silky red hair in my hand and pull her in for a filthy kiss that would absolutely earn me another punch in the face from her brothers if they saw it. After a minute I pull back, "Drive."

It takes about forty-five minutes to get from Knox's house out to Club Barely Over the Line. The entire way I have my hand planted on Delia's thigh, not teasing or stroking, but just keeping the connection between us crackling.

The metal gate chugs and squeaks open, both of us sitting in the car silently, with one of Delia's pop playlists humming in the background. I've never understood the old idiom *you could cut the tension with a knife,* but sitting in the car the sexual tension is a third passenger. Yeah, I get it. As if I could reach out and grip the need between us in one hand.

She parks close to the door and we're speed walking to the employee entrance without a word. There is a security guard posted at the door since it is their busiest night and he gives Delia a stern nod but pretty much ignores me. She swipes her security pass and grabs my hand, pulling me into the narrow hallway that connects to her office.

The walls thump with the beat of a song, the bass turned up so high I can't make out the words to whatever it is. Just as we turn the corner to the connected hallway where Delia's office sits across from a row of private dance rooms, another large, highly muscled security guard appears at the end of the hall.

"No, no, Mak. I am not here right now." She tries her best to ignore the guy walking quickly toward us.

"Miss Halsted, I'm sorry, but I was just about to call you when I heard from James that you were walking in. We have a situation."

I'm a fairly secure guy, a solid six foot four, and in pretty decent shape. But this guy makes me feel like a peon when he looms over us. He has to be at least seven foot and three hundred pounds of pure muscle. He has bronze skin and long black hair pulled into a ponytail at his nap. He is so attractive it has me questioning things about myself.

"Mak, go tell Harley. She's the one in charge tonight, not me."

Mak looks supremely uncomfortable and nervous for someone that could most likely bench-press both Delia and I at the same time. "Ma'am, Harley is part of the situation."

Delia leans her forehead against the door to her office, a defeated sigh deflating her whole body. "So fucking close."

Right in front of my eyes, Delia transforms from the woman who gives her brothers a hard time, rolls around on the ground with her friends' kids, and needs at least two cups of coffee in the morning before I can get her to make sense, to a badass boss who needs to handle business. It doesn't matter that she's wearing the same beat-up jeans and long sleeve t-shirt she has been in all night, I wouldn't want to mess with her now and pity whoever is.

"Okay, what's going on?" She follows Ty out to the main floor and I follow behind, keeping my attention on Delia and only Delia as we walk out to where there are several women already dancing.

Listen, I have absolutely zero problem with the career these women have chosen, but I know for a fact some of them also have kids that frequent the library and I want to give them the respect of not seeing them half-naked the next time they come in for Story Hour.

The music is so loud I can't make out what Ty is telling Delia, but her shoulders creep incrementally closer to her ears and she shakes her head in obvious disgust. They walk clear across the large room to a raised section of the club partitioned off with velvet ropes. On the platform is a group of men in suits that more than likely cost more than my annual salary at the library. Most of them stand back from where the real issue is, Harley in a body-hugging dress screaming at a tall white guy with silver speckled in his dark brown hair.

This guy can't be too bright, because instead of taking cover from Harley's rage, he is standing there smirking at her like she's a little girl he's humoring by listening to her. There are two security guards standing on either side of her, looking like they aren't sure if they should be protecting Harley or the guy she's more than likely about to open a can of whoop-ass on.

With confident strides, Delia climbs the three small steps and lays one hand gently on Harley's arm. Knowing I have no business trying to help, I stay just close enough to make sure Delia is good without seeming like I am hovering.

"Mr. Olsen, I thought I made my intentions clear during your last visit. What exactly are you doing back in my club?"

The guy turns the same condescending look at Delia, and if Harley doesn't slug the guy I just might.

"No one says no to me, little girl. I'm giving you the chance to change your mind. Five million is more than enough to cover this little—" he looks around the club, "—project you have going on here."

In my peripheral vision I see several of the dancers have stopped the show and are pulling on robes while they take in what is happening.

"I hate to break it to you, Mr. Olsen, but you could offer me five *billion* dollars and I still wouldn't sell it to you." Delia takes a step forward, planting her hands on her hips and staring the man down like he doesn't have a few inches and several years on her.

"Now, in just a moment, I am going to introduce you to my head of security, Mak, and he is going to remove you and your lackeys from the building. After that they will be putting you on our banned list. Should you step foot in even the parking lot again, I will have you arrested for trespassing. Stand there and stare at me like a dumb ox if you understand me."

The man looks taken aback, no clue how to respond. Watching as he tries to dissect what she said to him and that it was in fact an insult is highly amusing.

"But before you leave, let me reassure you that if you come back, I will let my partner here—" she indicates Harley, who is still seething behind her best friend, "—do whatever she wants to you and she has been known to do more damage than any of the very large, very well paid men around you right now.

"Makoa Masoe, may I introduce you to Mr. Olsen. He is the owner of some highly suspect clubs in New Jersey." The large man that intercepted us just moments ago steps in front of Delia, his large, impressive arms crossed over his chest. He looks down at the man like he might be made of pure shit. "Mak here is going to introduce himself."

Apparently Mak's form of introduction is picking the guy up under the armpits like he is nothing more than an unruly child and marching him out of the club.

"As for the rest of you," Delia says as she looks around at the men who seem to be the asshole's friends but are currently standing around looking bewildered. "You have a choice. You can walk out of here voluntarily or I can introduce the rest of my security staff. Up to you."

All four of the men quickly scurry off the platform and out the front doors.

Chapter 33

Delia

I swear, the drama in this place can be a lot sometimes. And it is never the women that work here causing trouble; it is always the men.

Speaking of which, I realize I have no clue what happened to Wes when I abandoned him to deal with the dickwad from New Jersey. One glance behind me and I see he is hovering at the bottom of the stairs up to the VIP section looking at me like I just created the stars in the sky. I shoot him a wink and a smile to let him know I'm fine and turn my attention to my best friend and partner in crime. Maybe sometimes literally.

"Har, are you okay?"

Her eyes narrow and I know immediately my plans for Wes and I baptizing my office are pretty much null and void for tonight. "Why the hell didn't you tell me that asshole offered you five fucking million dollars to buy this place?"

"Because it was a non-issue. I would never had said yes to him." Not enough money exists on this planet to basically sign over not only the deed to this club, but also the fate of every single woman that works here. I guarantee that guy is a big fan of the old clichéd casting couch.

"You still should have told me. Have you been considering selling to someone else? Is that what you've been hiding from me?"

"Harley, can we talk back in my office? Let everyone get back to work."

Harley rolls her eyes and crosses her arms in front of her waist, but starts walking back to my office.

With a regretful smile I approach Wes. "So, about our plans."

"I get it, I'll just hang out at the bar while you and Harley talk it out."

It is that moment that I realize Wes has his back turned on the club and the women who are starting up their routines again. His eyes are practically super-glued on me and his body stiff and unmoving.

"Wes, it's okay if you want to watch the dances. These women work hard on their craft, they are amazing, and I am not at all the jealous type." Really, I'm not. It helps that we have a strict no dating or hooking up with customers policy. But even if we didn't, I trust Wes. The realization that trusting him requires no thought on my part is more shocking than every-thing that just happened here tonight.

But Wes is shaking his head vehemently. Just as Sierra comes off the stage and struts by in a G-string to join a bachelor party at one of the booths, Wes slams his eyes shut. "Honestly, it's not about not wanting to make you jealous and more to do with having to see these women at the library with their kids and it feels incredibly disrespectful to see them like this when I'm going to be making book recommendations to them next week."

Okay, that is adorable. "I promise you, no one else will think it is disrespectful. You do realize that a not small number of people from town have come out here to hang out, often watch-ing their neighbors up on the stage."

"Good for them."

I can't help but chuckle; Wes is not budging on this. "Okay, well, you are going to need to open your eyes so you can walk to the bar at least."

"I have a plan." Wes slips his glasses off his face and opens his eyes. "There, I can see just enough to not run into anything, but not enough that I will recognize anyone."

"God, you are weird." I take his hand and walk him over to the bar, because even if he thinks he can walk across the room without his glasses and stay upright, I know better.

As soon as he slips onto one of the bar stools he slips his glasses back on. But then he sees the wall of mirrors behind the bar that allows people sitting here to still see the show and quickly pulls them back off.

"Order anything you want, I have it covered. I'll be back as soon as I can."

Back in my office, Harley paces back and forth along the length of the room like a caged lion. "Why didn't you tell me?"

"Because it was a non-issue. I'm not selling." I lean back against the door, giving Harley room to work her feelings out.

My best friend is amazing in most things, but having big emotions is not one of them. She doesn't know how to handle them, her parents never taught her what to do when she was so angry or sad or even happy that it is hard to contain. So she either bottles it all up until she is about to explode or avoids any situation that could result in big feelings.

"That asshole came in here and when he saw me in this dress—" she points to the gorgeous black bodycon dress that covers her from knees to collarbone, "—said it was cute that I was trying to play boss. That when he took over I would be on the pole, either the one on the stage or the one in a man's lap, my whole shift. No breaks. No playing dress-up."

She picks up one of the throw pillows on my couch and screams into it. I let her go. Over the course of our lives, I've learned when she is ready for me to chime in and when she needs to just spew her thoughts all over the room.

Her hand holding the pillow falls limply at her side and she starts pacing again, this time a little slower. "I tried my best to be civil. To tell him that the club wasn't for sale. But he said no one would turn down millions of dollars for a club in the middle of nowhere."

"And you believed him."

She stops a few feet in front of me and looks guilty. "Yeah."

"Har, I am not your parents. I'm not going to leave you or this place we have built together for money. It doesn't matter how much it is."

She nods, and I see the tears she never lets actually fall start to form along her lower lid. Right on cue, she tilts her head back, refusing to let them loose. She's told me things about her childhood here and there. I know the general picture, but I've always known she keeps the truly dark things to herself.

On my twenty-first birthday, we got so shit-faced she told me her mom had used Harley's social security number to open a bunch of credit cards, max them all out, and then never paid them. Her credit was fucked by the time she turned eighteen. It's why she couldn't be on any of the financial documents when we opened this place.

I know there is more. I've asked, a lot, but she insists she doesn't want to taint my worldview with her bullshit. It's a flimsy excuse and we both know it.

"Delia."

Okay, she's about to say something big. She never uses my full name. It's always Dee, Bestie, or Bitch, never Delia unless she's about to lay something big on the table.

"I've been trying to find a way to bring this up and have failed over and over again, so here it goes. I want to buy into the club.

Some of the other girls do too. I know you said you don't want to sell the club, but if you did, I want you to consider me. Us."

Whoa. I did not see this coming.

"Harley, I'm not selling the club to anyone that wouldn't continue what we built here. You know I have always considered this place as much yours as it is mine in every way except financial. If you want in, all you had to do was speak up and I would make it happen. You know that." I have asked her every year on the anniversary of our opening day. She has always said she didn't want to deal with the bullshit that went with owning a business. "But I'm not sure about bringing anyone else into the business. I would need a lot more information."

She takes a deep breath and grips the pillow she is still carrying in both hands. "I've been thinking about it a lot this past year. I think we should convert to a co-op business model. I've been researching it a lot, there was a pretty famous club on the West Coast, the Lusty Lady, that ran as a dancer-owned co-op for a decade. I think we could do it here, too."

"Wow. Okay." I step away from the door and pace a little myself. "I'm going to be totally honest, I don't know a ton about co-ops. We talked about them a little during my MBA classes, but never in this context."

Harley fidgets with the pillow, her face a stoic mask, but the way she twists the decorative tassels around the pillow tells a different story about her current state. "I know, but like I said, I've been doing research and the first step is forming a feasibility committee. I was thinking you, me, and Misty representing the dancers. Plus someone from the outside to guide us. Maybe Meredith, June's mom? She worked in finance for a long time, she might have some insight."

"You are serious about this."

She straightens her back and drops the pillow to her side again. "I am. I know this is a lot to lay on you tonight, but now that I know other people are sniffing around trying to buy the place, I feel like I can't wait anymore to bring it up."

"It's a lot. But it's interesting. Let's do it, the feasibility committee. Let's get it going. I'm on board with exploring it at least. Actually, there is something I need to tell you too."

"Oh god, I knew you've been hiding something from me." She goes back to fidgeting with the pillow.

"I got accepted to the University of Pennsylvania's law school. I haven't accepted yet, but I'm considering it. Maybe."

Harley drops the pillow on the floor and surges forward, wrapping me in her arms. "You brilliant stupid bitch, of course you're accepting! That is amazing!"

A startled laugh bursts out of me and I wrap my arms around Harley, too. "It's so scary though. I would have to move to Philadelphia for a while. You would have to step up a lot more around here. We might need to get someone to help you with the financial stuff. I don't know, it would be a lot."

"Woman, I literally just told you I want to be more involved here. I want to be part owner. This couldn't be more perfect. I can learn the business and you can follow your dreams of doing something that fits you so perfectly. A lawyer, wow." Harley places her hands on my shoulders and pushes me away to look me up and down. "I can see it, Delia Halsted Esquire."

"Haha, yeah that is a ways off still."

"What about the library hottie that looked like he might push Mak out of the way to beat down the twatwaffle from earlier? Does he know?"

I nod, looking at her sheepishly knowing she will hate not being the first to know. "He found the acceptance letter after dumping out my purse to find condoms the other night."

"Oh my god, that is amazing. And he is cool with it?"

A pressure settles over the bridge of my nose and the corners of my eyes. That first little tickle of happy tears. "Yeah. He said he doesn't care where I am, we are making this work no matter what."

"That man was always so gone for you." Harley releases me and collapses onto the couch. I follow quickly behind, both of us tucking our legs up under us and angling toward each other. "Don't get me wrong, if you decided you wanted to go on hating him forever, I would be right there with you hating him in solidarity. But this is better. You guys are disgustingly perfect for each other."

"Thanks. I'm actually feeling weirdly optimistic about everything."

"Oh, I forgot, fill me in on how Operation Mayor Sam is going."

Harley and I spend another forty minutes chatting in my office before we emerge to find Wesley still sitting at the bar red-faced with his glasses-less eyes glued to the surface of the bar and two of our best dancers on either side of him with their tits out for all to see. Sometimes I think they forget they are naked.

"I know cameras aren't allowed on the floor, but come on, I need to get a picture of this."

"No, Harley, I have to go rescue him. I'm pretty sure Misty takes her son to Story Hour every Tuesday. He's never going to be able to look her in the eye ever again."

Chapter 34

Wesley

The last two days have been barely organized chaos. I think I've talked to more people in this town as part of Operation S.A.M. (Sam Anderson for Mayor) than the entirety I've lived here. To say we got some confused reactions would be a vast understatement. Everything from, *Sam makes perfect sense* to *why should I even vote at this point if you guys are going to just keep adding more people to consider* to *fuck off I'm still voting for the goose.*

It's going to be close. I honestly have no clue which way it will go. But Sam did another deep dive into the town charter and discovered that if either Delia or I wins, we can refuse the office and then there would need to be a special election to decide the next mayor. So the plan is if either of us wins we will immediately step down.

But we're hoping it doesn't come to that, because that opens a whole other can of worms.

"Mmmmm, morning." Delia stretches next to me, her arms extending out above her head, hands balled into tight fists, her breasts plumped against each other as she lays on her side, her nipples relaxed and pale. Her hair catches the sunlight that streams in through her window, the red and blonde strands probably match the color of the sky outside as the sun just starts to peek over the mountains.

She has freckles all over her body, and I love tracing them, making shapes and words as we lay in that between space after we've completely sated ourselves but haven't gotten pulled under by sleep yet. Unable to resist that urge now, I drag my fingertip between my favorite constellation across the milky expanse.

The sleepy smile on her face pushes her cheeks up until her eyes all but disappear. There are so many things about her that I am only now learning. Things that sitting in a library as teenagers never revealed. Things I catalog in my brain to make sure I never forget them.

"What's that serious look on your face for? It's too early for big thoughts." She wiggles and nuzzles her way across the small bit of mattress separating us until her face is pressed against my neck and our bodies align from chest to toes.

"I was just thinking I'm so glad Burt made me run for mayor." It's something that's been turning over and over in my head in silent moments.

Delia pulls her face back to give me a disbelieving look. "What? Why would you be thinking something as silly as that?"

A strand of her silky sunshine hair falls across her cheek and I pick it up, rubbing the strands between my fingers before pushing it behind her ear. "If Burt hadn't badgered me into running, you never would have crashed that dinner. I never would have stormed the club and confronted you. We wouldn't have made out against the desk—"

Her face softens, eyes going dreamy.

"—And I might not have ever had the opportunity to wake up next to you like this."

"You don't think we would have gotten here eventually?" She gives me a soft kiss, lips just slightly pressing together since we both probably have horrific morning breath.

Now that question turns over in my mind, and I examine it from all sides. "I'd like to think so. But it might have taken a lot longer. And we were apart for long enough, so I'm glad Burt got me to where I am right now."

"Please, please don't make me feel gratitude for that man."

I give her a small smile. "There are a lot of horrible things Burt has done, including manipulating a grieving teenager. But he also took in a sixteen-year-old boy he had never met. Put food on the table and a roof over my head even though his sister hadn't talked to him for twenty years." A sudden fissure of fear tears through me. "Will you be okay with a life with me if it means

I can never fully cut him off? I'll never be close with him, but him being totally alone in life feels wrong, too."

"Believe it or not, your concern for him makes me love you even more." Another small kiss.

Love.

We haven't said it yet. I've felt it, thought about it saying, every second since that night in the club. Possibly long before that. All the way back to when a clumsy teenage girl in glasses crashed into me before class.

"I love you so much, Delia."

A wide smile overtakes her face and she burrows her nose back into the crook my neck. "I love you, too, Wes." She hooks one leg over my hip. I bend my own leg and press it between her thighs.

A sharp inhale cuts through the still morning.

"We should get ready." She kisses a line up my neck, whispering the words against my skin. "It's going to be a long day."

"Yeah, but nothing will fall apart if we're a little late." Trailing my hands down her bare back, I trace the line of her spine, like it is a road leading me to the round, perky ass I might be slightly obsessed with. "The rest of them can handle things for a little while."

I cup her ass and pull her tighter against me, my painfully hard cock trapped between as we move and slide against each other in a slow, languid grind.

"Oh my god, Wes. I was dreaming about this last night. How can I want you so much that I can't stop wanting you inside me even in my sleep?"

"I don't know, but if you figure it out let me know." Shifting my hand down over her ass, along the long, strong expanse of her hamstrings, I pull her leg up higher on my hip until I can feel the wet warmth of her against my hard length.

All those pole dancing classes have given my curvy, lush woman the most insanely powerful legs. The way they lock around my hips when I pin her against the wall makes me fucking insane.

"Yes, right there." We rock our hips slowly, my tip glancing against her clit with every forward thrust. "I'm going to come just from this," she pants into my ear.

Thankfully my stamina has greatly improved with the amount of time we've spent chasing orgasms together, but her words still put me right there on the edge of falling over a cliff.

Bowing my body, I bend down to suck on one of her nipples, biting it gently until it is peaked and red, glistening with moisture. Kiss my way back up her neck. "Come for me, Crash. Let me hear how much you want my cock first thing in the morning. Can barely function without coffee, but still need my dick first, isn't that right?"

"Yes, holy shit, yes." She claws at my shoulders and back as the pleasure builds to a crescendo along with her voice. "I need it, Wes, please. Pleeease."

All at once she's moaning and screaming, the rhythm of her hips stuttering as the first orgasm of the morning crashes over her. I don't change my pace, keeping the same consistent cadence, wringing every bit of her pleasure out.

"Need you inside, now." She reaches between us, gripping me in her hand. "See what you do to me, I got you all wet." She shuttles her fist down to the base and up to the tip, the easy slide aided by the orgasm I just gave her.

Giving this woman that I love so much pleasure will never stop giving me a surge of pride.

She notches me at her entrance, but I stop her with a hand gripping her wrist. "Wait. Condom."

"No need." She kisses my chin, then down my throat. "I have an IUD. I'm clean. And since you've been a monk for the past six years, I am guessing you are too."

I nod dumbly, the thought of being inside Delia with nothing between us making my brain go fuzzy. As if I just took a shot of the pure grain alcohol some of the old locals love to make in their basements and gift me at Christmas.

Everything is tighter in this position, with us on our sides, bodies pressed flush. It takes a little work, both of us pushing then retreating until I'm fully seated inside her. *Bare.*

Fuck, maybe my stamina hasn't improved enough. Already that heavy pressure settles at the base of my spine, the need to take and take until I'm spilling inside her.

No. Can't think of that yet. Do not think about coming inside Delia. Or of Delia walking around with a piece of me lingering deep inside her all day.

"Fuck, Delia, you feel so fucking good." I whisper the words against her shoulder, a reverence for this moment calling for hushed voices. "We fit together so perfectly. You were made for me, weren't you?"

"Yes, oh god, yes. All for you."

Slipping my hand into her hair, I grip it just tight enough to pull her head back so I can see her face as she moans and builds back up toward that peak. "Say it again, Delia."

Confusion settles on her face for a moment until understanding pierces through her growing orgasm. "I love you, Wes."

"Fuck." I roll her onto her back, hooking my arms under her knees and spreading her open beneath me. I plant my knees high, even with her hips so I can thrust hard and deep. No need to rush; at this moment we have nowhere to be, even if we do. When we are wrapped in each other like this nothing else exists.

"Wes, you're so deep, oh my god, I'm going to come again."

I love hearing her say it, but I already knew. The rhythmic squeeze of her cunt around my cock is all the confirmation I need to know that she's close. Raising up just far enough that I can slip a hand between us, I find her slippery clit, and with one swirl of my thumb around it she comes undone. Arms circle my shoulders, pulling me down on top of her. Legs wrapping around my waist and thrusting up to meet each of my strokes.

She tries to stay quiet, I'm sure wanting to hold on to the peace of the morning, but the pleasure raging through her body won't allow it, and instead she's screaming through another orgasm.

"Wes, pleasepleasepleaseplease." The words run together in one breath. A chant for something she needs from me but can't vocalize.

"What, Crash, what do you need me to do?" I would give her anything. Do anything.

"Come inside me. Please," she begs, her voice going smoky and quiet as the orgasm ebbs away again. But I know another is just a few seconds away. Another thing I've learned about Delia, after she cums once the rest are easily coaxed out of her. As if one is never enough, her body chases the pleasure over and over.

"You've only had two, you know the rule, three for you before I get one."

"Fuck the rule—" She bites down on my shoulder, hopefully leaving little marks there that I'll be able to run my fingers over later when I want a reminder of this moment. "I want your cum inside me. Want to be filled with it. Can't stop thinking about it."

"Trying to kill me, that's what you're doing." I won't make her ask again, and it's not like the request is a hardship. I've been riding that line of tipping over the edge since we started.

Gripping her hips tight in my palms, I pull her down onto my cock as I pump hard into her needy pussy. "This what you need, Crash? Need me to take this cunt hard and fast?"

"Yes, oh my god, yes."

Within seconds I'm falling over the edge, my vision going spotty and hazy as wave after wave of indescribable bliss surges through me and pours into Delia. She's coming again too, the squeeze of her milking every drop of my cum. There is nothing like this, nothing in this world that could be as important as what we are doing right now.

Gently, we float back down to earth. I try to roll off her so she can breathe, but her arms tighten around my shoulders and her feet lock behind my back. "Not yet."

I huff a laugh, and settle back on top of her. "I'm going to crush you."

"I like it. Like the weight of you. It makes everything feel more real. Permanent." There is emotion in her voice that has me scanning her face with concern.

"What's wrong?"

"Nothing. Everything is so right. It just makes me a little sad that we missed out on this for so many years." She gives me a wane smile and a little shrug.

"I think it's perfect because we were apart for so long. We know what it was like without this. It means we'll work all that much harder to stay together."

Tears appear in the corners of her eyes and drip down over her temples. "Say it again, Wes."

"I love you, Delia. Forever."

Chapter 35

Delia

"Holy shit." I come to a halt as soon as we turn the corner.

The line to get into the firehall and vote snakes out the door and down the sidewalk by the time we get there. An hour later than we were supposed to, but totally worth it.

After finally tearing ourselves from bed, we showered together in record time and raced out the door. We didn't even take the time to swing by The Bean to get coffee, which my brain is not happy about.

"Have you ever seen a turnout like this?" Wes tentatively takes another step closer, our arms stretching between us since I haven't moved and we are still holding hands.

"Never. Not once since I started voting almost a decade ago." I have voted in every single election since turning eighteen. Doesn't matter how small the race, doesn't matter if every single office has only one candidate. I show up and I write in someone if I don't like my options or lack thereof. "What do you think this means?"

"No idea." Wes tugs my hand, and reluctantly we start toward the line.

"Thank god you're here." Paula rushes up, a double-seater stroller carrying a sleeping Maggie and fussing Erica, three and one respectively. "We need help passing out the cards to everyone that explain exactly how they need to write in Sam's name."

She grabs two stacks of the small cards we had printed up. We aren't taking any chances after the CuGo debacle when no one could decide how to write the evil goose's name. I made so many trips back and forth to the closest print shop in Wellsboro that I think my car is still mad at me.

The line inches forward, and I notice several mugs from my mom's shop in people's hands. A hot spike of jealousy surges through me. We should have stopped.

"Okay, I have everyone up to Mrs. Winchester." She shoves the cards at us both and we drop our linked hands to grab them before they all scatter to the cold sidewalk.

It is absolutely fucking freezing, little clouds of breath floating from the people in line, making it look like a train chugging down a track instead of a queue of people waiting to vote for their next mayor.

"Do we know who they are all here for?" I scan the line, trying to figure out if I can predict votes based solely on how everyone is looking.

Paula's smile overtakes her whole face. "Judging by how many people have taken cards and asked to talk with Sam about their ideas? A whole fucking lot." Erica lets out a plaintive wail from between her little hat and pink puffy winter coat, looking super pissed that her mother has stuffed her into the warm clothes. "Okay, I have to take this girl and get her warm for a bit. Check diapers and all that. You two good?"

She looks back and forth between us, her smile growing a little more as the two of us exchange a glance filled with a whole lot of subtext.

"Awwww, you two are so cute. I'm so happy all the Halsteds have found their people." She pinches our cheeks like a grandma even though she was only three grades ahead of us in school. "Oh! I almost forgot, Murphy is runner for today since he can't vote, so if we need more of anything send him."

"Murph is here?" I go up on my tiptoes trying to look through the crowd to find the blonde idiot.

"What is a Murph?" Wes follows my gaze, trying to figure out what I'm talking about.

"Murph is Orion's best friend from the Marines." I glance back at the man who just rocked my world less than an hour ago. "He was a medic and now he's a veterinarian down in Baltimore."

"It's Navy Corpsman, not medic, pipsqueak." A large hand plops down on the crown of my head, ruffling my hair.

Swatting away his hand, I turn to glare at the guy that has essentially become another brother to me over the years. Every holiday, birthday, milestone, Murph shows up. Not to mention every single time he is in town he swings by the club and only requests private dances with one dancer. Harley.

"What are you doing here, asshole?" I give him an affectionate slug to the arm, which does absolutely nothing considering the man is like a million feet tall and built like a wall.

"Orrie called and said they might need some help making sure they don't give you any more power than you—" he boops my nose, "—already naturally possess, and I came to the rescue. Since I can't vote in this town, I make the perfect gofer."

"Wow, I appreciate it, man. Too bad the club is closed on Tuesdays, I can't treat you to a dance."

"Um, excuse me, a dance?" Wes takes one shuffle step closer to my side, his hand going to the small of my back in a possessive move I didn't expect from him.

"A dance with Harley. She's the love of my life, she just hasn't accepted it yet." Murph holds his hand out in Wes's direction, who reluctantly takes it. "You must be the man I have to thank for giving me my best friend. Wes, right?"

"Yeah, I'm Wes. But I don't know how I gave you—"

"If you hadn't been a twat in high school and got punched by Orrie, then he never would have lost his scholarship or joined the Marines. Then I would never have met him or the Halsteds or Harley. So I basically have you to thank for all my favorite things." Murph gives him a big goofy smile and drops their handshake, slapping him on the back. I'm impressed Wes doesn't move an inch at the force of that smack. "Okay, I am off to get more coffees. You guys want some?"

We both nod and Murphy is off as quickly as he came, just like always.

"Wait, isn't Harley gay?" Wesley rolls the shoulder Murph slapped and looks at me with a confused expression. "Does he know that?"

"She's pansexual. And extremely annoyed that despite her best efforts, she is in fact still attracted to men."

"Understandable, honestly. We are the worst." Wes leans down to place a sweet kiss on my lips. "How you will put up with me?"

"I'll figure it out." We kiss again, perfectly chaste considering we are in public, but gradually I become aware of murmuring around us. That strange itchy feeling on the back of my neck like I'm being watched.

We separate and look toward the packed line only to find every single head is turned in our direction, various expressions of confusion and shock that two of the candidates for mayor are now making out on the sidewalk on election day.

"Okay, let's go make sure neither of us gets elected." Wes grabs my hand and we walk toward the crowd together, not giving a single fuck about everyone watching us like a couple of strange zoo animals.

The morning goes by quickly. We talk to everyone in line, make sure they know Sam is the best choice and we both fully support him. Knox and June pass out refreshments from the farm to people in the line and all of us working on Sam's behalf.

The man himself shakes hands all day, to the point I'm worried he might actually get a stress fracture if he keeps it up. But it's working. Nearly everyone in line seems to be on his side, and I'm feeling strangely optimistic about the whole thing.

Halfway through the afternoon, Wes and I are taking a break, sitting on the wall of the fountain gifted by my family to the town. The statue in the middle is of my ancestors, the original settlers of this town. The fountain is off for the season, but there is an old tradition in town that if you kiss by the fountain then throw a quarter into its water, your love will last forever. It is considered a rite of passage in my family. I have a very good feeling Wes and I will be back here next spring.

"Young man, what is the meaning of this?" a very loud, very familiar voice calls from across the courtyard.

Wes squeezes his eyes shut, his hand wiping down his face. We knew this would need to happen, and more than likely today, but that doesn't make it any easier.

Wes stands from the fountain and turns to watch as his uncle storms across the leaf-covered grass. "Why are people in line talking about voting for Sam Anderson? Why are you here with—" he looks around his much taller nephew and sneers at me, "—with her. What in the hell is going on?"

Wow, I think that might be the first time I have ever heard Burt get even close to swearing. I rise onto my feet, standing behind the man I love so he knows I am here if he needs me.

"Burt, don't talk to her like that. I am with Delia because I love her and I plan to build a life with her." Wes reaches back to take my hand in his. "She has somehow forgiven me for breaking her heart all those years ago in a misguided attempt to protect her and her family. I didn't know better as a teenager, but you should have. You were an adult and you decided to use the power you had over a hurting kid to spread more hurt and suffering."

The man I have spent a lifetime loathing rears back as if Wes slapped him. "I never—"

"It's over now. The only reason I agreed to run for mayor was so I could undo everything you've done to this town. But Delia realized that there was a far better candidate who should be mayor not out of guilt but because he is truly a good man who loves this town." He squeezes my hand and I squeeze back. "We have both thrown our support behind Sam. Even if he doesn't win, we have both agreed to step down immediately if either of us win and then Sam will run for the special election."

"Wesley, you cannot trust a word anyone in that family says. They are all snakes who poison the minds of the—"

"Enough." He doesn't shout the word, but it is so filled with venom that Burt's mouth snaps shut, cutting off whatever bullshit he was about to spout out. "You will not talk about the love of my life or the family that has welcomed me despite everything. You no longer have any power over me. And in just a few weeks, you won't have any power in this town anymore either."

The air seems to seep out of Burt all at once, as if Wes saying the words has made him realize that he truly has lost everything he held dear. Unfortunately, the things he treasured weren't the people around him but his control over them.

"Uncle, I don't want to break every connection I have to you." Wes takes a small step forward, ducking his face down slightly so he is eye level with his uncle. "You are the only blood related family I still have, and I hold value in that. But if you can't find it in yourself to be civil to the family I am choosing, then I will not hesitate to cut you out of my life completely."

Burt opens his mouth to say something, but seems to think better of it. He tilts his chin up a fraction of an inch, as if trying to make himself feel bigger, then walks off in the direction of the firehall.

"Well, that went about as well as I could expect." Wes turns and gathers me into his arms, rubbing his hands up and down my back as if to warm me, but I think he is really just comforting himself, making sure I am still here with him.

Which I am and always will be.

"Come on, let's get back there. Polls don't close for a few more hours."

We turn, his arm around my shoulders and mine around his waist, and make our way across the square to make town history.

Chapter 36

Wesley

The Bean is more crowded than I have ever seen it. Every table and chair has a body occupying it. It's hard to move between the bodies milling about, trying to get closer to our new mayor and shake his hand.

Mayor Anderson has a great ring to it.

Only twenty percent of the votes have been counted, but it is looking like a landslide victory. We won't get the official tally for another day or two, but I would be shocked if Delia and I get more than a couple dozen votes each.

It is nearly one in the morning, the Anderson kids are all tucked in at home with their grandmother acting as babysitter so their parents can celebrate. And celebrating they are. Delia had Harley bring over a case of champagne from the club and mugs full of the effervescent drink have been making the rounds of the room, everyone clinking the ceramic vessels together as they talk about the historic vote.

A news crew even came out to cover the story of a small town with a last-minute write-in candidate that stopped a family legacy.

But all legacies have to fade eventually, and it was time for the Lickinbill era of mayors to make its way into the history books.

"Hey there, totally regular citizen that is not now or ever will be mayor." Delia squeezes between two of our neighbors to press her body against mine, looking up at me with that lazy, liquid look in her eyes that lets me know she definitely partook in her own libations. "How are you feeling?"

I look around the cafe. It is the first time I've ever been in here in the open. No sneaking in the back door when no one else is around. I can't wait to come in again during regular operating hours and just sit at a table and chat with Roxy. Or sit by the fireplace in the Den of Sin and read a book with Delia next to me.

"Lucky, I am feeling incredibly lucky."

It's true. I have had some pretty horrible things happen to me in my life, but I'm not sure I would change a single one if it meant I wouldn't be here in this exact moment. I would give up a lot of things to see my moms again, but giving up Delia isn't one of them. I'm not sure what that says about me, but I'm also not going to worry about it.

"Hey, now that you are most definitely not going to lead this town into a motorcycle gang haven, what are you going to do about law school?"

Delia's face lights up, joy and excitement surging through. "I'm accepting the spot. I'm going to law school."

"What?" Roxy rounds a table, her eyes going big. "It is incredibly loud in here, but did I just hear something about law school?" The woman who has been a good friend to me the last couple years places one hand on her daughter's shoulder and the other on mine.

"Yup." Delia raises her hands over her head. "I am going to motherfucking law school, baby!"

The whole place erupts in cheers. I'm pretty sure half the crowd doesn't even know what they are cheering about. But gradually every Halsted makes their way to us, Delia filling them in on the details about her acceptance. Harley, Sam, Paula, Murphy, they all migrate to the spot in the middle of the cafe that is quickly becoming a gathering of people that are becoming a family. We might not have all been born into this family, but we are just as strong as any blood connection.

"Wait, so does this mean one of my first acts as mayor is going to be hiring a new librarian?" Sam looks at me with unfiltered panic on his face.

I shake my head. "No, we love this town. The program is three years. We made it past ten years apart, three years taking turns braving the turnpike isn't too much of a burden. Don't worry, Mayor Elect Anderson, I'm not going anywhere any time soon."

"Plus, I don't start until next fall, so we have almost a year to figure out exactly how everything will work." Delia beams up at me once again, her hand in mine. "But you have to give up that tiny box of an apartment. It is such a depressing bachelor pad."

"Yeah, you going to move me in after we've been dating less than a month?" I tease her, but she gives me a look that says, *duh, stupid man*.

"I have a U-Haul you can rent," Simone, the town's mechanic and tow truck driver, pipes up from a few feet away.

"If we're moving shit, I expect free pizza and beer," Orion throws in, seemingly not at all concerned that his baby sister is moving in with the guy he once punched while defending her honor.

"I mean, someone is going to need to take care of Mr. Sparkles once she is gone," Harley adds.

"So help me, woman, if this is another wild animal you are harboring illegally, we are going to have words." Murphy glares at the woman he insisted just a few hours ago was his soulmate. She flips him off.

Everyone starts talking over each other, some making plans of attack for moving my things into Delia's place, some talking about the future of the town, others talking about the filthy books they found in the Den of Sin.

It's overwhelming and chaotic. After far too many years of quiet solitude, I fucking love it.

Epilogue

Six Months Later - Delia

"Delia, why do you have a Mason jar of watery slime in the back of your fridge? Can I throw this out?" Wes's voice echoes out from the kitchen, his words immediately striking panic into my heart.

"No!" I sprint through the bedroom, dodging boxes as I go, sliding into the kitchen just in time to pull the jar from his hands. "Do NOT throw out Mr. Yeast."

"Do I want to know what Mr. Yeast is?" He is wearing one of my favorite expressions: amused affection at my antics. It makes me want to kiss him silly, but my brothers will be back any minute with another round of boxes from Wes's old place.

"Mr. Yeast is my sourdough starter." I hold up the jar swirling the grayish liquid hooch that floats on top of the viscus starter. I *really* need to feed him. "I made him from scratch and he is incredibly temperamental. It took three tries to get my starter to work. I love this thing more than Harley loves all her pets combined." I point an accusatory finger in my new live-in boyfriend's direction. "So hands off."

Wes chuckles and goes back to digging through the fridge. "You got it, Crash. I will not mess with your wild yeast."

Cradling the jar against my chest, I march over to the counter and go about the routine of feeding my starter while Wes pulls out all the food I prepped to feed my siblings who I roped into helping Wes move into my place.

We weave and bob around each other, his hand grazing across the small of my back each time he passes by me. Ever since the election we have more or less been living together, but it wasn't official. His stuff stayed at his sad little apartment and he would go back every couple days to pack another bag, do laundry, grab his mail. He insisted we needed time to get to know each other as adults before officially moving in together.

Finally, that day has come. He is handing over the lease to his apartment to Murph, who has decided to move to town and start his own vet practice here. We are all thrilled to have Orion's best friend in town for good. Well, everyone except Harley, but she'll come around once he stops asking her to marry him.

Right on cue, Orion, Murph, and Knox all troop into the front door of my townhouse with the last of Wes's boxes.

"Dude, seriously, are the books at the library not enough? Did you need to have this many at your place too?" Murph drops a very heavy looking box next to the couch and collapses back onto the cushions. "I'm done, between my shit and your shit I won't be able to lift my arms for a week."

"Awww, poor baby can't lift the boxes with his matchstick arms?" Harley strolls into the front door carrying two cups of coffee, handing one to me.

"Wifey, you know these guns are far from matchsticks." Murph flexes, kissing one of his admittedly bulging biceps.

Harley fakes a gag, but I don't miss the double take she does at his muscles glistening with sweat. They are so ridiculous.

"Okay, we've got more food than all of us could possibly eat in a week over here. Everyone come dish up." Wes has arranged the salads, charcuterie boards, and pastries I've been making for days artfully around the table. Within seconds the guys are descending like locusts to strip everything but that lacquer from the table. "I take that back, apparently this was just enough food."

Wes's eyes have gone wide as he watches Knox, Orion, and Murphy devour their plates like absolute animals. He is still getting used to having lots of people around.

I grab a plate and start piling enough food on it to feed both Wes and I before the guys leave us nothing but crumbs for our lunch.

"Hey, Delia, why don't we go eat outside? Get some air?" Wes looks at me with an expression that says *I want to get you away from your brothers so I can kiss you without risking a broken nose.*

I shoot him a wink and we hustle out the front door and slow to a stroll for the two blocks down to the town square.

It is a beautiful, cool spring day. Flowers are just beginning to poke their heads out from the ground where they sat dormant all winter. The grass is still a little wet from an overnight rain, so we sit on the edge of the fountain dedicated to my ancestors, placing the plate between us and picking at the food as we relax in the sun.

"I have a present for you." Wes pulls out a small box from his pocket and my gaze flies up to meet his. "I swear, it isn't a ring. You said you wanted to wait until you finish law school and I am going to honor that."

I know myself; if Wes proposes now I will want to throw all of my attention into planning a wedding and starting our lives together. I don't want to juggle that and law school. Still, a little war wages in my chest between relief that he isn't about to pop the question and disappointment.

Gingerly, Wes opens the box and places it on the ledge between us. Inside are two shiny silver quarters. "Remember the day in high school you told me about the history of this fountain?" He tilts his head toward the statue of my ancestors, water pouring out in bubbling streams around their feet.

I nod. The memory of that day is as fresh in my mind as what I had for breakfast this morning. School had been canceled because of a weird fall heatwave and the air conditioning was broken. Burt had been out of town at a meeting with the state police, so Wes and I had taken advantage by walking around the square without having to worry about being caught.

"That day I went to the store and picked up a few things, I got these two quarters as change." He plucks them from the box, holding them in his palm. "They are both from the years we were born. I thought it was fate, something I never thought about before meeting you. So, I held onto them with the intention of throwing them into the fountain with you some day."

My chest tightens, eyes stinging with the onslaught of emotions rushing to make themselves known in the form of tears. "You kept them for over a decade?"

Wes nods. "They have sat in this box since we were sophomores in high school. I used to berate myself for holding onto them when I knew there would never be a reason to use them. But something told me to hang on anyway."

Gently, I pick one quarter up from his palm, rubbing the bumpy surface. "Wes, just so you know, I take this ritual more seriously than I do a marriage certificate."

The man I have fallen in love with twice in my life smiles so wide it crinkles the corners of his eyes. "Good. I want to be tied to you forever, whether it is through two quarters thrown into a fountain or a paper with our signatures."

Unable to hold myself back any longer, I lunge forward, wrapping my arms around his neck and kissing the absolute hell out of my live-in boyfriend. I am suddenly very angry our house is full of some of my most favorite people in this world, because it means I can't drag him back to our bed and make love to him for the rest of the day.

Normally I hate having to stop kissing Wes, but for this one moment, I don't mind. We each hold our quarters up, kiss the metal circles, and flick them into the clear fountain water. I watch as they float down to the bottom of the fountain, glinting in the sun.

For the first time, the money collected in the fountain at the end of the year won't be used to fill potholes. Instead Mayor Anderson, another of my favorite people, has convinced the council to use the money to start a grant program to bring in more businesses to the town. I'm thrilled that a piece of my story with Wes will be used to grow the town we both adore.

As for Burt, not much has changed there. He comes to every council meeting and complains about the changes Sam and the rest of the council are making. But with each meeting, he loses more and more of his vitriol. He and Wes have lunch occasionally, but they are usually short visits with awkward conversation since Wes refuses to shy away from our life together as a topic. Either Burt gets over his anger that Wes is in love with a Halsted, or he doesn't. That is up to him.

I turn back to Wes, who is already gazing at me with so much love it makes my heart skip a beat. "Well, now you have no choice but to love me forever."

"Oh Delia, I didn't need a quarter and a fountain for that. I've loved you for the minute you crashed into me in the hall, and I will continue to love you until my heart stops beating."

Another tear slips down my cheek as I climb on top of Wes, straddling him in the very spot my ancestors first made love. It might seem weird to most people, but I kind of wish we could make love right here in the town square. I think my great-great-great grandmother would love knowing even two hundred years later, her family is still finding love in this very spot.

The End

Bonus Chapter

Six Years Ago - Delia

Author's note: This was actually one of the first chapters I wrote when I started drafting Casting Shade. During the editing process it moved around in the manuscript until I finally decided it didn't sure enough of a purpose and seem to fit in any particular spot. But I still love the chapter, and I think it gives a little extra insight into the story of Delia and Wesley, so I am adding it here for you to enjoy.

Six Years Ago - Delia

"I'm so sorry, Delia." He sounds so goddamn earnest. Like he really means it.

"You shouldn't be here." It has only been six hours since I buried my father. Since my brother and I held my mother up while she sobbed as they lowered him into the ground. "I don't want you here."

"I'll go, I just wanted to bring you these." He places a bunch of lilies on the table nearest the cafe counter. "And to tell you, I've been here, the place where you are so fucking sad you don't know what to do with yourself. I felt that when my parents died. If you need someone to cry with, scream at, I'm here."

I can't bring myself to look at him. If I do, I'll break all over again. Instead, the espresso bar is getting the best cleaning of its life. The cafe served as the gathering place for pretty much the entire town after the service. People coming in and out, sipping cups of coffee, nibbling on pastries, all made and served by me. I didn't know what else to do. For the last three years all I've done is keep this place afloat. Made sure Mom ate, drank, slept, showered. How do I stop moving now that everything is just over?

"Losing a parent is a pain most have never known before. There aren't many people that can relate to that. I just... I want you to know I can relate and I'm here if you need someone to talk to." God, why does he have to sound like the Wes I knew at sixteen? Before everything went to shit.

Floorboards creak under his huge feet as he crosses to the door. Bigfoot. That's what Harley and I used to call him in gym class. I glance at the bunch of flowers lying on the table. They aren't white like all the other flowers people sent. They aren't sad. They are a riot of pinks, purples, blues, and yellows.

I told him once I hated white flowers. Nature produces so many amazing colors, why would you want the most boring one?

The fact that he remembered is what finally makes me crack. "It's different."

The creaking of the floorboards stops immediately. I look over to where he is frozen next to the door of the cafe.

"My dad dying, it isn't the same as your mothers. You were so young. They died so fast." My voice cracks, because thinking about teenage Wesley carrying this burden is almost too much to stomach. "We knew Pop was going to die. Even the day he was diagnosed, the doctors told us this is what would be his death. There is no cure for the type of brain tumor he had. It wasn't a matter of if, just when."

Wesley doesn't say anything, just turns around and walks silently back to the counter, his hands tucked into his pockets.

"There is a part of me that is happy he finally passed. He hadn't been himself for a long time. I think we all kind of mourned him while he was still alive." I'm surprised to feel tears slip down my cheeks, hot against my cold cheeks.

"I think that is probably natural. You're right, our situations are different. But losing someone is complicated. There is good and bad all mixed together." Wesley's voice is so soft, so comforting.

All day I haven't stopped to just stand and process. Hell, the last three years I've barely stopped to think. Why is talking to the man I hate most in this world the one I finally let everything pour out with?

"What could have possibly been good about what you went through?"

"They died fast," he says it in a rush, like ripping off the Band-aid will make it hurt less. "Before the ambulances could even get there. In the weeks after, that was the thing that I comforted myself with. They didn't suffer."

I nod, knowing exactly what he means. Because my pop did suffer. A lot. We all did. Even Orion who hadn't been here for most of Dad's illness. Surgeries, chemo, radiation, so many MRIs we lost count. He lost who he was at his very core.

"Want something to drink?" I'm as shocked as Wesley obviously is when I make the offer. But he nods and I start making two Morally Gray Heroes, Mom's spin on a London Fog. It's my favorite drink.

As I go about steeping the tea and steaming the milk, Wesley and I talk more. Like we used to back in high school. With no boundaries or history. Just two people telling their inner most thoughts to someone that just instinctually gets it.

We end up sitting on the steps that lead up to the apartment I've been living in since I took over managing the cafe. It's like the last five years never happened. Wesley never broke my heart so completely I have yet to date another guy. He never graduated and immediately fled back to New York where he grew up. His uncle never tried to shut down The Bean by reporting us to the health department for made-up bullshit. We've just always been here, sneaking around behind our warring family's backs.

"Why did you move back? I thought you said once you were an adult you would never come back here." The question comes dangerously close to the topics we've been avoiding, specifically our shared history. But I've been curious since the local town newspaper reported he accepted the position of children's librarian. The article went on and on about what a boon it was to get a Columbia educated local to help educate the youth of Amoresville. I'm pretty sure it was ghostwritten by his uncle.

Wesley heaves a deep sigh, leaning back against the next stair up and looking at me with so much sadness I almost can't breathe. "It's complicated. I thought I would feel closer to my parents in New York, and I did for a little while. I visited the theaters they had performed in. Walked down the street we lived on. But, everything changes so fast there I barely recognized anything. Here, I can see real evidence of my mom. I can feel her."

I can tell he is holding back, but not lying.

"Plus, that library was practically my second home when I moved here. It seems somehow appropriate that I am working there, trying to make it better for kids like us."

For the first time tonight, I genuinely smile. The library was neutral territory for us. Some place besides school that we could hang out without Burt or my parents knowing.

"Are there kids like us still? Making out in the corner by the legal section where the lightbulb is always burnt out?"

A heat I haven't felt in way too long trickles through my veins, warming parts of me I thought long dormant after the events of the past few years.

Wesley chuckles and turns to me with the biggest smile I've ever seen on his face. "No, but Old Lady Thurston warned me to keep an eye out when I got hired. First thing she had me do was replace the lightbulb."

I can't help but burst out laughing. Mrs. Thurston is a short, ancient thing and was afraid to climb the ladder to replace the lightbulb. Something we used to our advantage.

"Traitor." I elbow him in the side and he curls around the spot as he laughs.

As our laughing quiets, I realize exactly how close we are. Hip to hip, sitting on the second to last stair. I can't explain why I do it, why I lean in as if a tractor beam is pulling me closer to his lips. When my mouth brushes against his it's like coming home. A comfort so familiar a little sigh slips past my lips.

Wesley deepens the kiss, his hand coming up to weave into my long hair. Parting my lips with his tongue, tilting his head to get closer. Something low in my belly twists, winding tighter and tighter like a spring.

In the next instant I'm moving, swinging my leg over his lap and settling myself against him. He's hard already, the rigid length of him trapped behind his suit pants lining up perfectly with me through the plain black panties I wore for the funeral.

"Dee, we shouldn't," he says it in a groan as I rock against him.

Holy shit, does it feel good. When was the last time I felt this good? I know exactly when, but I can't think about that.

"Please, Wesley, I want to feel good." I rock against him again, resting more of my weight against him so that we're grinding together in such a delicious way it makes me gasp, and my forehead meets his shoulder. "Please."

"I never could say no to you." He pulls my head back up, continuing the kiss, only more frantic this time. As if he truly is giving into whatever horrible mistake we're about to make.

His hands roam my body, pulling up the hem of my loose black dress until he can palm my ass, helping me writhe against him in slow, rhythmic pumps.

"I can feel how wet you are already."

I should be embarrassed that he can feel the moisture through my panties and his slacks. But I'm not. I just want him so fucking bad. More than I have ever wanted another person.

Desperate to feel his bare skin, I pull at the crisp white shirt tucked into his slacks. After a second of my frantic tugging, he helps me pull it from the waistband, and unbuttons it in record time. My hands skate over his solid shoulders, pushing the fabric down off his arms. Wesley is lean, toned in the way runners and soccer players are. A sleeper build, that's what he has. On the outside he looks all innocent and nerdy, but get his clothes off and he is a freaking Adonis.

I grab the hem of my dress and pull it off over my head, tossing it behind me.

"Fuck, you are so gorgeous." His mouth finds my breasts, kissing and sucking along the edge of my bra, his hands gripping my waist in an almost painful hold.

Within seconds, I have the bra off and joining the pile of our clothes. He moves down to suck one nipple into his mouth, circling his tongue around the peaked tip. Every pull of his mouth on me has that spring twisting and tightening, heat spreading to my pussy until it feels like I might combust.

"So good, holy shit." I'm panting into his slightly too-long brown hair as he continues to feast on my breasts. I cradle his head in my arms, hair fisted in my hands as an orgasm of epic proportions builds. "Don't stop."

I release the silky strands, shoving my hands between us to get his fucking pants off. I need him inside me like I need air and chocolate.

"I'm not stopping until you're screaming the walls down around us. Even then I'm going to keep going." His hands join mine in pushing his pants down just low enough that his thick cock is finally released.

Rising up on my knees, I move my panties to the side. Wesley holds his cock still, pointing the head where I need him most. In one swift drop of my hips, I'm filled so completely it takes my breath away. Every muscle in my body tenses as he stretches me just a little past that line between pain and pleasure.

"Breathe, baby." He leans one elbow back on a stair, his eyes riveted to where we are joined, the thumb on his free hand circling my clit. "Ride me, Dee."

Those words break me free from the shock of having him inside me. My hips rotate experimentally. It feels so good. So different from the toys I use by myself. I grip his shoulders, steadying myself as I raise up and back down, grinding down on his thumb.

The orgasm teeters so close, I chase it with the movement of my hips, not using anything that could be classified as rhythm or grace. My whole existence has shrunk down to the area between my thighs.

For the first time in years, there is nothing happening in my head. Only the need to come.

"So fucking beautiful riding my cock. You're going to come all over it, aren't you?" Wesley Goldman: nerd on the outside, filthy dirty talker on the inside.

I nod frantically, so ready to feel that rush of pleasure.

He leans forward, wrapping both arms around my waist so we are pressed together chest to chest. He kisses along my neck and shoulders, murmuring praises and compliments between swipes of his tongue.

Finally, the spring tightens until it can't go any further, and everything explodes. I cling to Wesley, nails digging into his back while every nerve inside my body turns inside out. My cries and screams echo in the empty cafe. It feels like I'm falling apart, and the only thing holding the pieces together is Wesley's arms banded tight around my back.

Inside me, he explodes, the warmth of his cum filling me, setting off another orgasm as we cling to each other. Even through his own orgasm, Wesley continues to kiss along my shoulders and neck, telling me how beautiful and amazing I am.

Telling me how much he loves me.

I'm not sure he even realizes he says the words. But they make everything come crashing into reality.

What the hell was I thinking?

"Let go." I try to make some room between us, but Wesley either doesn't hear or is still so lost in his pleasure my words don't pierce the fog. "Let go!"

Panic rises in my chest, erasing every amazing feeling from just seconds ago.

The instant his arms loosen, I stand, hissing as Wesley's spent cock slips out from me.

"Delia—"

"—This was a mistake."

"Don't say that."

"What the hell was I thinking?" Frantically, I reach for my dress.

"Delia, wait, just calm down." Wesley stands on unsteady feet, pulling his pants back up and buttoning them.

I don't want to be naked in front of him anymore. I feel too exposed in every possible way.

"Delia, wait." He reaches for me, but I dodge his hands as I pull the dress over my head, pulling and tugging it down until I'm covered. "Delia, please, let's just talk."

"No. We should never talk again. That is how we got into this mess."

I grab his shirt and throw it at him maybe a little too aggressively.

"Delia, we need to talk." I can hear the frustration in his voice but can't stop my head from spinning long enough to wonder what he must be thinking. "Dee, we didn't use anything."

Yeah, I can tell. "I'll take care of it. I'll get tested for everything just in case. I'd appreciate it if you did the same." I pick up my bra and turn for the door.

"You don't have to—" but he doesn't finish his sentence because I'm out the front door desperate to escape whatever he wants to say.

And as if this moment could not get any worse, standing on the sidewalk in his usual khakis and sport coat over a polo shirt is Burt fucking Lickinbill. His beady little eyes move from me to a spot just over my shoulder and his face hardens.

"What is going on here?"

"Don't worry, Burt, I'm on my way to Wellsboro to get the morning after pill right now."

The mayor reels back, disgust painted all over his stupid, wrinkly face.

"Delia, just wait." I make the mistake of looking behind me. Wesley is standing on the porch, shirt still hanging limply in one hand, totally ignoring his uncle's presence and staring at me like I am the only thing in the world.

But it's all a lie.

I really wish I had learned that the first time around. "It was a mistake. It never should have happened."

I know from his wince that he recognizes the words he once said to me.

About the author

Brandy Ayers has been inventing stories in one form or another since childhood. Whether telling soap-opera-level-dramatic lies to her new neighbors at the tender age of six or daydreaming about how she would definitely run into and marry Keanu Reeves (her very age-appropriate crush in eighth grade), there was always something brewing in that weird little brain. After becoming a mother, Brandy decided she needed to do something other than care for her baby and go to work. Something for herself. That something ended up being writing down her crazy stories. More than ten years and fifteen books later, she's still at it.

When Brandy isn't writing, you can find her drinking way too much coffee, making jokes that produce groans and eye rolls from her kids, and growing her hodge-podge crew of pets. Lucky enough to have found two great loves in her life, Brandy lives with her second husband and fellow author James W. Farley in southern Pennsylvania.

https://www.brandyayersauthor.com/
Facebook: https://www.facebook.com/BrandyAyersAuthor
TikTok: @BrandyAyersAuthor

Instagram: @BrandyAyersWrites

Also by Brandy

Welcome To Amoresville
Pumpkin To Talk About
Up The Wrong Tree
Casting Shade

Rock Hard, Love Harder Series
Protecting His Brat
Chasing His Tease
Restraining His Runaway
Taking His Diva
Not Without You – Coming February 2026

Double Virgin Collection:
Only Us
Only You
Only Me

WQUZ News Series:
Standby
Breaking

Stand Alone Books:
Piece by Piece: A Modern Retelling of Jack and the Beanstalk
Wanted: No Strings
Unwrapping Her
The O Doctor
Taking Over

www.ingramcontent.com/pod-product-compliance
Lightning Source LLC
Chambersburg PA
CBHW051010180726
48291CB00006B/2055